EMPRESS OF THE SUN

Also by Ian McDonald

Planesrunner
Be My Enemy

IAN McDONALD

EMPRESS OF THE SUN

an imprint of Prometheus Books
Amherst, NY

Published 2014 by Pyr®, an imprint of Prometheus Books

Cover illustration © Larry Rostant
Cover design by Nicole Sommer-Lecht

Inquiries should be addressed to
Pyr
59 John Glenn Drive
Amherst, New York 14228
VOICE: 716–691–0133
FAX: 716–691–0137
WWW.PYRSF.com

18 17 16 15 14   5 4 3 2 1

Library of Congress Cataloging-in-Publication Data

McDonald, Ian, 1960–
    Empress of the sun / by Ian McDonald.
        pages cm. — (Everness ; book 3)
    ISBN 978-1-61614-865-2 (hardback)
    ISBN 978-1-61614-866-9 (ebook)
    [1. Science fiction. 2. Adventure and adventurers—Fiction. 3. Airships—Fiction.] I. Title.

PZ7.M47841776Emp 2014
[Fic]—dc23

2013036315

Printed in the United States of America

To Enid, as ever.

Author's Note: There is a Palari dictionary
at the back of the book.

1

A dot of brilliant light. In an instant the dot exploded into a disk. The disk of light turned to a circle of blackness: a night sky. Out of the perfect circle of night sky came the airship, slow, huge, magnificent. Impeller engines hummed. The Heisenberg Gate flickered and closed behind it.

"Voom," Everett Singh whispered, blinking in the daylight of a new Earth. He lifted his finger from the Infundibulum's touch screen. Another Heisenberg jump, another universe.

And the bridge of the airship *Everness* shrieked with alarms. Yellow lights flashed. Horns blared. Bells rang. Klaxons shrieked. *Impact warning, impact warning*, thundered a mechanical voice. Everett's vision cleared at the same instant as the rest of the crew's. He saw . . .

"Atlanta, Dundee and sweet Saint Pio," whispered Miles O'Rahilly Lafayette Sharkey, the airship's weighmaster. The Bible, particularly the Old Testament, was his usual supply for quotes. He had a verse for every occasion. When he called on the saints of his old Confederate home, it was serious.

. . . Trees. Trees before them. Trees beneath them. Trees in their faces. Trees reaching their deadly, killing branches towards them. Trees everywhere. And *Everness* powering nose down into them.

"This is . . . This shouldn't be happening," Everett said, paralyzed with shock at his station on the bridge. "The jump . . . I calculated . . ."

"Sen!" Captain Anastasia Sixsmyth bellowed. One moment she had been at the great window, striking her customary pose—riding breeches and boots, blouse with the collar turned up, her hands clasped behind her back, above her the soft velvet stars of Earth 1. The next moment she was staring an airship-wreck full in the face, shouting, "Take us up!"

"I's on it," her adopted daughter shouted. Sen Sixsmyth was as slight as a whippet, pale as a blizzard, but she was pilot of the airship *Everness* and she threw every gram of her small weight on the thrust levers. Everett felt *Everness* shudder as the impeller pods swivelled into vertical lift. But airships are big and long and lumbering, and it takes time, a lot of time, too much time, to make them change their course. "Come on my dilly dorcas, come on my lover . . ."

Impact warning, impact warning, the alarm shouted. It had a Hackney Airish accent.

"Belay that racket!" Captain Anastasia thundered. Sharkey killed the alarms, but the warning lights still filled the bridge with flashing yellow madness.

We're not going to make it, Everett thought. We're not going to make it. Strange, how he felt so calm about it. When it's inevitable, you stop fighting and accept it.

"Ma'am . . . Ma . . . I can't get her head up," Sen shouted. Captain Anastasia turned to Everett Singh. The great window was green, all green. A universe of green.

"Mr. Singh, Heisenberg jump."

Everett tore his eyes from the hypnotic, killing green outside the window and focused on the jump control display on Dr. Quantum, his iPad. The figures made no sense. No sense. He was frozen. IQ the size of a planet, as his dad had once said, and he didn't know what to do. Scared and unable to do anything about it.

"I . . . I . . . need to calculate . . ."

"No time, Mr. Singh."

"A random jump could take us anywhere!"

"Get us out of here!"

Sharkey glanced up at the monitors.

"Captain, we're grounding."

The bridge quaked as if shaken by the hand of a god. Everett clung to the jump station. Captain Anastasia reeled hard into a bulkhead. She went down, winded. Sen clung to the steering yoke like a drowning rat to driftwood. *Everness* screamed; her nanocarbon skeleton twisted to its limits. Ship skin tore with ripping shrieks. Everett heard spars snap one by one like bones. Tree branches shattered in small explosions. The hull shuddered to a crashing boom.

"We've lost an engine," Sharkey shouted, hanging on to his monitor screens. He sounded as if he had lost his own arm.

Everness drove into the thousand branches of the forest canopy. Green loomed in the great window. The glass exploded. Branches speared into the bridge. Captain Anastasia rolled away as a splintered shaft of wood stabbed towards her. Sen ducked under a branch ramming straight for her head. The bridge was filled with twigs and leaves.

"I'm giving her reverse thrust!" Sen yelled. Everett grabbed hold of the wooden rail of his jump-station as *Everness* shuddered right down to its spine. There was an enormous wrenching, grating groan. The impaling branches shifted a meter, no more. The vibration shook Everett to the fillings in his teeth.

"I can't move her!" Sen shouted.

"Leave her. You'll burn out the impellers!" Captain Anastasia cried.

"If we have any left," Sharkey said.

Captain Anastasia relieved her daughter at the helm. "Mr. Singh. Take us back to Earth 1. On my word. Everyone else, stand by. This will either cure or kill."

"No!" Sen yelled as she saw her mother's hand raised above the *flush ballast* button.

"Come on, you high and shining ones," Captain Anastasia

whispered. "Just once." She brought her hand down hard on the red button. *Everness* lurched as hundreds of tons of ballast water jetted from scupper valves. The airship strained. Her skeleton groaned like a living thing. Tree branches bent and snapped. A jolt upwards. Everett could hear the water thundering from the valves. It must look like a dozen waterfalls. *Everness* gave a massive creak and lurched upwards again. The branches tore free from the bridge in a shower of leaves. The airship was lifting. There was a crunching shriek of metal strained beyond its limits. *Everness* rolled to one side, then righted. All the power went dead. Screens, monitors, controls, lights, navigation, helm, communications. Dr. Quantum flickered and went dark.

Captain Anastasia took her hand off the *flush* button. The water jets closed. The silence was total and eerie.

"'And behold, there came a great wind from the wilderness, and smote the four corners of the house . . . and I only am escaped alone to tell thee,'" Sharkey quoted.

"I'd prefer a report on our status Mr. Sharkey," Captain Anastasia said.

"Status?" a voice bellowed from the spiral staircase outside. "I'll give you our status!" Mchynlyth, ship's engineer, burst onto the bridge. His brown face was flushed with emotion. "We're buggered. You know those big munchety-crunchety noises? Well, those were our engines coming off. That's why we've nae power. Circuit breakers cut in. And I near got half a tree up my jaxy. I'm sitting down there looking down at dead air in six different places. Our status Captain? How about buggered, bolloxed, and utterly banjaxed?"

Everness creaked, dropped two meters, and came to a final rest. Brilliant rainbow birds clattered up from roosts. They weren't birds, Everett realized. Those bright colors weren't feathers.

"Where are we?" he said.

Captain Anastasia whirled. Her black face was dark with anger.

Her eyes shone hard. She flared her nostrils, chewed her lip, waiting for the anger to subside enough to be able to speak civilly.

"I thought you knew, Mr. Singh. I thought you knew everything."

Everett's face burned with shame. He felt tight, choked, sick in his stomach. Burning behind his eyes, in his head, in his ears. Shame, but anger too. This was not fair. It hadn't been his fault. He had calculated perfectly. Perfectly. He didn't make mistakes like that. He didn't make mistakes. There was something wrong with this world. That was the only explanation. He wanted to shout back at her that he didn't make mistakes, that she was as much to blame. He shook with anger. The words burned hot and hard in him. Captain Anastasia turned to the rest of her crew.

"Let's get her lashed down and back to airship-shape and Hackney-fashion again."

2

The crew harnessed up in the cargo hold. Captain Anastasia tugged Everett's harness, checked the fastenings and buckles. Everett couldn't meet her eyes. The damage was all around him. The skin had been pierced in half a dozen places; splintered branches like wooden spears. There was an entire top part of a tree in Mchynlyth's engineering bay, a giant Christmas tree rammed up through the hull. Except the leaves were red and smelled of something spicy, rich that Everett knew but could not place. He could see ground through the hole. It was a very long way down. *Everness's* nanocarbon skeleton was mighty, but it could not take such an impact unharmed. Struts had shattered. Cracked spars showered flaked layers of nanocarbon. An entire cross member had sheared through; it creaked ominously above Everett's head. The spine was intact. If the ship had broken her back, there would have been no option but to abandon her.

Everness had lost three of her six impellers in the impact. Engine struts had snapped; command lines and power cables were ripped through like severed nerves. The number two impeller had torn free, pylon and all, leaving a hideous wound in the ship's skin. *Everness's* mad descent through the treetops had strewn the engine pods across several kilometers of deep, alien forest. Captain Anastasia was mounting a search and recovery mission to the forest floor, three hundred meters below. The trees were taller, and his feet felt less firmly glued to this world than any Earth Everett had visited. Less gravity? How did that work? And then there was the sun. It wasn't moving right . . .

"Sen!" Captain Anastasia bellowed.

Sen's voice came from above. "Just getting some togs on."

She rode the drop line down from the spine walkway to the hold floor. That's an entrance, Everett thought. *Everness* had jumped from an Earth 1 Oxford winter to this Earth's tropical warmth and humidity, and everyone had dressed appropriately: Mchynlyth had peeled off the top of his orange coveralls and tied the arms round his waist. His singlet showed impressive abs and a lot of pink scars on his brown skin. Sharkey had ditched his coat for a sleeveless shirt. He wore his twin shotguns in holsters across the back of his white shirt. Captain Anastasia was lean and muscular in capri tights and a tank top. Everett remained smothered in winter layers. They covered up his guilt. He had no right to show his body, expose his skin to the sun.

Sen's warm-weather togs were as little as she could get away with. Grippy-sole ship boots, rugby socks, work gloves, gold short shorts, a boob tube, and a headband to keep her wild white afro under control.

"Go and put some clothes on!" Captain Anastasia bellowed. Sen sashayed past her adoptive mother with a defiant flick of her head. Mchynlyth was chewing his face from the inside out trying to keep the laughter in. As Sen strapped into her harness she flashed the briefest smile at Everett. It was sun on his face. It said, *I's all right, you's all right, omi friends forever.*

"So, we get these engines or what?"

Then Sen stepped off the edge of the loading bay, hit the lift control on her wrist, and vanished with a whoop into the deep red foliage below.

"Sen, we don't know . . ." Captain Anastasia roared. "Bloody girl." She leaped after her daughter. Mchynlyth, then Sharkey followed, winch reels screaming. Everett watched them drop down through the branches until he could no longer see them through the foliage. It would be all right. That was what Sen's little private smile to him had said. Everett stepped off the platform and felt the sudden tug as the winches took the strain.

Red leaves and a chaos of branches beneath him. Above him, the hulk of *Everness*. Everett let out a small cry of pain and shame. When he was a kid he had seen an old film of a whale hunted, killed, dragged onto a factory ship, and peeled of its blubber. He had cried himself to sleep and cried himself awake again. His mum had talked him through it, told him that it was old, old film, that no one did that kind of thing anymore. The great whales were safe. *Everness* was like that whale; a beautiful thing hauled out of its natural element, speared and harpooned and spiked, tied down, its skin ripped open. Hunted, helpless. Hideously wounded.

Everett knocked painfully into a branch. Look where you're going. He hadn't, that was the problem. Every Heisenberg jump was calculated guesswork. He made assumptions. But for some reason, there was a forest where there shouldn't have been. How? Why? He'd plotted a straight point-to-point jump, from one set of coordinates on Earth 1 to a set on the world where the Panopticon had recorded a jumpgun trace. Simple spherical geometry. Simple, for him. The only way it could have gone wrong was if the geometry of this world was different.

"No," Everett whispered, then he saw through the leaves beneath his feet the crew clustered around a massive, strange, cylindrical object wedged in the fork of a tree. Torn branches, splintered limbs: it took Everett a moment to identify what he was seeing—one of *Everness's* impeller pods, come to rest a hundred meters above the ground.

Leaves brushed his face, and now he knew the musky, rich perfume. Hash. Resin. The forest smelled like the mother of all sixteen-year-olds' parties.

"Tharbyloo!" came a voice from up among the branches. Moments later the forest rang to a splintering crack and a branch speared down through the dapple of deep red foliage, aimed straight at Sharkey's chest. At the last second he stepped to one side. The branch drove deep into the soft, fragrant forest leaf mould. Sharkey nonchalantly adjusted the trim of his hat.

Power tools shrieked, chainsaws screamed up in the canopy. Sawdust and woodchips fell on the anxious crew.

"I got her!"

Once the ground base had been set up, Sen had been sent up on a line with chainsaws, nanofilament cutting lines, pry bars, and a lube gun to free the number three impeller. Everett had questioned the wisdom, but Mchynlyth had quickly put him in his place. Sen was small, agile, and could get into tight places no adult could.

He wished she was down on the ground. The forest floor was sweltering and steamy but the atmosphere was frigid. Sharkey would not speak to him. Mchynlyth had let him know that it would be a long time—a very long time—before he forgave Everett for what he had done. Captain Anastasia gave off such an air of personal hurt that Everett could not bear even to look at her.

"Lowering!" Sen shouted, a voice among the leaves. Mchynlyth hit a button on his wrist control. The groaning creak was so loud Everett feared the whole tree was coming down on top of him, all three hundred meters of it. Then the rounded belly of the impeller pod pushed the leaves and smaller branches apart. Down it came in a web of lines. Sen rode it down like a bronco.

"Mah baby, mah baby!" Mchynlyth embraced the engine like a friend. "What have they done to ye?" Clever tools opened panels. Mchynlyth and Captain Anastasia were bent over the hatch. Everett ached with guilt.

"Is there something I can do . . ."

Mchynlyth and Captain Anastasia turned at the same time. The looks on their faces froze him solid. He died . . . there, then, in a clearing in an alien rainforest in a world that didn't make senses, in a parallel universe. Died in his heart. He stepped back.

He had never been hated before. It was an emotion as strong and pure as love, and as rare. It was the opposite of everything love felt, except the passion. He wanted to die.

"By your leave, ma'am, I've never had a skill for fixin'," Sharkey shouted. "'Better is a dinner of herbs where love is, than a stalled ox and hatred therewith,' as the word of the Dear teaches, but sometimes a man hankers after a chunk of stalled ox. I'm going to see what our neighborhood offers the aggressive carnivore."

"I'll . . ." Everett began, but Sharkey whirled away, whipped the shotguns out of the holsters he wore across his back, and stalked out of the clearing into the hooting, whistling, chirruping, singing, forest shadows.

"Sen . . ."

She had tied her hair back and pulled her goggles down. She was a steampunk funk queen and Everett's heart broke looking at her at work in the hatch, toothpick skinny, sweaty, grease-smudged, totally absorbed in repairing her ship, her home. Her family. He had never felt so alone, not even when he had hijacked Paul McCabe's Heisenberg Gate and sent himself to Earth 3. There he was an adventurer. Here he was a survivor. There he had a plan. Here all his plans were impaled upon tree branches. And everyone hated him.

Everett tried to think of the people who loved him, his friends, his family. He froze when he realized he couldn't see his mum's face anymore. He could see her hands, her clothes, her shoes, but not her face. He couldn't see Victory-Rose's face, or Bebe Ajeet's, or the faces of his many Punjabi aunts and uncles; he could hardly remember friends like Ryun and Colette. All that remained of her were pink Doc Martin boots and purple hair. He had only been away from them for a few weeks, but so many worlds and people and so much fear and excitement and strangeness had come between Everett and the people he loved, like screens of frosted glass that showed shapes and outlines but hid details. The only face he could see was that of his dad, in the final moment in the Tyrone Tower when Charlotte Villiers had turned the jumpgun on him. He saw that too clearly. It was as if the sharpness and brightness of that final glance washed out all the other faces.

He had never felt more alone.

He couldn't stop his tears. They were the simple and most natural and right thing to come, but he would die rather than let the people working on the engine see them. He turned and ran into the jungle.

The river stopped Everett. The trees ended abruptly and the bank gave way so suddenly and steeply that he went skidding down between boulders and exposed tree roots. He had let his body carry him without any conscious thought. Just running. Just hurdling branches and huge tree roots. He could have run on and on until he wouldn't have been able to find his way back. Here, at the river's edge, he could faintly hear the sound of Airish power tools and lifting tackle. There was a way back. There was always a way back.

Trees taller and grander than any on Earth soared above Everett. He could see the sky. A small fall of water between two boulders had hollowed out a pool. The water was deep and clear, cool and calling. Sun and water touched the hurt and guilt and loneliness. In a moment he was kicking off boots, wriggling out of ship-togs. He splashed into the pool, lolled back. Cool, deep water rose up over his chest. Everett took his feet off the bottom, kept himself upright with tiny movements of his hands and feet.

The water blessed him. He was alone, but not lonely. He had never been skinny dipping before. He loved the sensual feel of water touching every part of his body. I have swum like this before, he realized, before I was born, naked in the waters inside my mum.

It was a bit of a freaky thought.

Everett paddled round to where a ray of sunlight fell through a gap in the canopy of red leaves. Sun fell on his face. He closed his eyes. Opened them with a shock.

The sun.

There was something wrong with the sun. It was still full in his face. It shouldn't be. It should have moved across the sky. It hadn't.

It was lower, closer to the lower edge of the gap in the branches, but it was still full in his face. The sun didn't move on an arc from east to west. It was moving straight up and down.

His calculations. He had calculated for a jump from a spherical planet to another spherical planet. The geometry of the world . . .

"No way!" Everett shouted, surging straight up out of the water. Winged things burst upwards in panic from the trees. "No! This is insane." But the numbers were running in his head; numbers connecting with other numbers, with theories and physical laws, painting a picture of the world that fitted—that was the only explanation of the facts.

He had to get back to the crew. They would listen to him when he told them what he had worked out about this world. They had to listen to him. He waded to the river bank.

His clothes. Where were his clothes? He'd left them on a rock, neatly folded, weighted down with his boots in case the wind got up and blew something away.

Everett heard a noise. There, behind a root buttress. A rustle. A movement. A . . . giggle? Everett cupped his hands over his groin. Water streamed from him.

"Sen?"

It was a giggle.

"Sen! Have you got my togs?"

No answer. No movement.

"Stop playing around . . . There's something important you need to know. Mega."

"Come and get them!"

"Sen!"

She could wait all day for him to come out of the water.

"Okay then, since you think it's so funny . . ." Everett waded out of the river. He let go his covering hands. He heard a whoop from behind the tree root. Everett imagined himself from Sen's point of view. He looked okay. Better than okay; he looked pretty good.

"Remember when I dressed you at Bona Togs?" Sen shouted. "Well, I's going to dress you again." A hand draped two socks over the sloping root. "Come and get 'em!"

"I will," said Everett Singh. He heard a squealing shriek of delight and laughter, then a flurry of moving foliage. He pulled on the socks: heavy knit, thick rib top, like the ones Sen wore. He felt dumb in just socks.

"Come on!" Sen shouted from behind a brake of silvery cane. She waved his boots at him, one on each hand.

"Sen, this is important. The world . . . It's . . ."

"That scar's really healing up good," Sen called from deeper in the forest.

Everett had almost forgotten about the scar that had been scorched across his side at the Battle of Abney Park Cemetery by his alter's laser. Sen's careless comment knocked him back into the pain and humiliation. He had been badly beaten. He would wear the mark of his enemy for the rest of his life. Everett had unfinished business with alter-Everett.

Now Sen hung his ship shorts from a low branch.

"Sen! Don't mess around!" Everett shouted as he struggled to get his feet through the legs.

"You wear too many clothes!" Sen called from a new hiding place. "It's bad for you." She draped his T-shirt over a spiny shrub. She had cut the sleeves off and shortened it. It was not quite her crop-top level, but shorter than any Earth 10 omi would be seen in. Bare-chested, Everett strode to retrieve it.

Something splintered softly under his left boot, and his ankle went deep into something soft and wet and sticky. A scent of rot and sickness wafted up. Everett looked down. His left foot was embedded in the ribs of a mouldering human corpse. Empty eye sockets stared up at him from a skull clothed with rags of skin. Vile liquids and rotting organs leaked from the blackened, burst skin. Everett tried to extricate his foot. Decaying things glooped and sucked.

"Sen!" he yelled. "Sen!"

"Uh uh, Everett Singh, you come and get it."

"Sen!" His tone said *no jokes any more.*

She came running, hurdling lightly over roots and fallen branches.

"Everett, what is it? Oh, the Dear."

Everett had followed the trace truly and accurately. Someone had been banished to this world by the jumpgun.

Sen held two hands out to Everett.

"I's got you, omi. Walk towards me. Come on Everett Singh."

He took her hands and pulled his foot out of the dead thing. He could feel gross corpse stuff on his skin. He would never be able to get it clean again. But that was not the true horror. The horror, terrible, all-devouring fear was who that corpse might be.

"Sen, can you look at it? Is it?"

Sen understood at once.

"It's not him. Do you hear me? It's not him."

Everett shook with released tension. He thought he might throw up now, not from the vile rotting nausea of the corpse, but from relief at who the corpse was not. His dad. He heard Sen mumble something in Palari. He knew Palari pretty well, but Sen was speaking so low and fast, with so many dialect words, that he could not make her out.

"Sen, what is it?"

"He's dressed Airish style. I think I knows it. I think it's 'Appening Ed."

At first Everett could not place the name, then he remembered. Charlotte Villiers had led her Sharpies into Hackney Great Port to try and seize the Infundibulum by force. She had been met by a mob of roused, anarchic Airish who had no truck with police on their territory. They had been led by a short, angry man—'Appening Ed. Charlotte Villiers had pulled a gun and made him disappear. It had been the first time Everett had seen what a jumpgun could do. So this was where he had been sent. And something in this red rainforest had killed him. This red rainforest in this world where the sun didn't obey normal physics; the world didn't even obey proper, spherical geometry.

"Sen, I need to get back to the crew. There's something you need to know about this world. Something really important."

3

Charlotte Villiers drew on tight calfskin gloves as she surveyed London from the thirty-second-floor window of the Tyrone Tower. Snow crowned the angels that stood atop the Gothic skyscrapers. Snow draped cloaks and capes and stoles around the shoulders of the crouching lions and griffons and mythological beasts that gazed down from the tower tops onto the bustling streets. Snow sheeted from the hulls of the airships as they cast off from the great iron tower of Sadler's Wells skyport and turned onto their flight paths. Snow on train roofs made them winding snakes, slinking along their elevated lines. Snow piled in drifts and banks at the sides of the streets, far far below, burying bicycles and rubbish bins and electricity charge points that would not return until a thaw. Snow trodden to treacherous ice slicks on the walkways, citizens tripping and tottering in tiny, nervous steps, coat collars turned up and hats pulled down, breath steaming.

"I'm sick of winter. Could we not for once move the Praesidium somewhere warm?"

Charles Villiers, Charlotte Villiers's alter and Plenipotentiary from Earth 4, lifted a forefinger to Charlotte Villiers's cigarette in its ivory holder. A flame lit from his fingertip. Charlotte Villiers winced in distaste. Thryn technology, of course, but the Thryn would never have designed anything so crass. Restrained. Poised. Enigmatic. Charlotte Villiers admired the Thryn much more than the humans of Earth 4, her alter included. Earth 4 had glutted itself on Thryn technology so greedily that its people had not developed a technology or made a scientific discovery of their own in thirty years. They were addicts. Charlotte Villiers despised addiction. It was a vile weakness, whether alcohol, narcotics, sex, power, or alien technology.

"Earth 8 is pleasant in its northern hemisphere at this time of year, my cora."

"Earth 8 is an ecological wreck with runaway greenhouse effect," Charlotte Villiers snapped. "I do not suit favela chic." She pulled the fur stole tight around her neck, not because of the cold beyond the window but because of her alter's use of the word *cora*. Earth 5 had given the Plenitude the terms of familiarity and endearment between alters—a twin in a parallel universe, closer than siblings or lovers; you, but so very, deeply, completely not you. Hearing the word on her alter's lips made Charlotte Villiers shiver. She frequently wondered how Charles could be her alter at all. He was in no way her intellectual equal. And so childishly simple to manipulate. He was her *coro* in name only. Out of all her fellow Plenipotentiaries, she respected only the Earth 7 conjoint Jen-Heer-Fol and Ibrim Hoj Kerrim. The Earth 2 Plenipotentiary might not possess her sheer edge of cold intellect, but he was a consummate diplomat and politician in a world where those were so often contradictory qualities. She had almost betrayed her hand to him once, in the heat of action, when she had seen that Everett Singh intended to send himself through the Earth 10 Heisenberg Gate, and she had pulled a gun on him. She had talked her way out of the incident, but Ibrim Hoj Kerrim was wily, graceful, and completely incorruptible. It would require her very sharpest, cleanest, most deadly plan to neutralize him in the Praesidium. But she had no doubt that she would succeed. Her only equal, the only one to best her, time and again, was her enemy, Everett Singh. Her enemy, her prey. In the end, you will give me what I desire, with your own hand. Let us match my will to your wits, Everett Singh. Charlotte Villiers took a draw on her cigarette, breathed a coil of smoke into the air.

A knock at the door.

"Enter."

A bellboy in the high-collared, embroidered jacket of the Service Corps entered and clicked his heels respectfully.

"These are diplomatic boxes you want transported, Excellency?"

"They are, Lewis," Charlotte Villiers said.

"Shall I move them all or are there any you wish to take personally?"

"I trust you, Lewis. I will be carrying personal effects only."

"We will have everything prepared for you."

"Thank you, Lewis."

Every six months the Praesidium of the Plenitude of Known Worlds rotated to a new parallel Earth. The theory was that doing so would promote equality and democracy. Charlotte Villiers considered it a sop to political correctness. She would have been quite happy to have a permanent headquarters on Earth 2—the weather was good, the shopping excellent, the clothing and cuisine outstanding—or even Earth 5: those horses and carriages, and the elegant, well-proportioned architecture and fashion, were graceful and picturesque. The settling in was tedious and disruptive, even if she could commute home to Earth 3 by Heisenberg Gate. Charlotte Villiers had endured four moves since ascending to the Plenipotentiate and it still seemed that no sooner were all the files unzipped and shelved than it was time to zip them, box them, and ship them on again.

"I shall have to brush up my Anglische," she said. "It's such an ugly language. It sounds like retching."

"You want one of these, cora," Charles Villiers said. He opened his hand to show a thumb-nail-sized chip. "It comes with a special frame; you wear it like a pair of glasses. Beams the language into the back of your eye. Brilliant."

"Call me old fashioned, but I prefer not to have a language burned into my forebrain by some memory chip." The idea of someone else's voice, words, thoughts in her had filled her with disgust. Charlotte

Villiers's brain was guarded, untouchable, entirely her own. Dark secrets were locked within. "Anything from the tracker?" She had sent her agent, Everett Singh's Earth 4 alter, on a highly illegal Heisenberg jump to the forbidden plane of Earth 1 to plant a quantum tracking device on the airship *Everness*. He had been sent with one of the Thryn Sentiency's most powerful personal combat units. He had come back with nothing but a suit liner and a backpack.

Charles Villiers checked his mobile phone.

"No data yet."

"Are you sure it's working?" Charlotte Villiers asked.

"It's Thryn," her alter said. "It's infallible."

Charlotte Villiers raised an eyebrow. Earth 4ers were so trusting of their technology. Charlotte Villiers preferred working with people. Especially people she could manipulate or threaten. Scared people were trustworthy.

"Has he even planted the thing?" He could have ditched everything—Thryn battle suit, hedgehoppers, tracker—and run for home at the first sight of the Nahn. Charlotte Villiers knew enough of the nanotech plague that had engulfed Earth 1 to have doubts about her bravery in the face of the Nahn. Invading you, dissolving you, incorporating you, taking your body, your mind, smelting them into an alloy of all the others it had absorbed: the Nahn was the same horror as the Earth 2 language implants, a thousand times magnified. The Nahn was violation.

"He says he has," Charles Villiers said.

"There are liars, gross liars, and fourteen-year-old boys," Charlotte Villiers said. "But I still have his family. His real family."

O vernight the snow had melted into the endless wet grey of January. Everett M. Singh looked out at the procession of car headlights in the morning gloom as the Roding Road schoolrun began. Car exhaust steamed in the chill. He still didn't understand the logic of running a transport system on liquid-fuel/internal-combustion engines.

On the window sill the Nahn buzzed in its glass prison. Everett bent down to peer at the thing in the jar. Laura had almost caught him last night. He had stayed awake, the Nahn spider clutched tight in his hand, until all the lights went off and the noise of television and radio and teeth being cleaned came to an end. He had gone quietly downstairs. The new Thryn implants meant he could move quickly and quietly. Not quickly and quietly enough. Laura had come down-stairs, woken by the noise, to find Everett M two-thirds of the way through a jar of peanut butter.

"Everett, I know guys your age are always starving, but I mean, spooning it into you . . ."

Everett M had grinned sheepishly and tightened his grip on the Nahn spider in his left hand.

"You know, since you came back there's been no filling you. Did they give you a pair of hollow legs or something? And there's not a pick of weight on you. Put the light out when you're finished."

The peanut butter went some way towards filling the cold, gnawing hunger that never went away, but what Everett really wanted was the jar. He rinsed it out and before the Nahn spider could make a break for freedom, clapped his hand over the opening and shook the nano-device inside. In an instant the lid was on. That was the reason for the peanut butter. It was farmer's market organic Fairtrade crunchy peanut butter (it had been pretty good, by the spoonful) and it had a metal lid. Every other jar in the kitchen had a plastic lid. The Nahn would have been able to feed on that plastic, grow, and escape.

The Nahn spider was aware of him. It scuttled around the jar to turn what passed for a face to him. Sensor eyes the size of pinpoints opened up to analyze him. The spider thing scrabbled at the sides of the jar, but not even Nahn technology could get a grip on the smooth glass.

"I should have done this last night," Everett M said. With one thought, his right arm opened and unfolded an EM pulser. The electromagnetic pulse would fry every modem and wireless router and mobile phone on this side of Roding Road, but it would kill the Nahn stone dead. Kill dead something that was never properly alive. He would make this world safe. It wasn't his world, but he would be its hero. They would never know. Everyone on the planet would owe him, Everett M. Singh, and they would never know.

He shaped the thought that would send the pulse of energy from the Thryn power cells. And stopped. There were memories in his head. Hyde Park in the snow, with the shattered shapes of Nahn hellhounds and death-birds in a ring around him. Himself—his nanotech Earth 1 alter: how the oily black of the Nahn shifted into the brown of his own face. The eyes. They couldn't fake the eyes. The eyes of the Earth 1 alter were insect eyes, shimmering and multifaceted. Everett M almost cried out as he remembered the Nahn tentacles snaking out of the ground faster than he could blast them, tangling the legs of his Thryn battlesuit, wrapping him and binding him and smothering him a meter deep inside a mound of heaving Nahn stuff. He had come close, so close to something worse than death.

He remembered the deal he had offered to save his life and get out of the hell plane of Earth 1. Give the Nahn a way of escape, a way past the quarantine the Plenitude had put on that plane.

All the Nahn wanted to do was survive, like him.

"Did you put that thought there?" Everett whispered at the spider thing scrabbling the jar. He had carried the Nahn spore from Earth 1 to the Thryn citadel on the far side of the Moon and then to Earth 10, hidden inside his own body. Had part of it remained there? Was it already sending nanotech tendrils and feelers through his brain? "Are you still inside me?"

"Everett!" The shout and the sudden bang on the door made him jump. He knocked against the peanut butter jar. It fell towards the floor. Only Everett M's Nahn reflexes stopped it from shattering. "Going now. Not ten minutes, not five minutes, not one minute: now!"

Shaking, Everett M set the jar back on the shelf. Grey sleety rain fell beyond the window.

"Coming!" Everett M pulled on waterproof and his Tottenham Hotspur backpack. He turned to the spider in the jar and whispered, "I'll kill you later."

The gates to Abney Park Cemetery were still locked and draped with yellow warning tape. The official story was gangs of youths, cheap cider, and cheaper glue. It wouldn't stand up to even a moment's examination—the explosions, the clean cuts of lasers, whatever weapon that Earth 3 girl had been using, and the downed the tree branches. Sixteen-year-olds off their tits on white cider and glue just smashed things. But the local newspapers and radio were so short of staff they just repeated whatever press release the police fed them. Charlotte Villiers's cover story would never be questioned.

Everett M's shortcut through the cemetery was closed and the detour made him ten minutes late for school.

"Don't often see you getting one of these," said Mrs. Yadav, the school secretary in charge of the late slips. She swapped it for his note of absence. "Social Services?" She looked pityingly at Everett M.

No, I've been in a parallel universe battling nanotech horrors and my alter, Everett M thought. *And I have the end of your world in an empty peanut butter jar on my bedroom window sill.*

"It's just routine." Another part of Charlotte Villiers's deception.

"Social Services is never just routine," the secretary said. "Does Mrs. Packham know about this?"

"Yeah, she does," Everett M lied.

"I'll drop her an email," Mrs. Yadav said.

As he took books from his locker Everett M felt the metal door vibrate under his fingers, a dull buzzing. He stepped back. No, not the locker, all Bourne Green School was humming, as if the steel girders that held it up were vibrating like the strings of a guitar. Everett M dared to open up his Thryn sense for a moment. He listened deep; he opened his eyes to electrical and magnetic fields. Nothing. The hum, the vibration, was in his head. He knew what it was now: the buzz of the Nahn in its glass prison. Buzzing. Buzzing in the jar. Buzzing in his head. Buzzing in the corridors of Bourne Green. Buzzing in math class.

"Mr. Singh, are you with us or are you just visiting this planet?"

"Sorry, sir."

Buzzing at the Coke machine at break. Chesney Jennings and Karl Derbyshire came up on either side of him. In Everett M's world they had been second-rate bullies and enemies. Persecutors of the geek.

"Social services, then."

So, no different on this plane.

"So what is it, they take you away because your mum's a pedo or what?"

The buzzing became a deafening roar. Everett M felt energy channel into his lasers. Cold clutched him, the Thryn technology drawing on his own body's reserves. Against his will, the panels in his forearms were opening. It took every last drop of will to force them shut.

"Leave it," Everett M said.

"What if I don't want to?"

Everett M thought power into his right hand. He snatched Karl Derbyshire's unopened Coke can from his hand. He put his thumb underneath the bottom, his little finger on the lid. He squeezed. Seals popped, aluminium crumpled and split, soda exploded all over Derbyshire and Jennings. They jumped back. Their white school shirts were speckled with brown.

"You shouldn't have had a go at my mum," Everett M said. He dropped the flat disk of crushed metal into the trash.

By lunch the word was all around the school, by SMS, Facebook, Blackberry PIN, word of mouth. Even the cool kids, the ones who never seemed to do anything, but did that nothing in the most stylish way possible, looked at him. Just a look, for a moment, maybe a tilt of the chin, but acknowledgement.

"Did you do that with your bare hands?" Nilesh Virdi, a friend in both universes, asked.

"No, I'm an alien cyborg who's taken over Everett's body," Everett M said. "How do you think I did it?"

"Have you been buffing up?" Gothy Emma Queen of the Emo girls asked. Her lieutenant Noomi handed Everett a Coke can.

"Can you do it with diet?" she asked. She got out her phone. "This is so going up on YouTube. Like twenty million hits."

Everett M handed it back to her.

"I don't do tricks."

"We'll come and see you in goal!" Noomi shouted after him as he walked away.

If the word had reached all the school, it had reached Mrs. Packham. She popped her head into Mr. Boateng's English class.

"Everett, can I have a quick word? In my office."

Mrs. Packham's office smelled of windows and sandalwood. A jar of aromatic oil with little dip sticks lancing out of it sat on the window ledge. The room was painted a golden yellow, and the perfume and the light made it seem like a little warm haven in the dour grey winter outside. That was part of the plan, Everett calculated. As was the box of tissues on her desk.

"Did Mrs. Yadav tell you?" Everett M asked. This was the lesson he had learnt from the Battle of Abney Park Cemetery and the fight against the Nahn. Strike first.

"Before everything else, Bourne Green is a caring community," Mrs. Packham said. "We're a family. So it's natural for us to look after each other, to let each other know if something isn't exactly right. So if we hear that Social Services are involved, that involves us too. There are synergies here. Would you like a cup of tea, Everett?"

"I'd prefer coffee."

"I've only decaf."

"I'll leave it."

"You've been through a lot recently Everett, and we haven't really dealt with it, have we? First your dad going missing, and the police involvement—that's never a nice experience, Everett. And then, well, over Christmas when you went missing. You've never really talked about it. I know, I blame myself partly, and it did happen at a bad time . . ."

"When would have been a good time?" Everett said.

Mrs. Packham ignored the snark. Everett guessed she was in her mid-thirties though to him everyone over twenty-three looked the same. To mark herself as separate from the teaching staff she wore loose clothing in bright colors.

"That's all right, Everett. This is a safe place where you can talk about anything. No one will judge you."

"Really?"

"Really."

"Okay then. I am not really Everett Singh. I'm a cyborg double from a parallel universe. I'm a secret agent from a group of politicians from the Plenitude of Known Worlds. What happened in Abney

Park? That thing in the news? That was me. I could level this entire
school if I wanted."

Mrs. Packham stared at Everett M for the space of two slow
blinks.

"When I said anything I meant anything about how you feel. I
hear what you're saying, but how does that make you feel?"

"How do you think a cyborg double from a parallel universe
feels?"

Mrs. Packham's mouth twitched. She leafed through a plastic
folder.

"I heard about your stunt at break time. It's not just the physical aggression that's making me concerned; there's verbal aggression as well. What you just said to me, for example. I mean, do you
think that maybe what you said there, and you disappearing over
Christmas—how can I put this? You're the oldest in your family,
by quite a long way. Your sister, what is she, three, four? In a sense,
you're like the only child. And now you're the only man in the family.
You were very close to your father. I'd like you to explore the thought
that maybe you're looking for other ways to get the attention he used
to give you."

"I thought you said no one would judge me here."

"Now you're being defensive, Everett. And as well as the defen-
siveness, I've been hearing reports of inattention in class. That's not
you, Everett."

"Is everyone spying on me?" Everett M shouted.

"No one's spying on you, Everett. Why, do you think people
are?"

Careful, Everett M said to himself. *Make too much trouble, say too
much, or even too little, and she might send you to the doctor. And you can't
have doctors working all over you, outside and inside.*

"No, I don't. I don't . . . I just . . ." But he had to keep her sweet.
Then he knew what to do. And it was obvious and easy, and the words

came out straight and true. He talked about his dad, his real dad. His dad who had died in a bike accident on the way to work, suddenly and stupidly and without any hope of appeal or a second chance. He talked about anger. He remembered being angry that his dad had died without thinking of any of them, just leaving them with no idea and no plan for what to do. He talked about pleading. He remembered going over and over in his head all the tiny things he or his Mum or Vickie-Rose could have done to prevent his dad from being at that place on that bike at that moment when the Sainsbury truck turned left. He talked about abandonment. He remembered the realization that dead was forever, that his dad would never come back, never be there, never *be*. He talked about pretending. He remembered the exaggerated normality of life after Dad had died, everyone doing all the little everyday things in a big way so that there could be no moment, no crack in the busyness of everyday life, where the awfulness could well up like dark water under ice. He said and remembered all these feelings, but he made them about the other Everett's dad. He wasn't dead, but the feelings would be the same. And Everett M understood that other Everett Singh.

Then Mrs. Packham was glancing at her watch and saying, "I'm afraid we're out of time for today." When Everett M stood up he found he was breathing more deeply and easily than he had since the accident, and the air in his lungs tasted clean and pure. For the hour he had been in Mrs. Packham's room, he hadn't heard the buzzing of the Nahn. In the corridor it returned louder than ever.

Everett M knew what he had to do now.

"Everett!"

Everett M glanced over his shoulder. School out: school kids pressing towards the gates and the waiting for cars. Breath steaming. Loud chatter and ringtones. A face looking at him: the geek guy Ryun. The other Everett's friend. Everett M ought to stop, say something. Ryun's suspicions had been raised by the SMS message and

Everett M's obvious lie that he had lost his phone. The message had tipped Everett M off that the other Everett was on this world, which had led to the Battle of Abney Park Cemetery. The message, and the viral video everyone had passed round of the airship over White Hart Lane football stadium. Everett M had joked that it was obviously a commercial cargo airship from a parallel universe, but now he wondered if he'd been too clever: had Ryun guessed that the obvious lie was in fact the truth? How much did he know from the other Everett; how much did he suspect about Everett M? Get clever. Stay clever.

"We're going out," Everett M shouted back. "Catch you tomorrow!"

"I'll be on chat!" Ryun shouted back.

"Maybe!"

Everett M slid into the center of the crowd streaming out onto the street. He saw Jennings getting into a car. Fat bullies always get picked up by their mums. A moment's thought summoned a twitch of power through Everett M's EM pulsers. A targeted pulse shorted out the car's ignition system.

Get out and push, fat boy.

5

Everett M ran all the way down the Dog's Delight, along Yoakley Road and the detour via Stoke Newington Church Road around Abney Park Cemetery. He allowed himself a tiny flicker of Thryn augmentation, adding 20 percent to his running speed. Enough to get him home quick, but not so fast as to make him look like a superhero. Still, the runners in their winter-weight tights and thermal tops stared at the kid in the school uniform, sensible shoes, and Spurs backpack effortlessly overtaking them. By the time he got to Stoke Newington High Street he was freezing and ravenous but Everett M pressed on.

He banged through the back door and up the stairs to his room.

"Hi Everett hello how was your day, good and how was your day Mum?" Laura called from the kitchen.

The jar. The jar was not on the windowsill.

Everett M felt his brain turn to a pool of stupid, of *WTF?*

The jar was gone.

Something, he had to do something. Look for it, maybe it had been knocked to the floor and rolled under the bed. It's still in the room. It has to be in the room. Everett M looked under the bed. He looked in the waste basket. He looked in his drawers, along his shelves, pulled all the clothes out of his wardrobe, checked behind the desk and fittings, all the places an empty peanut butter jar could not have got to by itself, could not possibly fit.

The jar was *gone*.

Everett M's heart banged in his chest. The run home from school had not even stretched him, but now his breath was short and panting and panicky. Everywhere. He had looked everywhere. It wasn't in his room. It had to be somewhere else. Get yourself together. You can't let them see you like this. The Thryn had given him technolog-ical enhancements for everything except human emotion. Everett M fought down the fear. Breathe. Calm. Breathe.

He went downstairs. Laura crouched in the blue light of the open freezer door, frowning at the choice of frozen meals to microwave for dinner tonight. Victory-Rose was at the table, painting something in pinks and purples. The radio burbled DJ Simon Mayo on Drivetime. Laura was singing what she thought were the words for "Poker Face."

"We're not eating till six, but if you're starving there's a new loaf in and sandwich stuff in the fridge," Laura said, picking through the ready meals.

"There was a peanut butter jar . . ." Everett said.

"I replaced that. I know you're just having a growth spurt and all that—you put on two inches over Christmas, I'm going to have to get you a new school uniform—but, straight from the jar, Evvie. There's a lot of fat in that stuff. I'm worried about your cholesterol."

"The old one, the empty one."

"The jar?"

"In my bedroom. I was doing something with it. Did you take it?" Even as the question left his lips, he saw the answer. Victory-Rose lifted her paintbrush and swirled it in a jar of water, turning the con-tents mauve. A jar. Of water. An empty peanut butter jar.

"Mum . . . that jar, was there something in it?"

"Oh, like a spider or something. What were you keeping it for?"

All Everett M could see was Victory-Rose's paintbrush, rinsing in the water.

Look at me, Vee-Ar, Everett thought at her. *Let me see your eyes.* There was the terrible possibility that if Victory-Rose looked at him, he wouldn't see human eyes. He would see the black shiny spider eyes of Nahn invaders. The little girl kept her head down, tongue out in concentration, focusing on her painting. *Look at me,* Everett thought. He had to see. He had to know.

"What did you do with the spider?" Everett M fought to keep his voice normal. He could feel the blood beating behind his eyeballs. But he had to remain normal, he had to remain casual, he had to remain a fourteen-year-old kid.

"Oh, I threw it out into the garden," Laura said. "It's bad luck to kill a spider. It makes it rain. Which do you think, the rogan josh or the teriyaki?"

Everett M saw that Laura expected an answer from him.

"The teriyaki," he said. "Unless it's Grandma Ajeet's rogan josh. Hey, what are you painting Vee-Ar?" The little girl beamed and held up her pink and purple world. Her eyes. Her eyes were round, dark, brown Anglo-Punjabi eyes. Now Everett M thought his heart would burst from relief. Victory-Rose/Victoria-Rose, Laura Braiden/Laura Singh, there was no difference between them. They were his family now. He would fight to the last watt of energy in his body to keep them safe.

"No, it's Sainsbury's 'Taste the Difference,' from Jamie Oliver," his mum said.

The Nahn spider was out there, and every second, every polite word, it was gaining distance. Yet Everett M had to keep cover, though he felt sick, sick like everything inside him had rotted into slime.

"How long will it be?" he asked.

"I said there's bread and stuff for sandwiches if you're starving."

"Just want to do something before dinner."

Everett M dashed to his room and quickly pulled on anything that might make him look like one of the runners he had so effortlessly beaten on the way home from school.

"I'm going for a run," he announced in the kitchen. Even Victory-Rose stopped daubing fluorescent pink seagulls on the paper sky at that.

"You're going for a run?" his Mum asked.

"I've got a game tomorrow. I need to get ready for it. And you said I was eating the house out, and like, I have to burn up all that food somehow. Run."

"You're going for a run."

"People do. Like me."

"Oh," Laura said, drawing the word out long. "It's for someone, isn't it? There's someone, isn't there? You're buffing up for her. That is so sweet, Everett."

"Mum!" But Laura's guess was a perfect cover story, so Everett M worked the lie. "I have a game tomorrow. Really."

"You know, that really is kind of romantic. Buffing up for a girl. Are you going to run past her house? That's a cute beanie."

"Mum. I'm gone. The teriyaki. A lot of it."

And he was gone. The cold hit him deep. Everett's energy levels were still low and he was ravenous. He should have had one of Laura's sandwiches, a dozen of them, because he knew he would need power, but the image of the Nahn spider hurrying hurrying on too many legs through the frosty grass was like barbed wire in his brain. He knew what the buzzing in his head was now. When he had been trapped in the Madam Moon battle suit, when he thought he was going to die the worst death he could imagine, his Nahn alter had said that it would take several months for the Nahn to learn Thryn technology and assimilate it. And on the inside of the suit, Madam Moon had whispered that she was analyzing and assimilating Nahn nanotechnology. The buzzing was the sound of his own implanted Thryn augments responding to the presence of the Nahn. He had his own inbuilt Nahn radar. Everett M turned on to Roding Road and into a slow run and opened up his augmented hearing. His ears opened into the electronic, the electromagnetic. Radio and cell-phone signals deafened him. A hundred satellite channels poured into his head. One by one Everett M screened them out. Next came the chatty buzz of wifi networks, the shoutiness of Bluetooth, the minicab channels and Tesco home-delivery network. A pirate dubstep station was broadcasting on the edge of an emergency services frequency. Television and radio, and high above, like night birds, the voices of aircraft around London's airports. The world was a cacophony of silent voices that passed through everyone except those who needed to hear them. Everett M heard them all, every single one, and one by one he tuned them out until he found what he was listening for, the small mosquito buzz of the Nahn.

Everett M followed the Nahn buzz down Roding Road, onto Northwold Road. For a moment it was lost in the music of car radios and mobile phone chitchat. Jogging up and down, breathing out great clouds of steam, Everett banged his gloved hands together for warmth and skipped over the treacherous extending dog leads of the dog-walking-service woman. So, she was a feature in this universe as well as his own. There. Faint, but once he picked it out, there was no mistake. The Nahn thing had dodged the drive-time traffic along Northwold Road and crossed into Stoke Newington Common. The park was a triangle of darkness among the street lights. People, cars, homes, shops were less than twenty meters away but Everett M felt alone and isolated. Movement. Snuffling around the back of a park bench. Everett M flicked up his night vision. Dog: a bull terrier cross, the kind you could buy for two hundred pounds from the Guinness Trust flats to make you look hard, was rooting around among discarded fast-food boxes. A bull-cross. On its own. It was trailing a leash.

Where was the owner?

The dog looked up from its rummaging. It looked Everett M straight in the eye. Everett M looked the dog straight in the eye. What he saw there was not big, sad, soft dog eyes, but the hard black speckle of insect eyes. The dog growled. Everett M thought power down his right arm. His palm opened. Metal and clean white Thryn nanoplastic unfolded like a cyborg flower. The dog gave a yelp and fled. In a thought, Everett M was after it. The dog could go through shrubs and railings, but Everett M was faster. The dog burst from Stoke Newington Common and raced up Rectory Road. It zigzagged through the nose-to-tail traffic on Stoke Newington High Street.

Everett M had encountered the traffic on Stoke Newington High Street before. It had been painful. He still carried its scars.

"Not this time," Everett M hissed through his teeth. He opened both EM pulsers and with a burst of power repeated the trick he had played on Fat Jennings's car. Every engine on the street went dead. Everett M threaded himself through the stationary traffic to see the dog slip through the railings into Abney Park Cemetery. "Okay then," Everett M said. "If that's what you want. Battle of Abney Park, round two."

Forty cars were stranded on Stoke Newington High Street but the drivers were too busy shouting and phoning people and banging horns that didn't work and looking under hoods and standing in the cold asking each other *what what what happened here?* to notice the teenager in the running gear point a finger to unleash a brief, brilliant spike of laser light that cut through the chain locking the gates together.

And in.

The cold and dark closed around Everett M like a fist. His night vision showed him the destruction he had caused when he had fought his alter here. Stone angels reduced to headless, wingless bodies; cherubs blasted to pairs of legs. Tombstones and Victorian memorial pillars lay in shattered chunks. Tree branches littered the ground. A dumpster stood half full of shattered wood and stone, as if the contractors had given up in despair at the size of the job.

Everett M wasn't proud of any of it.

He tuned his Thryn sense to listen for any traces of Nahn activity. A trace, fainter than a fly's heartbeat, but enough for Everett M to follow.

"I can see you," he said. The trace led him off the main path into the winter-killed brambles and dead bracken. It wove between tombstones and tree trunks choked with ivy to a circle of Victorian grave markers—pillars, cherubs, ornate stone scrolls, weeping angels. The dog lay on its side in the center of the circle. Everett opened the pulsers in the palm of his hands and went cautiously up to the dog. It was not breathing. He poked it with the toe of his running shoe. The dog's body collapsed in on itself. It was an empty shell, sucked dry of life.

"Okay," Everett M said, looking around him. He listened for Nahn activity. No contact, no clear trace leading from the dead dog deeper into the graveyard. But there was something, a vague hum, a hiss of activity with no direction and no center. Everett M closed his eyes and concentrated. Beneath him. In the ground. He stood above a circle of Nahn activity.

Everett M's eyes flew open at the first earth tremor. Water drops fell from the branches. Again, the ground beneath his feet shook. The Nahn noise was a roar now, and in motion, moving upwards through the soil towards him. A tombstone lurched and cracked. Trees shook. Movement. Everett whirled. The grass in front of the grave stone bulged upwards, as if something was punching up from beneath. A hand thrust up through the grass. Stunned, Everett M watched the long-dead hand reach into the night air. Writhing black fibres wound around the wrist, bound the bony digits in shiny black sinews. With a titanic heave, the skeleton wrenched itself out of the grave. Nahn muscles wrapped around the old rotten Victorian bones. The skull, still wearing a few wisps of hair, turned to Everett M, its empty eye sockets filling with the black orbs of insect eyes.

"You have to be joking," Everett M said. The earth shook again, hard enough for him to lose his footing. As Everett M went down, the Nahn skeleton lunged at him. Goalkeeper reactions rolled Everett M out of the way as he opened his right arm and extruded the laser. He was dangerously cold and hungry, but he needed every weapon Madam Moon had installed in him. The laser sliced the skeleton's head from its body. Black Nahn tendrils writhed from severed neck bones. The headless skeleton kept coming. He took its legs from under it. It crawled towards him, dragging itself along on bone fingers. "Oh come *on*." Laser in the right hand, pulser in the left. One EM blast froze the Nahn stuff infesting the skeleton and shattered it like black ice.

Now Everett understood the earth tremors. All around the circle of tombstones, the graves had burst open. The dead leapt out, their bones strung with Nahn muscle. They were fast and strong. Everett ducked under outstretched bone hands, rolled and slashed a Nahn corpse in half, top to bottom. The two halves of the body twitched, sending Nahn tendrils out towards each other. He em-pulsed it to nothing even as a zombie still dressed in the rags of a Victorian mourning dress spat black Nahn stuff from its bone jaws. He beheaded it with one laser blast, counted the seconds until his pulser recharged. Come on, come on, *come on!* And fire. You're proper dead now. Everett M spun. A scythe of laser fire toppled Nahn zombies like wheat stalks. He hacked them to bits and, as they squirmed and crawled towards him, took then out blast by blast.

All was still. All was quiet. Everett M opened up his augmented senses. No Nahn hum. Job done. Zombie invasion taken out quick and neat and early. He stepped over the ring of shattered bone and rotting Nahn stuff. That would be fun for the park keepers in the morning. And something shot up out of the mash of dirty bones, opened its dead jaws in his face, reached for him with claw hands. A baby—the skeleton of a dead baby, animated by the Nahn. Everett leaped back in shock, then his augmentations took over. The em-pulse caught it mid-air, froze all its Nahn stuff to black ice. It fell to the ground. The black ice shattered like glass under Everett M's running shoes. One final scan. Nothing. Planet made safe, and all before dinner.

"It's teriyaki time."

6

Her alter following two steps behind her, Charlotte Villiers stepped out of the Heisenberg Gate, heels ringing on the metal ramp. The Earth 7 hosts waited at the foot of the ramp; identical smiles, identical handshakes.

"Welcome, Fro Villiers," said Jen Heer to Charlotte Villiers. He was a stout, middle-aged white man, greying early, wearing creased pants and a frock coat over an elaborate brocade shirt.

"Welcome, Her Villiers," said Heer Fol simultaneously to Charles Villiers. Heer Fol was physically indistinguishable from his counterpart and was dressed in identical clothes.

Charlotte Villiers knew the Earth 7 etiquette—only acknowledge, shake hands, speak with the person speaking with you; if your language had a plural form of "you," like French or German or Spanish, use the singular form; don't be surprised if the other person completes what the first one begins to say; forgive them their moments of unspoken communication. It is twin telepathy.

Jen Heer and Heer Fol were identical twins. Every operative in the Earth 7 jump room was an identical twin. Every person on Earth 7 was an identical twin. More than identical twins; closer even than clones. They were one mind in two bodies. What one felt, the other felt; what one saw, the other remembered; what one thought, the other heard. They could communicate mind to mind, instantly, silently, completely, no matter how far apart they were. Researchers on many worlds had studied Earth 7's twins intensely, and their best theory was that they were quantum entanglement on the everyday scale.

Entanglement was one of the most beautiful mysteries of

quantum theory to Charlotte Villiers. Take two particles and, using a laser, place them in the same quantum state. They become entangled, connected to each other. In some ways, they are like one particle in two places. No matter how far you separate the entangled particles, in distance or in time, any effect on one will be mirrored immediately in the other, whether a wavelength of light distant or the width of the observable universe. Everything is connected. That truth filled Charlotte Villiers with a sense of wholeness and peace.

Quantum entanglement was routine on the scale of atoms, not so common on the scales that register to the human senses. That ghastly little man from Earth 10, Paul McCabe, had told her his team had succeeded in quantum entangling two bacteria. He had presumably thought she would be impressed by such an achievement. He had yet to meet the Earth 7ers, who achieved quantum entanglement on the scale of brains, and no one knew how it worked, except that it seemed to be a natural phenomenon.

Whatever the explanation, Earth 7 twins—they disliked that term, Charlotte Villiers remembered—made superlative diplomats, reporters, investigators, secret agents, and spies, with an undetectable line of communication across universes. Their only weakness seemed to be that they grew increasingly cranky, bad tempered, and depressed the longer they were apart.

And there with the Jen Heer Fol twins—him, Charlotte Villiers reminded herself (they liked to be referred to as one person in two bodies)—was that same ghastly little man, skulking in that scruffy private detective's raincoat. Behind him was the Harte woman. Atrocious hair color, quite inappropriate for a cross-planes diplomat; but in every other way she was much more capable than her university boss. She couldn't be trusted. Charlotte Villiers would never forgive her the blow that had struck away the gun she'd aimed at Everett Singh, which had allowed him to escape to Earth 3 and thence to the entire Panoply of All Worlds. But Charlotte Villiers would study her closely. The Plenipotentiary practiced the old maxim of keeping your friends close but your enemies closer. The sooner the arrangement with Earth 10 was taken out of the hands of bumbling scientists and put on a proper diplomatic basis the better.

"Charlotte!" Paul McCabe's handshake was like a dead fish.

"Miss Harte." Charlotte Villiers nodded to Colette Harte.

"This is an extraordinary world," Paul McCabe said, not at all discouraged by Charlotte Villiers's snub. "Extraordinary!"

"Yes, some worlds are more ordinary than others. How do you find Heiden, Colette?"

"It's very beautiful."

You answer carefully, Charlotte Villiers thought. *I do not trust you, but you trust me even less.*

Heiden's beauty, like everything else on Earth 7, was twofold. The first beauty was its location: it stood at where three rivers joined. On Earth 3, these would have been the Thames, the Seine, and the Rhine. On Earth 3, those rivers ran into the English Channel and the North Sea. On Earth 7, the English Channel and the North Sea were gently rolling chalk downland cut by the wide and wandering rivers. Britain was not an island, but a peninsula on the western edge of Europe. Where the three rivers joined, Heiden stood on a cluster of islands amid rivers and canals. It was a city of bridges and embankments, gracious squares lined with steep-pitched roofs; church steeples hung with the city's famous thousand bells; narrow, twisting streets loud with the hum of electric moped cabs and the horns of tandem bicycles. It thrummed to the rhythm of barge engines echoing under the elegant bridges and the swish of taxi boats slicing through the three rivers' calm waters.

"Heiden is the culinary capital of the Plenitude," Charlotte Villiers said. "I have a favorite restaurant on Loudengat in the Vereel Quarter. Bijou and charming."

"I was at a place in Raandplass last night," Paul McCabe said.

"Good, but the portions were enormous."

"They find the concept of cooking for one person disturbing," Charlotte Villiers said.

Brilliant light illuminated the jump room: a Heisenberg Gate opening. Ibrim Hoj Kerrim descended from the gate. One step had taken him from the strange England-off-the-coast-of Morocco to this England-not-an-island-at-all. His brocade coat was immaculate, his turban pinned with a silver plume, his beard precisely trimmed, and his nails perfectly manicured. He greeted his fellow Plenipotentiaries from the Plenitude and from Earth 10, which was now an accession candidate.

"Good, we are all here . . ." Jen Heer began.

"I will show you the Plenipotentiary suites," Heer Fol finished.

Earth 7's Praesidium buildings occupied the whole of one of the many small islands that lay at the confluence of the three rivers. The building had been a monastery—Heiden's strange, two-headed saints and angels looked down from pillars and paintings as the Jeen Heer Fol twin led the Plenipotentiaries through shaded courtyards and under baroque domes.

Charlotte Villiers fell into step beside Ibrim Hoj Kerrim.

"I hear you're thinking of standing for the Primarchy," she said.

"Direct as ever, Ms. Villiers."

"I consider it a virtue," Charlotte Villiers said. "The Plenitude of Known Worlds would be graced with you as its head."

"You flatter me."

"I understood that Al Buraqis value flattery."

"We like it to be genuine, Ms. Villiers."

"Surely if it's genuine then it's not flattery?"

"Exactly so, Ms. Villiers."

"I just want to reassure you that you have my unqualified support, Ibrim," Charlotte Villiers said. Earth 7 workers scurried in pairs with trolleys and electric carts, shifting the daunting piles of equipment and documents that accompanied a move of the Praesidium and all its many offices and ministries.

"And your Order?"

"We are only concerned with the security of the Plenitude."

"Yes, I've seen your concern, Ms. Villiers. It cost me forty spahis. Forty men were sent through that gate, and nothing ever came back, not even a rumor. They had families, wives, lovers . . . No, I've seen what you're trying to do on Earth 10. I've seen your Order at work. I do not require its support."

"That's direct, Ibrim."

"But not flattering, Ms. Villiers."

Charlotte Villiers and Ibrim Hoj Kerrim paused a moment on a covered stone bridge over a canal to allow a group of Plenitude staffers to pass.

"You may not need us as supporters, Ibrim, but you certainly don't want us as enemies," Charlotte Villiers whispered.

"What are you saying, Ms. Villiers?"

Jen Heer Fol and the rest of the Earth 10 Plenipotentiaries were waiting at the end of the bridge.

"There is damaging information we can keep to ourselves, Ibrim," Charlotte Villiers said.

"This is blackmail."

"It is."

"What do you want?"

"You don't want to join the Order, that's fine. But don't interfere with my—our—work."

"Are you all right, Fro Villiers . . ." Jen Heer began.

"Her Kerrim?" Heer Fol finished.

"Just catching up," Charlotte Villiers said with a smile. The party moved on through the labyrinth of the Praesidium Palace.

Jen Heer Fol stopped abruptly at a pair of vast, ornate doors.

"We will be using. . ." Jen Heer began, swinging open one half of the doors ". . . the Ambersaal," Heer Fol concluded, opening the other door.

The room beyond took away even Charlotte Villiers's breath. Every centimeter of wall was covered in amber. Decorative panels showed the miracles of angels inlaid in amber, from palest yellow to dark brown. January light pouring through window panels of translucent amber was turned to gold. Everything was golden. It was like drowning in honey.

"Exquisite!" Charlotte Villiers said. As the other Plenipotentiaries gazed up in amazement at the delicate tracery of the roof vaults, all carved from paper-thin sheets of amber, Charlotte Villiers slipped in alongside her alter. "He's not with us," she whispered. "But he's not against us."

7

"Flat?" Captain Anastasia said.

"We're on the surface of a disk," Everett said. "Either the upper or lower; I'd need to see the stars. To be honest it doesn't really matter."

Mchynlyth left off fastening the lifting cables to the impeller pod. The engine had been lowered from the tree fork to the forest floor. He looked stern disbelief at Everett and took a rotor disk from his pocket. He put his finger through the hole at the center.

"You're telling me that my wee finger is the sun?"

"Well, the hole would be a lot bigger, and the sun would be a lot smaller, but yes, that's what I'm saying," Everett said. "We're on an Alderson Disk."

"Explain please, Mr. Singh," Captain Anastasia said. "Slowly and clearly, if you please."

Everett read the faces around the impeller pod. Sen tried to look interested to please Everett. Mchynlyth was surly and disbelieving: everything Everett said was a challenge to him. Sharkey was still out hunting. But Captain Anastasia's face asked the most from Everett: will this help or hurt my ship and my family?

"An Alderson Disk is a mega-structure," Everett said. "It's a solid disk of material that surrounds the sun, I'd guess from inside the orbit of Venus to just beyond the orbit of Mars. Or it would if those planets existed in this universe. Say ninety million miles from inside to outside, and an outer circumference of half a billion miles. That's a lot of surface area."

"And I'll just bet you've worked it all out," Mchynlyth said.

Snark if you like, but you're paying attention to me now, Everett thought.

"I've done some mental arithmetic," said Everett. "It's about a billion Earths. Both sides are habitable, you see. An Alderson Disk could support a population of one thousand trillion people. With a thickness of two thousand miles, it would give about two-thirds Earth-normal gravity—you might have noticed that you don't feel quite as firmly connected to the ground as usual."

"But the sun's at the center, right?" Captain Anastasia said. "So how would you get night and day? The world turns—our world, I mean—to and away from the sun. But if the sun's always at the center . . ."

"You move the sun," Everett said. This was the insight that had come to him in the pool in the river. This world must be this way because it was the only way it could fit what he had observed. The words, the ideas sounded insane, but the numbers said there could be no other way. They had crash landed on a massive artificial disk, like a giant DVD, that surrounded its sun. And the sun was moving. "It's actually easier to move the star than it is to move the disk. In fact, the sun's how I worked it all out. I saw that the shadows were getting longer but the sun wasn't moving across the sky. The sun was setting, but it was vertical. Straight up and down. And the only way you can get that is if the sun is moving. The math's quite straightforward; it's a form of simple harmonic motion, like a pendulum. The sun bobs up and down. The mass of the disk . . ."

"I think our minds are sufficiently boggled, Mr. Singh." Captain Anastasia said.

"So a day here is about thirty hours. And once you know that we're on a disk with the sun at the center, you start to notice other things, too. The trees, the branches, all lean in the same direction. All the leaves are tilted at the same angle. And I know why we crashed, too. It's because we went from a rotating sphere to a stationary flat disk . . ."

"Is there any way this . . . Alderson Disk . . . could be a natural phenomenon?" Captain Anastasia interrupted.

"No way," Everett said.

"I was afraid you'd say that. How would you go about building something like this?"

"It would take a technology millions of years in advance of us. Maybe tens of millions of years."

"Well, then they should be able to give us a wee helping hand with our terribly old-fashioned totally bolloxed airship," Mchynlyth said.

"Tens of millions of years," Captain Anastasia said. "So: not us. Not . . . humans."

"No. Humans haven't been round long enough," Everett said.

"People—things—that can build something like this," Captain Anastasia said, "do we really want to meet them?"

A shout from the edge of the clearing: "Scarper! Get on your lally-tappers and scarper!" Sharkey burst from the trees. His guns were slung in their holsters on his back. Draped around his chest was a dead creature, the quarry of his hunt. Everett only got a glimpse of it because Sharkey was running for his life: long, lithe, lizard-like, rainbow colored, small eyes and sharp claws. Behind him, flowing and leaping and bounding over roots and logs and branches, came a living tsunami of creatures that looked just like the one he wore around his neck. Very, very alive. Very, very angry.

"Drop lines!" Captain Anastasia shouted. "Quick's the word, sharp's the action!" Sen and Mchynlyth buckled and in an instant were up into the branches. Everett fumbled with the harness.

"Mr. Sharkey!" Captain Anastasia bellowed. Both she and Everett could see on his face that Sharkey knew he would never make it. Get to the empty harness, buckle in: impossible.

"Sharkey!" Everett yelled. He extended a hand. Sharkey grabbed his hand, hauled himself forwards, and seized fistfuls of Everett's harness. The forest erupted in a stampede of hurtling bodies, long necks, darting heads, iridescent rainbow skins, raking clawed feet. Then Everett hit the button. High above the winch screamed then jerked him and Sharkey into the air. Captain Anastasia was a split second behind him. Lizard things leaped and snapped at Sharkey's heels, then the drop line took them up out of range. The herd broke over the impromptu camp, snapping and surging over the impeller.

"Mah engine!" Mchynlyth shouted from high above. Captain Anastasia tapped her wrist control. Lizard things slid from the pod's slick skin and fell into the swarm of surging bodies as the winches bit and hauled the impeller into the air.

Sharkey clung for life to Everett's harness. They spun slowly as the winch lifted them higher. Their faces were centimeters apart.

"Indebted, Mr. Singh," Sharkey said. Everett grimaced at the dead creature, pressed up close against his body. The animal was the length of Everett's arm, four-legged, long-tailed, with yellow reptile eyes with a vertical slit of a pupil. Lithe as a weasel. Ears were tiny holes far back on the long, curved skull. Pointed teeth were bared. The front paws had five digits, and the pale skin was as smooth and creased as a baby's hand. The fingers were long. The skin was smooth, but arcs of rainbow color, like oil on water, ran across it. Peering close, Everett saw that the smoothness was an illusion. The creature was covered in scales; smaller and smoother even that snakeskin. The spectrum colors came from the play of light along the edges of the scales. There was something in that skin that made Everett not want to touch it, and a shadow in its open eye Everett did not like, something too knowing.

"What is that thing?" he asked.

"Supper," Sharkey said. "'For I was an hungred, and ye gave me meat.'"

"Nae offence," Mchynlyth said, "but I'll take the vegetarian option."

He passed the dish to Captain Anastasia. The crew sat elbow to elbow around the small table in the cramped galley. The smell of onions, garlic, cumin, chilli and curry leaves, and coconut milk could not quite mask the smell of the meat. Captain Anastasia looked into the bowl and passed it to Sen. Sen gagged back a little sick in the back of her throat. Everett passed it straight to Sharkey. Sharkey had skinned, gutted, and cleaned the creature, taken off its head and tail, but left it to Everett to turn it into dinner. Everett had barely been able to touch the flesh. It's thin bones cracked and splintered under his knife. He scooped the meat into the onions and frying masala paste, poured on coconut milk, and clapped the lid on. Even after an hour it was still rubbery when he prodded it with a fork.

Every eye was on Sharkey. He spooned out a large serving and took a mouthful. He chewed. He chewed for a long time.

"Bona manjarry. Nothing wrong with it. Kinda textured. Tastes like alligator."

"Is that naan?" Mchynlyth said. "Gie us a whack of that."

Everett passed the bread, still hot from the oven.

"I stuck it on a stick and held it over the hotplate to puff it up," Everett said.

"My gran used to do that with the coal fire," said Mchynlyth. "Just a wee show of the heat. Bugger all tandoori ovens in Govan. I'd take some of your dhal, Mr. Singh.

Everett passed the bowl of lentil curry. He was being forgiven. Not fully, not immediately, but the process had begun. They were all together on a wrecked ship on a world more alien than they could possibly imagine, with death and danger beneath their feet. They were family.

"My Bebe gave me her halva recipe," Everett said. "Any special occasion, she'd make halva."

"Oh aye, it was the same when I was a wain," Mchynlyth answered, "Holi, Christmas, good exam grades, dog has puppies, third cousin twice removed gets engaged; lash round the halva. Hers was different from yours; she made it from baisen flour so it was more like fudge, and it was green, and it had this kind of herb taste. It was only after she died I found out she made it with bhang—that's cannabis to you goras. No wonder all those wee-uns were rolling around grinning, they were off their tits."

"I didn't know your family were from Govan," Captain Anastasia said.

"Aye well, there's things I tell you and things you never ask about," Mchynlyth said. "I must have been the only desi boy in Govan couldn't cook. Always a matter of some regret."

Everett thought, *I could teach you*, but he did not say it. Mchynlyth had his own world of engines and electrics, and there he was master. He would not go back to being an apprentice in another world.

"Mr. Mchynlyth, I notice you have your shush bag with you," Captain Anastasia said. "Any chance of a bijou tune?"

Mchynlyth opened the elaborate brass clasps of the cracked leather case and took out a set of bagpipes. The galley was too small to deploy all the pipes so he stepped onto the catwalk, blew up the bag, and adjusted the drones comfortably against his shoulder. Then he blasted into "Scotland the Brave" at a volume that rattled plates in their racks and cups on their hooks. Mchynlyth followed with "The Bonnie Banks of Loch Lomond" and "The Tangle of the Isles." Captain Anastasia thumped her fist on the table in time to the music.

"Tune, sir, tune!" she said.

"I used to pipe the Master and Commander of the *Royal Oak* in to formal dinners," Mchynlyth said to Everett. "And none o' them Och Aye the Noo music hall tunes: proper pipe music. Pibrochs and everything."

"Thank you, Mr. Mchynlyth," Captain Anastasia said. "Sen, the floor is yours."

Sen leaned over the table to Everett.

"Is you watching closely?" she asked. She held the fingers of her right hand in front of Everett's face and snapped them. An Everness tarot card appeared in them: a man in a striped circus costume on a unicycle, juggling planets. Sen held up a finger on her left hand. When Everett looked back the card had vanished from her right hand.

"You'll bring it back," he said. "It's only half the trick, making it disappear. The clever bit is bringing it back again. The prestige. I saw the movie. See? I's watching closely."

Sen snapped her right hand. She produced not the card, but Everett's iPhone.

"Not closely enough, Everett Singh." The rest of the crew applauded. Sharkey looked pale and in pain. "But you're right. It has to come back again. Look in your pocket."

Everett grinned—properly fooled—and from the pocket of his ship shorts produced the card. Everyone applauded. Sen curtseyed. "That's for the Hackney train," she whispered to Everett as she went back to her seat. "If I'd really wanted, I would have had your dilly comptator and you would never have known. Prestige *that*."

"Mr. Singh?" Captain Anastasia said. "The floor is yours. Entertain us."

Everett got to his feet. From the moment Mchynlyth picked up his bagpipes he had been dreading this moment. He could make the funniest joke sound like a term report, make people peep through their fingers if he danced, could clear a room if he sang. But Captain Anastasia's stern expression said that *Everness* expected every omi and polone to zhoosh up and let the bona temps roll. It was part of the forgiving. Captain Anastasia had orchestrated this whole dinner and these party pieces to bring everyone together, knit them back into a unified crew. Disunity could kill. But what to do? Apart from cooking, there was one thing, two things he was good at. And he had an idea.

Everett swapped places in the corridor with Mchynlyth. He stripped off the T-shirt Sen had mutilated. He tied it into a soft, firm ball, like the ones he had seen kids play with in his father's village in India.

"Okay," he said. "Count with me." And he flipped the T-shirt ball into the air, caught it on his knee, bounced it into the air again, flipped it up with his foot, catch flip catch flip catch flip. Ten eleven twelve thirteen. Keepie-uppie. Twenty-three twenty-four twenty-five. "Now someone ask me to multiply two numbers. Big numbers."

"Twenty-four and fifty-three!" Sen shouted.

"Big numbers. Like, three thousand two hundred and twenty-seven." He caught the ball on the right side of his head, flipped it over to the left.

"Five thousand and three!" Sen said.

"Sixteen million, one hundred and fourteen thousand, six hundred and eighty-one," Everett said, without ever taking his eye of the ball or dropping it.

"You just made that up," Sen accused.

"No, that's the right answer," Everett said.

He flipped the ball onto the back of his neck, caught it there, dropped it into his hand. Mchynlyth was writing furiously in a small notebook.

"Just a wee minute . . . Aye. He's right."

"How did you do it?" Sen asked.

"There's tricks to it," Everett said. "Like rounding things and rounding things down. Five thousand is a lot easier to multiply by than five thousand and three . . . then I just add three times the first number at the end. And three thousand two hundred and seven is just over three thousand two hundred and five. Fives are easy to multiply. Lots of tricks, but mostly I'm just good with numbers."

"Impressed, Mr. Singh," Captain Anastasia said. "Mr. Sharkey, a rebel tune, if you will. Rouse us—all that carbohydrate has made us lethargic."

Sharkey got to his feet. His eyes bulged. His face went grey. He reached for the edge of the table to steady himself. He swallowed hard, trying not to throw up. His face contorted. He bent double, stabbed by stomach pain.

"Permission . . . to be . . . excused, ma'am," he said and ran out of the galley.

"Mr. Mchynlyth, maybe one of those pibrochs now," Captain Anastasia said. "And play it loud."

Mchynlyth played loud indeed, but not loud enough to mask the groans and retching and other more liquid noises from the ship's jax. Sharkey returned pale and sweating. Everett tried not to giggle.

"Both ends," he said. "'The morsel which thou hast eaten shalt thou vomit up, and lose thy sweet words,' Proverbs 23:8. Meat is definitely off the menu."

Everett woke in his latty; eyes wide, every sense electric, his body alert and awake and ready for activity. Pitch blackness. He looked at his clock. Seven thirty, half an hour later than his usual waking up time. The day on this flat world was six hours longer than on the round worlds. The sun would not rise for another two and a half hours.

Diskworld, he thought, and giggled in his hammock at the joke. Everett was a big Terry Pratchett fan. His Dad had hovered impatiently, waiting for Everett to finish each book so he could pounce and snatch it, whisk it away into his study and read it in a single evening, giggling away. No one else on the ship would get the joke. That was all right. It was a thing between Everett and his dad. Wherever he was, out there among the worlds.

He had been almost sick with relief when he found out that the corpse in the forest had not been his dad. He had been both glad and sad that it had been 'Appening Ed, someone he had seen, almost known. Disappointed but hopeful, because the search would have to go on. Scared and tired because stumbling into what was left of 'Appening Ed had made Everett realize that there was no guarantee that his dad was alive. Lying in his hammock in the creaking dark, Everett saw his dad vanish, taken out of the universe by Charlotte Villiers's jumpgun. The last thing he remembered was the look of surprise.

He saw that other Tejendra Singh from Earth 1, who had lost everything he had ever loved to the Nahn. He saw the look on his face as the Nahn took him, a few short steps from the top of the Imperial College bell tower and safety. Peace.

He saw his mum. That day that seemed so long ago, but was only just over a month, when he had gone out to school and taken that other turn that led him to Charlotte Villiers and the Heisenberg Gate and all the worlds beyond it. That tired but strong smile. *Take care, love.*

He saw his face, that was not his face, but the face of his alter, that other Everett Singh, whom Charlotte Villiers had taken and twisted into the opposite of him. He saw him in the snow and the evening light at the gate of Abney Park Cemetery, looking straight at Everett as the weapons unfolded from his arms. But worse was what he saw in his imagination: his mum giving that same *take care love* strong-but-tired smile to Anti-Everett, as *he* set off to Bourne Green. He saw the Anti-Everett turn and return the smile, not to his Mum, but to him. It said, *are you so sure you're the hero here?*

Everett leaped out of his hammock. He stood panting. Sleep was impossible now. He pulled on clothes and stepped out of his latty. The corridors and walkways of *Everness* were lit soft ghostly green by emergency lighting. Noises and groaning from the jax. Sharkey was still suffering. Everett took the staircase up to the High Mess. The beautiful room had been wrecked by the crash. Windows were smashed in, ship skin ripped by branches. The great Divano table was overturned.

A patch of light focused on a torn section of hull then rose up and turned on Everett. Everett shielded his eyes. The light went out.

"Everett?" Captain Anastasia's voice. Everett's vision returned through blobs of white and blindness: the captain, with a headlamp and a knife in her hand. A knife that could heal as well as cut. A skin-ripper: a scalpel for the nanocarbon skins of airships. She had been repairing her ship. Guilt, bitter and thick, welled up inside Everett, so strong it made him shudder.

"Captain . . . Annie." *Call me Annie*, the captain had said, in this very room, before the fight against the Nahn. *You'll know when you can.* "The ship . . . your ship . . . I'm sorry."

The words were wrong. The words were stupid. The words could never be enough. Words were all he had.

The room was dark, but he saw Captain Anastasia flinch, as if he had touched her with a needle of ice.

"We'll fix her bonaroo," Captain Anastasia said. "We will."

"Have you been here long?

"Long enough. I can't sleep. I should sleep—the Dear knows I've enough to do in the daylight—but I can't sleep, not while she's this way."

"I don't think I'll ever be Airish enough to feel the way you do for your ship."

"It's not an Airish feeling," Captain Anastasia said. "What do you feel when you think about your father?"

Again Everett saw his dad, hands outstretched, knocking him out of the focus of the jumpgun. He saw again the look on Tejendra's face. Surprise, but Everett now recalled another expression: triumph. He had saved his son.

"It's like that," Captain Anastasia said, and Everett knew that his face had said all he could not. "It's the heart of you. Everett, make me some of that hot chocolate. The special stuff."

"Yes, ma'am."

"Everett." Captain Anastasia's tone said that he was not yet fully forgiven, but that he would be when everything was healed and whole again. Her family was; her ship would be. "You don't have to rush off. You don't have to rush anywhere. I've been up here for hours. Listen." She held a finger to her lips.

Everett held his breath. Sound by sound, the night made itself heard. Whoops, whistles, chirps, metallic rasping, long dwindling hisses that morphed into tweets, hiccups and burps and barks and sounds like human sobbing. Voice upon voice it built. And not just noises. Winged things darted and dashed past the smashed window.

Leaves thrashed, lights pulsed, like glow worms the size of footballs. Swarms of sparks flocked like starlings in a winter evening sky, a whirl and dance of tiny lights. From the far distance came a deep moan like the voice of a migrating whale.

"Look at the dark," Captain Anastasia said. "There's no moon. The stars are beautiful, and I know them like I know my own skin, but the moon, that's part of me. I miss it."

"They couldn't really have one," Everett said. "I think they must have used up every planet and moon in the solar system to build this. Even then, it wouldn't have been enough. Because I was thinking, whoever built this place, they would have to have been around a long time, like a lot longer than human beings have on our world—worlds. And the things that hit the camp . . . I mean, I only kind of saw them for a moment, but what they looked like most was dinosaurs. And that got me thinking; what if the dinosaurs hadn't died out? What if that asteroid hadn't hit the Earth, or whatever—I don't totally believe that it was one big catastrophe, but, anyway, what if the dinosaurs hadn't died out, but just kept evolving? And what if one of those dinosaurs had a big brain, and could use its hands, and discovered tools and language and fire, and got really, really smart? Smart dinosaurs, they could build something like this. They'd have a sixty-five-million-year head start on us."

"Everett, you don't have to try to explain everything," Captain Anastasia said. "Sometimes being there is plenty. I'll take that hot chocolate now, I think."

"Yes, ma'am."

"Make it, Mr. Singh. And bona breakfasts for everyone. Including Mr. Sharkey. I imagine he'll be pretty hungry."

8

Hunting again. Not meat. Sharkey would not make that mistake again. He had been up all night, groaning and heaving. It was metal they were hunting. Engine. Sharkey hacked a path through thorned vines and feathery fronds that curled away at the touch of his machete blade. Everett was three steps behind him. They were following the line of *Everness*'s descent, away from the river where Sen had hidden Everett's clothes, and the forest was dense and confusing. Everett couldn't see more than a handful of meters in any direction. There were no patterns, no shapes, nothing to steer by, just layer upon layer of vegetation. And sounds. Whistles and twitterings and musical trills and deep whooping noises that rose up into high screeches; clickings and tickings and scritchings and scratchings and hummings and bummings. All around them, but they never caught a glimpse of the things that made the sounds. There were movements high in the tree canopy, or the flicker of what looked like the wings of a butterfly the size of a dog, or a shape moving against the unmoving background of the trees and leaves, glimpsed in the corner of the eye. But when Everett looked, there was never anything there.

Compasses were useless—Diskworld had no magnetic north and south poles like a spherical planet. The compass needle spun all over the dial. An Alderson Disk had two directions, towards the sun and away from the sun.

"You'd think something that big would have left an equally big hole," Sharkey said, squinting up into the dazzle of sunrays slanting through the leaves.

"I think things grow pretty fast round here," Everett said. He climbed over the ridge of an exposed tree root and dropped down into the shadow. Something lunged up at him, something pale and eyeless and silvery that raised a frill of translucent flesh, and spat. Everett dodged a jet of green. It struck a leaf, which immediately began to brown and wither. Sharkey swung a shotgun butt and struck it hard. It gave a hissing shriek and vanished into the dark.

"I've an idea. Let's stay out of the shadows," Sharkey said. "Look after yourself, Mr. Singh." He threw Everett his other shotgun. "You know how to use that."

They pressed on, carefully detouring around the shadows that never changed. Everett's skin prickled. He felt as if he was being watched, not by a single set of eyes, but by the whole forest.

"So tell me, Mr. Singh, do you truly believe that this world was made by lizard men?" Sharkey said.

"Evolved dinosaurs. They mightn't look all that different from you and me; walking on two legs, eyes facing forwards, hands and thumbs and all that. Maybe a bit scaly."

"Sounds mighty like lizard men to me. Now, I don't hold with such things myself, but it strikes me, lizard men or not, any folk smart enough to build a thing like this Diskworld, well, you'd think we'd've seen some evidence of them by now."

"It's a big place," Everett said. "You could lose entire civilizations on this world."

"Perhaps," Sharkey said.

"When you say that you don't hold with such things, what does that mean?" Everett asked.

"When the Dear made the world, his design was perfect, but these lizard men saw fit to take and turn it to their own design, not just this world but all the other worlds of this sun. That I call hubris—Satanic pride."

Everett knew better than to argue with people on matters of personal belief.

"However, I've seen things that the Word of Dear don't accommodate," Sharkey continued. "And I believe that where there is no direct guidance from scripture, a man may interpret according to his own wisdom." Sharkey held up a hand. "Quiet." Everett froze. Sharkey circled slowly. "There's something between us and the drop zone."

"What?" Everett whispered. His hands tightened on the shotgun.

"I have absolutely no idea," Sharkey said. He stopped in his slow turning. "Ah! 'Seek and ye shall find, knock and the door shall be opened unto ye.'" He pointed with his shotgun. Fallen branches, white splintered wood still exposed. A hole in the forest.

The impeller lay on its side, taller even than the tip of the feather in Sharkey's hat. The branches had broken its fall, but the casing still looked battered and dented. Sharkey peered into the open end.

"The fan blades look intact," he said. "Mchynlyth would know better." Sharkey opened up the inspection.

Out in the forest, branches crashed. Everett looked away from the fallen engine. The sound of thrashing foliage was moving towards him. Louder. Closer. Everett's every sense was alert. Something was moving, something that did not disappear when you looked at it. Something big.

"Sharkey, that something . . ."

Everett saw it in the split second before it burst through the screen of leaves and creepers. It was blue and big. Very big. Proper Jurassic Park carnosaur big.

Sharkey looked up.

"Run!" he yelled. Everett was three steps ahead of him. Everett glanced behind to see the hunter explode into the little clearing in an explosion of twigs and leaves. That one glance told him everything. Big as a house. Long neck, tiny beady eyes. Two strong legs. Claws like sabres on the short forearms. Teeth. Way too many teeth. Shimmering electric blue. And coming fast.

"Where?" Everett shouted.

"Anywhere!"

Everett looked at the shotgun in his hands.

"Do you think . . ."

"You'd only annoy it," Sharkey panted.

"It looks pretty annoyed anyway . . . whoa!"

Everett's boot caught an exposed root. He went over and down, hard. He came up to see a head the size of a family hatchback bear down on him. Jaws opened. There could not be that many teeth in the universe. The stench of rotting, half-chewed, undigested flesh gusted in his face. Then Everett saw a halo like a crown of golden thorns appear above the carnosaur's head. The halo spun, glittering in the sunbeam striking down through the canopy of leaves. The carnosaur's eyes went dull. The head pulled back. It drew itself up to its full height, shook its head as if trying to dislodge a fly from an ear hole, then turned around and stalked back into the deep forest, still shaking its head.

The halo lifted from the carnosaur's head and disappeared.

A face looked down into Everett's. Wide eyes, with wide golden pupils and a black slit of an iris. A transparent membrane flicked across each eye. Two slits where a nose would be. The mouth a wide gash with almost no lips at all. Ears like little commas set low on the long, backward sloping skull. The skin was silvery, with the powdery consistency of the minute scales of moth wings. The hair was a thin Mohican from just above the eyes over the top of the skull to the nape of the neck. Long, thick hairs lay flat. The eyes flicked their membrane eyelids again and the hairs rose and Everett saw they were very fine quills. The crest ran with rainbow colors and lay flat again. The nostrils flared. Not a human face. Never a human face. But it looked Everett up and down with purpose and intelligence. The lips moved. Music like birdsong came out.

The thing repeated the snatch of birdsong.

"Are you trying to talk to me?" Everett said.

The creature's crest rose again. The air around its skull sparkled: the same halo that had appeared around the carnosaur's head now appeared behind the creature's head, a crown of living gold.

"Everett, on my word, roll away. I have a clear shot," Sharkey called. From the edge of his vision Everett could see Sharkey, shotgun levelled. At the same instant the creature saw him too. The creature pointed, the golden aura flickered, something flashed in the light and Sharkey had a twenty centimeter blade hovering at his throat.

"Okay," Sharkey said, but he did not put the shotgun down. The creature snapped its attention back to Everett. It sang a trilling set of notes.

"I am Everett Singh, from Earth 10," he said. The creature whistled a phrase that might have been Everett's words played on a flute. The creature gave a low burble, blinked its translucent eye membranes again. The outer parts of the golden halo unravelled, flowed down the creature's arm, and formed a rotating ring around Everett's face.

"What the . . ." Sharkey shouted. The creature flicked one of its long, slender fingers at him. The hovering knife blade moved a fraction. Blood seeped from the tiny nick it made in Sharkey's throat.

"It's okay," Everett called. "It's . . . I think it's . . . oh wow."

"Are you okay, Everett?"

He could hear voices in his head. Voices that were all one voice. His voice. Everett as a fourteen-year-old, Everett as a toddler forming his first word—Tottenham, his Dad said, though his mum told him it was really "Teddy's eye socket"—Everett as an excited nine-year-old after a show at the London Planetarium, Everett the smart kid always giving the clever answer in Year Six. Everett speaking Palari, Everett's few words of Punjabi. A thousand voices, all talking at once, all one voice. The creature lifted another finger and the golden halo lifted from Everett's face, ran up the finger, up the long arm to rejoin the slowly spinning halo behind its head.

Everett thought that it looked like a Ganesh, or a Shiva Nataraja, with haloes that burned with golden flames.

The creature made a noise that sounded like a parrot saying *Everett Singh*. It made it again, clearer now.

"Everett Singh. Earth 10," the creature said. Its voice was bird-like and more music than language, but Everett could understand every word.

"Oh my God," Everett said.

The creature cocked its head one way, then another.

"Oh my God," it said. "You are Everett Singh from Earth 10." It looked at Sharkey, crooked a finger. The knife pulled away from his neck, flashed back to the halo, and dissolved into glittering dust.

"Did you just learn my entire language?"

Again, the one-way-then-the-other look. Birds do that, Everett thought. Jackdaws and magpies. Clever birds.

"Yes," the creature said. Its voice was becoming less birdsong and more Stoke Newington with every word. Its crest flicked up and turned deep electric blue. "I am Kakakakaxa."

"Sharkey," Everett said. "You believe in lizard men now?"

9

The thousand bells of Heiden rang out from the city's steeples, peal calling to peal, bell answering bell, from spire to spire, carillon to carillon, farther and farther until last of all the chimes of the Zeeferrenkerk on the Island of Chains rang faintly in the yellow evening air. Soft wet snow had begun falling, the white flakes lingering for only a moment on the cobbles of the courtyard beneath Charlotte Villiers's window. Golden light shone from the leaded windows around the court.

"How many are staunch?" Charlotte Villiers asked.

"In our section, Aziz, de Freitas, Tlalo. The Earth 10ers."

"Not enough, Charles. Not enough. But at least Ibrim Hoj Kerrim is secure."

"You asked him to join the Order?"

"In as many words. He informed me he would not need the support of the Order. Unfortunate. But he understands his position. The fact that he helped us in the past could be severely damaging to his chances of becoming Primarch of the Plenitude of Known Worlds."

Charles Villiers helped himself to a bonbon from a porcelain dish.

"Have you ever thought that he might just decide not to run for the Primacy?"

"Ridiculous. Quite ridiculous."

"Not everyone is as ambitious as you, cora," said Charles Villiers, helping himself to another sweetmeat. "These really are very good. I still don't get the twin thing, but they really know how to cook."

A knock at the door. Lewis, Charlotte Villiers's Earth 3 valet, entered with coffee. He noticed the uncomfortable silence as he poured two cups.

"Thank you Lewis." Charlotte Villiers took a sip. It was exquisite, as she expected. How do they make it taste the way it smells, she wondered.

Charles Villiers's phone chimed. He tapped up the screen then opened the office door and looked up and down the corridor. He locked the door behind him.

"I've got a trace from the tracking device," he said.

"It works!"

"*Everness* has made a jump. We know where they are."

"Good. We'll have the Infundibulum by morning."

"I don't think so," Charles Villiers said. "It seems your jumpgun may not have been as random as you think."

"Explain."

"The plane he's gone to; it's been visited before," Charles Villiers said. "It was tagged by the Earth 1 random survey." Before the Nahn had assimilated 90 percent of Earth 1's humanity into an oozing nanotech group-mind, that world had pioneered the Heisenberg Gate and sent drones on random jumps to parallel Earths, mapping the tiniest hairsbreadth of the immense variety of the Panoply of All Worlds.

"Which plane?"

Charles Villiers showed his alter the screen of his phone.

The coffee cup fell from Charlotte Villiers's fingers. Black coffee splashed the pale carpet.

"God help us, each and every one," Charlotte Villiers breathed.

10

The strike was beautiful. From the edge of the penalty area, it lifted and curved in defiance of wind, weather, physics. Team Red defenders stood gaping as it went past them; Team Sky Blue strikers, Mr. Armstrong the referee, even Mr. Myszkowski the groundsman, all stopped to stare. Even Cora Sarpong who had hit it stood astounded. She had never hit a ball like that before and knew she never would again. It was the strike of a lifetime. Beckham would have killed to have bent a ball like that. It was inswinging, unplayable. It arced down towards the top left corner of the Team Red goal. Everett M hadn't seen it.

Cora, Team Sky Blue, Mr. Armstrong, Mr. Myszkowski, all had *gooooaallll!* on their lips.

At the last instant it came into the edge of Everett M's peripheral vision. It would have beaten any human goalkeeper. Everett M fed a surge of power into his enhancements. Thryn cybernetics kicked in. He leapt. At full stretch, he caught the ball with the tips of his gloves, knocked it behind for a corner.

The roar died. No one moved as the ball rolled across the goal line. Cora's mouth was open in disbelief. She looked about to burst into tears. Her girlfriends rushed to fold her in hugs. Something utterly unbelievable had summoned up something even more unbelievable.

Everett M felt a little tinge of guilt as he went to retrieve the ball and roll it out to the Team Sky Blue player for the corner kick. He could as easily have punched it clear. That would have been too super. He gave a shy half nod to Noomi and Gothy Emma. Noomi took a photo.

"We're making a Facebook page!" she called.

Since the coke-can-crushing incident, Noomi and Gothy Emma had been spectators at all Everett's Bourne Green Year Ten League games. They had been the only spectators. The two of them haunted the dead-ball line, directly behind Everett M in his net. They weren't in his sight line, but Everett M was always conscious of them, behind him. He didn't like them there. They made him feel watched. He suspected they were photographing his ass.

Jake Hughes took the corner for Team Sky Blue. The ball went out to a soft header on the edge of the six yard box. Everett M needed no Thryn technology to scoop the ball up in both hands and roll it out to Aysha Haddad, who was making a long run up the right wing.

Team Sky Blue's spirit was cracked. Team Red overran them for the final ten minutes of the game. It was a rout. Everett M had broken them. Every goal that went in, Everett M felt worse about his cheat. And it had been a cheat. He couldn't help himself. Every time he used the Thryn power, he wanted to use it again, use it more. By the time the final whistle blew he felt condemned by Cora Sarpong, Cora's friends, Team Blue, the whole of the Year Ten League. The gods of football sneered down at him.

"Save, Everett!" Noomi called as Everett picked up his water bottle and towel from the back of the net.

"We're calling it Geek Goalies!" Gothy Emma shouted.

"No! Everett's Hot Ass!" Noomi yelled. "Everettshotass, all one word, at Facebook dot com."

Everett M blushed as he hurried to the changing rooms. The truth was he quite liked having a small fan club. Small, but loyal. Noomi Wong had started appearing a lot in corners of his vision. She was there when he was at his locker, on the far side of the hall where the vending machines were, outside the door of the next classroom, leaving one class as he entered another. Just there for a moment's glance, and gone. Everett wondered if it was confirmation bias, like when the family got a new car and he'd started seeing that make of car everywhere. He had started to use his enhanced Thryn field of vision just to catch sight of her. He liked the sense of power, that he could see her without her knowing. She looked at him a lot. He flicked up his extended vision. There she was, still on the goal line. Gothy Emma had gone back indoors, but Noomi waited, wrapping her arms around herself to try and trap some warmth. That was a stupidly short skirt she was wearing. And over-the-knee socks didn't keep you warm. They didn't need to. They were a great look on her.

"When did you do that?"

Everett M knew that Ryun had been his alter's best friend. Those were the hardest lies. Parents—Laura—were easy; they always thought that anything out of the ordinary was their fault, or you punishing them, or something to do with drugs. Best friends knew you better. They knew the true you, however strange, and the fake you, however bland.

Ryun was frowning at the scars on Everett M's forearms as he towelled his hair into a manga quiff after the showers. The hot water had made the suture lines stand out, thin pale lines on dark skin.

"I ran through barbed wire. Stupid."

"Where did you do that?"

"Up at Enfield."

"You got up to Enfield?"

"Like I said, I forgot a lot. I'm remembering it now."

"I'd remember running through a barbed-wire fence," Ryun said.

All Everett M wanted was for Ryun to stop asking questions. He pulled his shirt over the lines where flesh met flesh; the wounds felt like lines of molten glass. He shrugged, looked away from Ryun. Conversation over. *You know I'm lying*, Everett M thought. You think I'm a cutter. He didn't like Ryun thinking of him like that. He didn't like Ryun imagining him sheltering in some roller-shutter doorway in an Enfield industrial park, taking a piece of glass, rolling up his

sleeve, the flesh goose-puckering in the cold, testing the edge against
the soft pale skin on the inside of his forearm until he knew what
pressure would make a cut, drawing it up from wrist to elbow, the
glass edge opening up the flesh cleanly and easily, the blood gathering at the end of the cut line to drop dark and steaming onto the
concrete. It made him clench tight inside. A heart shiver. *I'm not what
you think I am*, he wanted to say. I'm not a cutter. He could never say
that.

He walked home feeling cold and dirty, filled with unclean
things, as if the sterile white Thryn technology had become infected.
Abney Park Cemetery was more warning tape than open space these
days. The Council had reopened the paths, but the new Shock! Head-
line in the Islington Gazette was SATANIC CULT DESECRATES
GRAVES. He had left a spectacular, horror-movie mess of bones and
shattered skulls after battling the Nahn. The local Wiccan priestess
had been on local radio to explain that the opened graves and scattered
bones were more likely the work of dogs, badgers, or males under the
age of twenty-three than Satanists (who didn't exist) or witches and
Wiccans (who were a very respectable religion, with several covens in
Hackney Borough that counted a couple of councillors as members).
He had saved the world, but today he took no pleasure in it. He was a
freak, a patchwork of skin and plastic. A scarecrow. Alone.

His phone beeped. A picture message. His ass, in Team Red football shorts and compression tights, bent over, scooping up a ball. The
same gear he was wearing now, with school blazer over his football
shirt.

BETR W/ LESS ON, said the message.

Everett M gasped. He tapped a reply. These Earth 10 phones
were rubbish.

U SXTING ME?

U WISH, came the reply, then, after a link to a Facebook page:
EVERETT'S HOT ASS.

"Oh my God!" Everett M felt a hot blush move up his neck and over his face as looked at the collection of photographs of his ass in a variety of sportswear, through the goal netting on Bourne Green playing fields. A dog-walking woman stared as she whirled her charges past: Everett M, rooted to the spot, hand to mouth, grinned. A new SMS pinged in.

NOOMI SEZ; CUD U TAKE UP CYCLING?

Everett felt a needle of hurt at the memory the SMS called up: his dad, heading off on the bike that was worth a family holiday in Turkey, in all that gear, but struggling to get his feet into the pedal cleats. His real dad. His dead dad. Only a needle of hurt, only a moment.

Y?

The answer came straight back. BEST SHORTS.

Everett M floated back to Roding Road in a fog of pride, humiliation, cool, and the excitement that someone, *someone*, thought he was hot.

He burst in through the back door of Number 43.

"Boots!" Laura shouted. Everett M kicked them off and left his claggy football boots by the back door. He dumped his backpack by the table and slid across the kitchen floor in his sock-feet to the fridge. Bread mayo turkey breasts tomato those pickles that made everything taste like it was from McDonalds, salad dressing ditto . . .

"They don't wash themselves!" Laura shouted after Everett M as he slid back across the floor to the hall and thudded up the stairs to his bedroom. Where had he left it? All the gear from the night of the Second Battle of Abney Park. Balled up on the floor. He pulled it on, laced up running shoes.

"Two runs in a week?" Laura said as he came back into the kitchen. She watched in mock amazement as Everett bundled his football kit into the washing machine. "The age of miracles is not past." Everett M's real mum had said that too. Everett M had always wondered when the age of miracles had been, and what it had been like to live in it, and whether anything had ever followed any consistent logic, or if sense and science had just been turned on their heads by random acts of senseless magic.

"Is that so weird?" he asked.

"There *is* a girl," Laura said.

Everett M gave the side-to-side Punjabi head wobble that could mean anything from *absolutely definitely* to *perhaps perhaps perhaps*. This one meant *maybe*. He wanted her to know, but he didn't want her to know who.

"I knew it!" Laura said. "Who is she? Do we know her? Are her parents on the Residents' Committee?"

Everett M was already halfway down the rear alley.

It was pleasure to run. Everett M turned off the Thryn enhancements and let his body use its own muscles and sinews. Muscle fibres throbbed. His heart hammered. January night air, thick with car-exhaust fumes, burned his lungs. They were good. Nothing added, nothing enhanced. Everett M. Singh pure and simple. The rhythm of his feet was sure and steady. He did not have to think about it. His feet took him across Stoke Newington High Street, along Stoke Newington Church Road, onto Albion Road. Noomi lived here. Number 117. She'd told him. Every window was bright with lights. He could see silhouettes moving behind the sheer curtains. His Thryn vision could easily show him whether one of them was Noomi, but he didn't want to do that. Better to imagine she was there, peeking out as he ran past—moving well, looking fit. He ran slowly down Albion Drive. Five houses down he turned and ran back up Albion Road. A car was pulling out from the side of the road. A moment of madness: Everett M flicked Thryn power into his legs and in one leap hurdled the car. He landed agile as a cat in the middle of Albion Road and kept running. He whooped with delight. The car blared its horn, but Everett M was already a hundred meters away.

Did you see that, Noomi Wong? Put that on your Facebook page.

And you, Charlotte Villiers. I took that car sweet. You'll never get me again with a trick like that, knocking me down in the street. Never again. You may think I'm working for you, but I'm working for me. You owe me, Charlotte Villiers.

His phone buzzed against his ass. Everett hooked it out of the tricky little zip pocket at the back of his running gear.

The SMS said simply ???!!!???

Everett M opened up the Thryn power and blazed home, grinning as he dodged through the evening traffic. He felt warm and stupid and lost inside, a little sick, a little uncertain, a little dizzy, as if he had looked over the edge of the tallest building. It felt marvelous.

11

Noomi and Gothy Emma had rated it. All Gothy Emma's emo and vampire friends had rated it. The Bourne Green Harajuku girls had rated it. Even the girls who talked about nothing but makeup had rated it. All of Team Red, Team Lilac, Team Gold, and Team Sky Blue had rated it. The really sporty guys who never talked to geeks, all the teachers who coached sports teams, and one hundred and twelve random strangers had rated it. Ryun Spinetti's mum had rated it. Ryun's Spinetti's dad had rated it. And that scared Everett M the most.

"Your dad has rated my ass," Everett M said. "Your dad thinks my ass is hot." He and Ryun Spinetti were down in the basement den at Ryun's house. Television played, iPads glowed, smartphones shone. Ryun's mum was fixing something to eat. Everett M understood that this was a very good thing. The smell working down the stairs into the den was certainly a very good thing. It didn't have that slightly acrid smell of microwaved plastic food tray that Everett M associated with food at home. Everett M had accepted the invitation back to Ryun's place reluctantly, but inevitably, like a trip to the dentist. Ryun had just got FIFA 13 for the Xbox, though Everett M suspected Ryun had questions concerning all the ways Everett M seemed so different since before Christmas. He didn't know what he would do if Ryun questioned him too closely. His Thryn superpowers didn't run to lying.

"My dad thinks it's funny, is all," Ryun said.

Everett M liked Ryun Spinetti's dad. He seemed about to burst into laughter at any moment, and it seemed like he could find something funny in anything. Something on the television or on his phone or in the *Islington Gazette*, or something his cats just did.

"'Satanic cult desecrates graves,'" he read, quivering with laughter. "If only." He had given a five-star review to a picture of Everett M with his hand down the back of his shorts, giving it a good scratch. So had everyone else. By the time Mrs. Spinetti called that the dinner was on the table, which meant it was ten minutes from being ready, there were five hundred likes. Everett M's ass was well on its way to going viral.

"I wouldn't read the comments if I were you," Ryun said.

Ryun's mum called again, and this time there *was* food on the table. Moussaka. Homemade. Hot enough to burn the skin off the roof of your mouth. Everything Laura's home cooking was not. Everett M waited as little as he politely could before inquiring about seconds. And after that, because it would be wrong to send the serving dish back to the kitchen with a little left in it, he asked for thirds.

"Now that is a vote of confidence," Ryun's mum said. "Everett, when you were here last time, you didn't see my rings?"

"Sorry, Mrs. Spinetti?"

"Ooh, you've got posh," Ryun's mum said.

Tiny traps lay everywhere. Everett M realized he didn't know Ryun's mum's first name. She steered him away from danger by continuing, "It's just, I always leave them in exactly the same place because I've got a head like a drain and I know I'd forget if I put them anywhere else."

"No, I definitely didn't."

"Maybe one of those stupid cats knocked them down the drain."

After dinner Ryun's sister Stacey wanted the den to play a dancing game on the Kinect with her friends, so Everett and Ryun went up to Ryun's room. Everett M had never been in a geekier place in his life. Screens and computers everywhere. He was getting used to clunky

Earth 10 hardware, but this was like living in a museum of dead tech. Dust everywhere. Everett M still couldn't understand what his alter had seen in Ryun Spinetti.

Everett M found space on the unmade bed. Ryun perched on a swivel chair in front of the big hi-def monitor. He chewed his lip. He flared his nostrils. He shook his head. He glanced at Everett M and then away. He looked in every way uncomfortable.

What are you going to do, Everett M thought. *try and snog me or something?*

Everett M realized he had no idea what alter-Everett's relationship with Ryun Spinetti had been.

There were no Thryn enhancements for this.

Suddenly Ryun blurted out, "You went, didn't you?"

"What?"

"You went. I know it. It's the only thing that makes sense."

"I don't know what you're talking about." But Everett M did. He didn't want to know; he didn't want Ryun to keep talking and with every word put himself in more and more danger, because Everett M didn't know what he would have to do if Ryun Spinetti revealed Everett M's secret.

"Man, I was there. You showed me the videos. Right here, on this screen. All those parallel universes."

There is a feeling: like the backs of your eyes dropping off. Like your belly opening and everything inside you falling out. Like all the blood in your veins turning to mercury and pooling in your legs. Like your brain emptying and your heart collapsing inwards like a dying star turning into a black hole. It's the feeling of the worst thing in all the worlds happening.

And yet Everett M found he could think, found words on his lips.

"Yes," he said. "I did."

They were only three words, and not even clever ones, but the sheer shock of them bought Everett M time to think of his next words. He would have to choose them carefully. Everything he would say and do from now on would be shaped by them.

Ryun's eyes were wide. Wider than horror-movie wide, wider than porn-on-your-iPad wide. Most-astonishing-thing-you-have-ever-experienced wide. The shock turned into a huge grin.

"I knew it. I knew it! Industrial park at Enfield: never! Big fat lie!"

"I went through," Everett M said.

"What was it like?"

"It didn't hurt a bit," Everett M said. It was true. "There's a bright light, then you see what's on the other side and you step through and you're there. It doesn't take any time."

"Through one of those . . . gate things?"

"Heisenberg Gates."

Then the full weight of what he had guessed, of what Everett M was telling him, fell on Ryun. His mouth opened. He hugged himself. He shook.

"Oh my God. Oh my God! You went to another universe. You went. To another. *Universe!* How? I mean? Where? Who?"

"My dad had a friend at Imperial. She did the coding and everything."

Then the even bigger question, beyond the big question, loomed over Ryun, like a thunderstorm beyond a raincloud.

"Where did you go?"

"Earth 3," Everett M said. There was no purpose in lying about this. "There are nine parallel worlds—ten if you include yours—ours."

"Is that the one where Britain is like near Spain and Morocco?" Ryun asked.

What had alter-Everett shown him?

"No, that's Earth 2," Everett M said. "Earth 3 has no oil."

For a moment he thought Ryun might fall off his chair.

No oil, he kept saying. *No oil!*

"So how . . ." Ryun asked, and then answered his own question. "Coal! Sweet. Steampunk!"

"Cooler," Everett M said. "Electricity. Tesla-punk." He'd never been to Earth 3, but he dare not mention the world he did know: Earth 4. The fact that the main difference between it and this Earth was the presence of the Thryn and their technology—and the fact that Earth 4's Prime Minister Mr. Portillo seemed to be a television presenter in this universe—might put suspicions in Ryun's mind Everett M did not want there. "And airships."

"That video!" Ryun shouted. He turned to the computer and hit keys. The video was still up on YouTube. Jerk.

The image was jerky, the zoom zoomed in so fast it made Everett M feel sick, the soundtrack was people asking incredibly stupid questions, as people do when faced with something completely beyond their experience. *It's for the Olympics*, someone kept saying over and over. *Gorrabee. The Olympics*. Ryun froze the image on the crest on the airship's prow. He shrugged: *tell me.*

"It's a Type 27 air cruiser of the Royal Air Navy," Everett M lied. He had his story now. "It's protecting me."

He really thought Ryun's eyes might explode, they were so wide and staring.

"I found my dad," Everett M said. "They took him because they didn't want his work falling into the wrong hands. If you want to jump between worlds, you have go from Heisenberg Gate to Heisenberg Gate. But my dad found a way to go from any point in any world to any other. Just like that. And there's an evil empire out there that wants to get a hold of it. And if they do, they can invade everywhere at once. Including our world, right here. So there's like a special forces unit, keeping the thing safe." The biggest lies are the ones nearest to the truth. Like snowflakes falling on a mountain ridge, they could end in different oceans. Truth, or an ocean of lies. And like a snowflake, it gathered others around it, rolling into an avalanche of lies. Everett M found it was easy to lie to Ryun Spinetti. And *fun*. "They're keeping my dad safe, but they sent me back. They gave me the ship. It's not here, of course, it's just like a universe away, but if I get in trouble, I can call it." He took out his phone.

"That's your phone," Ryun said.

"There's an app for it," Everett M said.

"So when it was here?" Ryun asked.

"Dropping me off," Everett M said.

"That was the first day of term," Ryun said. "I thought you came back before that?"

And then there is the place where that avalanche of lies can sweep you to disaster.

"That was part of the cover story," Everett M said.

"So did you send that text?"

"What text?"

"This one."

Everett M remembered it as Ryun flicked it up on his Blackberry. *Get this 2 Mum: am OK. Dad OK. CU soon.*

"Well, duh, who else?" Everett M said. "Did you send it to my mum?"

Ryun shook his head.

"But you said you'd lost your phone," Ryun said. "Just before I showed it to you. So what's that one you've got?"

One lie feeds another, fatter and fatter.

"Okay, so it's not just the app," Everett M said. This was sliding away from him. He could not say, *hey, what's with all the questions?* He had admitted he had been to parallel universes and back. How could you not expect questions?

"But you sent it from your old phone."

"They transferred the number."

"Onto a phone from a parallel universe?"

If they can build me a phone to call a parallel universe, how difficult do you really think it is to transfer my number over? Everett M was about to say. Then the avalanche hit him. He was beginning to believe his own lies. At the moment Ryun's dad, on his way to the bathroom, glanced in. He nodded at the image of the airship, frozen on the screen.

"Is that thing still viral?"

"That's last week," Everett M said, grasping a chance to change the subject. "This week it's my ass."

"Seven hundred hits on your ass," Ryun's dad said.

Everett M winced.

"Mr. Spinetti . . ."

"You lads are so easy to wind up," Ryun's Dad said. "There's almost no fun in it."

"She is hot on you," Ryun said, when he heard the bathroom door lock.

"Weird kind of hot," Everett M said. "More like stalking."

"Stalking's modern," Ryun said. "So, are you going to ask her out?"

Everett M had been enjoying the attention so much that he hadn't thought about its endpoint; snogging Noomi Wong. The thought made him feel a little warm and a little wild and a little hard. Noomi was weird, no argument, but cute. He had always liked weird girls, on his world and on this world, especially if they were cute with the weird. And he was pretty weird himself. Nanozombie slaying savior of this universe. But how close could he let her come, with his secrets and his lies? Would he always be aware, when he was kissing her, that she was kissing an arsenal of Thryn biocircuitry and implanted weapon systems? Could he ever be real enough to have a girlfriend? He wanted to.

"I'll keep her stalking for a while yet."

"Well, I know they get bored quick if you're not obviously interested," Ryun declared. He shook his head. "I can't believe that you've been to a parallel universe and here we are talking about Noomi Wong being hot for you."

Much more questioning like this and Everett M's edifice of lies would fall apart. He had to get out.

"Up to seven hundred and fifty likes," Ryun's dad said, coming back from the bathroom.

"Were you on Facebook on the toilet?" Ryun said.

"Isn't everyone?"

"That's crass even for you."

In the few seconds between Ryun and his dad, Everett M slipped out his phone and called up an app. A real app, not a made up one that called airships in from other universes. A small, silly one he had never seen a use for until now. He tapped the icon and slipped the phone back in his pocket.

Ten seconds later, it rang. An app that calls your own number. Everett swiped the screen and took the call.

"Hi, mum. Yeah, yeah. It's not a problem. I'll be about ten, fifteen minutes. Yeah, I can make my own way. See you . . . see you."

"Mum's not feeling too great," he said. "I got to go. Do you think your dad could . . ."

"Sure, sure."

He was home in seven minutes. Ryun's dad took pride in knowing all the shortcuts and rat runs. Everett M waved as Ryun's dad drove off from 43 Roding Road. He liked Ryun's dad, even if he had rated Everett M's ass. It was all right to like other people's parents.

He didn't like the lying. Lies and girls. As if his life as an Earth 4 alter secret cyborg agent wasn't difficult enough.

The rat startled him. They were all too common in Stoke Newington, but what drew him up short was that it was sitting in the middle of his front doorstep. Bold, unafraid, little paws folded like hands, black eyes watching him, whiskers twitching.

"Shoo," Everett M said. The rat stayed unshooed. "Go away, rat."

He took a step towards it. The rat gazed at him.

What were they putting out in the trash that rats had got so bold these days?

"Gaah!" Everett M waved his arms. The rat groomed its whiskers with its paws.

This was insane.

Everett M ran at the rat. He was right on top of it when it leaped away and dashed under the hedge.

Lies and girls and rats with attitude.

12

The bells of Heiden rang ten o'clock and the wind shifted and a new snow blew in, a fine, dry, cold snow carried on a wind from the east that swirled and gusted through the city's squares and narrow streets. A snow that gathered in the corners and against the tall buildings that lined Sant Omerhauplass, that caught in the curves of the wooden carvings of the old Bund houses and lodged in the stone folds of the statues of the Cathedral of the Brothers Christ. The staff of the Bear Blond Café would have closed up but for their one customer and her insistence that a guest would be joining her. Charlotte Villiers turned up the collar of her Earth 3 coat and cupped her hands around the bowl of hot chocolate. It had been twenty minutes since she had last seen another human being in Sant Omerhauplass. The twin waiters stamped their feet and tucked their hands into their armpits and stood as close as politeness allowed to the gas heater.

Ibrim Hoj Kerrim crossed the square from the Grootskanal Bridge. He was dressed for a northern winter, muffled up in thick coat and scarf, the ear flaps of his hat pulled down and knotted under his chin. He sat down at Charlotte Villiers's table.

"Could you not have found a table inside?"

"I find it invigorating. Shall I order you some hot chocolate? Nowhere else in the Known Worlds makes it better."

"I would love some, thank you."

The carillon of the Cathedral of the Brothers Christ played a snatch of a hymn tune, the quarter hour.

"I find Christianity a baffling religion at the best of times," Ibrim Hoj Kerrim said. "So messy and gory, and everything is so personal. But the Earth 7 variant . . . Two Jesuses, one of whom went up to heaven, the other who went down to set up the embassy of the Kingdom of Heaven at the gates of hell . . . Bizarre."

"I'm not a believer myself," Charlotte Villiers said. "I find all religions have some core of irrationality that I simply cannot accept, but, given the nature of Earth 7 society, it makes eminent sense to me."

"You have an alter," said Ibrim Hoj Kerrim. The waiters, in neat white aprons, served him a drinking bowl and a pot of hot chocolate.

"Everyone has an alter," Charlotte Villiers said. "Somewhere. You just haven't met yours yet."

"Perhaps. But mine is one of the more . . . distinctive worlds."

"The Principle of Mediocrity would suggest otherwise."

"Well, I agree with you on one thing, Ms. Villiers."

"What a novelty!"

"This is the best hot chocolate in the Ten Worlds. But you didn't bring me out here in a blizzard to drink hot chocolate in an empty café."

"No, I brought you out to this empty café to drink hot chocolate and frighten you," Charlotte Villiers said, taking a sip from her bowl.

"Frighten me?"

"My alter Charles planted a tracking device on the Singh boy's airship."

"Of course, you did not have the time to inform the Security Council about this."

"Of course. It tracks the Heisenberg jumps he makes and where he goes after the Heisenberg jump. It's quite accurate."

"Where has he gone?" Ibrim Hoj Kerrim asked.

Charlotte Villiers set down her chocolate bowl.

"Everett Singh has discovered the Jiju."

Ibrim Hoj Kerrim spoke softly in his own language. *Is that a prayer?* Charlotte Villiers thought. *Did you ask your God to protect you? You should.*

"You have succeeded in frightening me," Ibrim Hoj Kerrim said. "Who knows about this?"

"Only Charles. And that fool from Earth 10, McCabe. The boy is a family friend. He knows if I keep information from him."

"If the boy has jumped to the Jiju Worldwheel, then every planet in the Plenitude is in clear and present danger. The Jiju, in control of the Infundibulum and the Heisenberg Gate. We will all die in fire."

"We have a small window in which we can act," Charlotte Villiers said. Snow blew across the cobbles of Sant Omerhauplass. "We send a task force to the Worldwheel. We recapture the Infundibulum by any means necessary. The tracking device allows us to insert a squad precisely. Surgically."

"Surgical. That is a word with blood in it," Ibrim Hoj Kerrim said.

"If we have to kill everyone on that airship to get the Infundibulum, so be it."

"'We'?" Ibrim Hoj Kerrim asked.

"The Security Council will be dithering and prevaricating right up until the moment the Jiju city-ships appear in our skies."

"It seems I'm forced into an alliance with your Order," Ibrim Hoj Kerrim said. "But I cannot commit any more Earth 2 soldiers."

"We use my own people," Charlotte Villiers said. She pulled her coat collar closer around her.

"On two conditions," Ibrim Hoj Kerrim said. "First, if they fail, I inform the Praesidium."

"Of course. The security of the Known Worlds is paramount. They won't fail."

"My second condition: Your soldiers have never been off their own world. Until a few months ago, they had no idea there were other worlds. They lack interplane experience."

"What is it you want, Ibrim?"

"You lead them."

And you are a very clever man, Charlotte Villiers thought. *I can't refuse. If I succeed, no one will ever know. If I fail, you will have removed your rival. But I will not fail, and war is openly declared between us, and when I return, I shall have dealings with you, Ibrim Hoj Kerrim.*

"I'll require proper equipment. Heavy weapons. Access to a military jump gate. And a recall relay. If things go wrong, I want my people out of there."

"You will be carrying the recall relay?"

"I am everything you think I am, Ibrim, and worse, but I do not needlessly waste human life."

"So glad you said 'needlessly'." Ibrim Hoj Kerrim pushed his bowl and saucer away from him and stood up. "Of course, you won't want to delay. Every second wasted puts the Plenitude in peril."

"The Plenitude will not find me wanting," Charlotte Villiers said. She watched Ibrim Hoj Kerrim vanish into the swirling snow. She left some schillings in a saucer and crossed Sant Omerhauplass to the Nenin Bridge. The snow was sharp on her cheeks and lips, and the bells of the Kristenbrooder Cathedral chimed the half hour. Behind her the twin waiters took in the chairs and pulled the shutters over the Blond Bear Café.

13

Everett would never understand people. A real, genuine alien; a living dinosaur; and not one member of the crew was excited.

Mchynlyth was dismissive.

"How many Kas?" He shook his head as Everett repeated the name. Kakakakaxa squatted on one of the branches Number Two impeller had brought down in its fall through the canopy. It looked up at the sound of its name, a very human reaction. It blinked its eye membranes. A very inhuman reaction. "Buggerello to that. Kax." Mchynlyth went back to examining his engine, running his fingers over the casing and either hissing in horror or cooing in love. Kakakakaxa—Kax—studied him, head cocked first to one side, then the other.

Captain Anastasia was suspicious.

"What do we know about this creature? Person? How did it learn our language? What is that thing around its head? What's it doing here? Where did it come from?"

Captain Anastasia left no room for answers, for which Everett was glad because he realized that in the time he had spent waiting for the crew to arrive with shifting gear, Kax—the name was stuck now—had found out a lot about him, and he had found out almost nothing about Kax, except that its people called themselves the Jiju, a two-tone, bird-like whistle. And the thing around Kax's head—the Jiju name was three descending trills—was some kind of swarm of micro-robots that could take the shape of anything that Kax willed. And could affect minds, like the carnosaur, and read minds—like his. The heat in the forest clearing was incredible, but Everett felt a stab of cold in his stomach. What else had Kax taken out of his mind?

Sen was hostile.

"Is it a boy or a girl?"

Kax turned a blade of its halo into a little robot fly and sent it buzzing around Sen's head.

"What? I don't know. Does it matter?" Everett said. "It saved me from getting bitten in half by some kind of T-Rex. That's what matters."

"Matters a lot more than that," Sen declared. She swatted the robot fly away.

"Bona riah," Kax said. Not only had it absorbed Palari, it spoke it in a Stoke Newington accent.

"It'd better not be a girl, 's all," Sen said sullenly.

Kax wore sturdy boots that reached the knee and several belts festooned with pouches and pockets attached. Nothing more. Everett wasn't familiar enough with reptile sex to know where to even start looking, let alone what he was supposed to see. Supposing lizard men (or lizard women) had visible parts. Supposing after sixty-five million years of evolution they even reproduced like the lizards in the biology lab tank. Kax in return was very interested in human sexual features, what the Jiju could make out beneath the layers of clothing.

The robot fly buzzed over to land on Captain Anastasia's breasts. Mchynlyth and Sharkey tensed. Sen was a heartbeat behind them.

"What are these physiological features?" Kax asked. Its halo was rotating. Everett had a theory that that the halo was absorbing information and feeding it to Kax.

"At ease, omis. And polone," said Captain Anastasia. "They are female human sexual features. They enable us to feed our babies with milk. We call them willets, in our Palari speech. Breasts, in King's English. There are a lot of slang names for them. Most of them made up by men, who historically have found them attractive and fascinating."

"Willets," Kax said. "Will. Ets."

"It touches my willets, it gets a knife in its whatever-its-got," Sen hissed.

Now the fly buzzed in Mchynlyth's face. He flicked at it; it buzzed away, then danced in closer. With a furious roar, Mchynlyth lunged, caught the fly in his gloved hand and crushed it. A sudden cry and a Govan oath. Mchynlyth opened his fist. Blood leaked from the slashed palm of his heavy work glove. A golden blade dropped from his open hand and flashed across the clearing to rejoin the halo around Kax's head.

Kax whistled a cluster of fast and furious notes at Mchynlyth.

"Aye, tweet tweet my friggin' lovely to you, too," Mchynlyth glowered back.

Kax raised its crest of fine quills and uncurled from its perch. The halo rippled. Everett moved in between Mchynlyth and Kax, hands raised. *Back off, people.*

"Stand back, Mr. Singh," Captain Anastasia ordered. She pushed Everett sharply out of the way and took his place. "I'll have no fighting here. Mr. Mchynlyth, let's get this back to the ship. Kax . . . put them blades of yours to some use. Can you clear us a path through the undergrowth?"

The Jiju flared its nostrils, blinked membranes across yellow eyes. "I shall do that."

Mchynlyth's scheme was simple. Hook the impeller pod to cables. Fix each cable around the trunk of a tree. Ratchet ratchet ratchet ratchet. Impeller moves five meters. Repeat one hundred times.

Everett's biceps burned. His shoulders ached. His chest throbbed at every twist or turn. Even his stomach muscles twitched painfully. But again Mchynlyth yelled *Pull!* and Everett pulled on the ratchet. Pulled with all his strength. Pulled until his hands were raw. Pulled until the red dots swarmed in his vision.

"Haul off!"

Everett collapsed, lay on his back panting, staring up at the dappled light through the red leaves.

Only sixty left to go.

He got back on his feet again.

Kax tilted its head from one side to the other in that curious-bird look it did.

"But you're exhausted, Everett Singh," it said. "You need to recover your strength."

I need to do right, Everett thought as he unshackled the ratchet from the tree, slung the cable over his shoulder, and hauled it to the next tree. *I need to do more right than anyone else. I need to be ten times the crewperson of anyone on* Everness, *and maybe then I'll be able to live with myself.*

He hauled the cable around the massive tree trunk and hooked it on to the hasp. Everett hissed in pain as the metal ratchet rasped the raw skin of his palms.

"Cha break, Everett." Captain Anastasia stood at his shoulder. Her black skin shone with sweat. Everett pulled on the ratchet. "That's an order, Mr. Singh."

She gently pushed Everett away from the ratchet.

"You don't need to prove anything," she whispered for Everett's ear alone. Then, aloud, "Sen, on break as well."

"Ma . . ."

"Take a break. Kax!" The Jiju uncoiled from its perch, flared its nostrils at Captain Anastasia's tone of command. "Get clearing."

"What's the little word?" Kax said.

Captain Anastasia's eyes were wide with outrage. Her nostrils flared.

"Get clearing, *please*."

"Yon lizardy's got way too much Everett in it for my liking," Mchynlyth muttered.

It's not just got the accent and the vocabulary, it's even starting to sound like me, Everett thought. Captain Anastasia was right: how much did Kax know?

Kax clearing undergrowth was worth watching. A thought turned the halo into a disk of whirling knives, shredding everything before them, scything a clear path between the trees. Leaves, stems, briars, and thorns, even whole branches were reduced to a whirlwind of woodchips and red sap. Fragments of leaf fell like red snow around Everett and Sen. Sharkey, Mchynlyth, and Captain Anastasia fell to the ratchets.

"Why can't it build an engine and do the hauling for us?" Sen said. She was unashamed of her dislike of Kax. "Do something useful."

"She is doing something useful."

"*She?*"

"*It*, I mean."

"You said *she*," Sen hissed. "What do you know? What do you know? What did she tell you?"

Everett did not know why he had called Kax *she*. It was a vague sense in his head, maybe put there by Kax herself during the scan of his mind that had given her both English and Palari, that this Jiju was female. And young. Startlingly young. He didn't want to be drawn into one of Sen's jealousy games. He knew what those were like from the girl cliques at Bourne Green school. There were rules you had to guess and people you could and could not talk to, but you had to guess that, too, and it was all about whose side you were on, not what was right or wrong.

"Never mind that," Everett said. "What I want to know is where the power comes from. Nothing runs on nothing. It's not physics."

Bad science ruined science fiction movies for Everett. Starships that could go someplace in under six parsecs. Why did that starship make a whooshy noise when there was no air in space to carry sounds? When Luke Skywalker pulled all those moves and turns in the X-wing, why didn't the G-forces rip his spine out of his back?

Those zappy space fighters—what did they run on? A parsec was a unit of distance, not time. Momentum was conserved. Space fighters and nanorobots didn't run on invisible magic power. There was no magic.

He still didn't understand how the Heisenberg Gates worked, though.

Sen was practical about it. "Does it matter?"

"It matters because the only way I can get them to work without breaking the laws of physics is if they pick up electricity. Like it's beamed in. I'm thinking, if they can pick it up from anywhere, then it has to be everywhere. Like, right under our feet. If you're going to build a whole Alderson Disk, you might as well wire it at the same time."

"And? God, Everett Singh, the stuff that runs around in your head."

"If the Jiju can tap it, so can we."

"Oh," Sen said. And, "ah!"

Shouts. Sharkey came sprinting up the cleared avenue between the trees, Mchynlyth behind him, Captain Anastasia on his heels.

"They're back!" Sharkey shouted. "Sauve qui peut!"

"Oh the Dear!" Sen shouted. She went sprawling to the ground as Kax pushed past her. "What?" Everett hauled Sen to her feet, but the infestation was on top of them. Everett saw teeth, lots and lots of tiny, sharp teeth. And claws.

Kax stood before the wave of creatures. She raised her arms, snicked in her thumb claws, whistled a long, melodious tune. The whole of the great red forest seemed to pause and listen to her song. The reptile swarm stopped dead. Each lizard thing went up on its hind legs, curled its long tail around it, and raised its front paws. Everett almost giggled. They looked just like meerkats. Alien rainbow lizard meerkats—and thousands of them. The forest rang with song, from Kax, from the lizard swarm. Then, in flicker of rainbow color, they were gone.

"You were lucky," Kax said. "They were my sisters."

"Can't see the family resemblance," Sharkey said.

"My hatch sisters," Kax said. "We are different broods, but we are all eggs of the Empress of the Sun."

"I knew she was a girl!" Sen blazed. "You is completely utterly totally and forever banned from doing anything with her, ever, Everett Singh."

"They're all . . . like young versions of you?" Everett asked. He ignored Sen.

Kax blinked, ruffled her crest. The quills ran shades of red, then settled again.

"Ick. All that . . . sex stuff. No. Nasty." Kax hid her face in her hands for a moment.

"Where did she . . ." Captain Anastasia asked.

"From me," Everett said. He touched a finger to his head. "What do you do?" he asked aloud.

"So many hatch sisters, but only one survivor," Kax said. Everett found it disconcerting listening to his own accent and intonation from the thin lips of the Jiju. "We go through many shapes, but there is only one rule: the strong rule. You've crashed your dilly ship in the middle of a Crèchewood. Of my hatch, only two of us remain now. I will find my hatch sister, and I will challenge her to single combat. Then I kill her and then I shall become Heir to the Sunburst Throne of the Sunlords."

"I knew it," Sen hissed, "And a princess, too."

"Some princesses are made, not born," Everett whispered.

Sen flared her nostrils in rage. "Are you saying that I'm a princess?" She tailed off. The rest of the crew were looking at her in a way that said *you're being a princess*.

"You're safe now," Kax said. "Word's passed among the Sunlord hatchlings. They're not intelligent the way I am, or even you are, but once it gets into their little heads, it stays there. There is a problem . . ."

"You're not the only ones in this . . . crèche forest," Everett said.

"All the great Clades have hatcheries in this Crèchewood," Kax said. "And if you're a friend of the Sunlords . . ."

"We're the enemy of everyone else," Everett said.

"It's the Jiju way."

"Well, it's decided then," Captain Anastasia interrupted. "There's nothing keeping us on this world, so we'll be off it quick smart. Thank you for your hospitality, Kax, but we've places to be and things to be at. I want that impeller ready for lifting by sundown. All hands to the ratchets. Includes you, Mr. Singh, and Ms. Sixsmyth. Kax, shred."

"Here's an idea," Sen whispered as she and Everett went back to the ratchets, "let's never tell her that we ate one of her sisters."

"I didn't actually eat it," Everett protested.

"No, but you curried it," Mchynlyth said, overhearing. "Here, wear these." He threw Everett a spare pair of heavy engineering gloves. Everett thought he caught a glimpse of a smile. The forgiving had begun. Everett pulled on the gloves and grasped the ratchet. Fifty-nine left to go.

Cicadas? Those things that go whirr and click in the night in the warm bits of the world? They're big. Bigger than you think. A family holiday villa in Turkey, just outside Kusadasi. One main bedroom for Laura and Tejendra, a put-up bed in an alcove by the open fire for Everett. He loved it, a little nest hidden in the stonework. Victory-Rose hadn't been there, hadn't even been thought of. Everett had fallen asleep in his little hidden place listening to the chirr whirr of a Mediterranean insect that signalled warm evenings, the smell of sage and rosemary, and a turquoise sea at the end of the lane. On such thoughts Everett drifted into sleep. Woke up screaming as whatever made that noise dropped out of the stonework onto his face. Legs and crisp chittery bits and little pricking spurs and spines, clawing at him. And *big*. Everett was still screaming as he ran with his mattress into Mum and Dad's room, threw it and himself to the floor, and skidded to a stop against the wall. A cicada, he later learned. Giving a name to the horror didn't make it any less horrible. He still got the shivers at the thought of crispy, chitinous bugs with long thrashing legs.

So when the thing dropped onto his face, Everett Singh woke up. Yelled. Fell out of his hammock. Yelled again at the impact, yelled as muscles agonized from the Big Haul protested, yelled at the skittering bug thing still in the latty. Everett hit the lights and saw a golden spider with too many legs running along the crack between latty door and frame, trying to find enough of a gap to squeeze through.

"No you don't," Everett said and grabbed it by a leg. He lifted it, its legs thrashing, up to eye level. Not an insect. Not. An. Insect. Then he gave another yell and dropped the golden spider thing. It had nipped him. As it headed across the floor, hunting for a way out of the latty, Everett seized one of Mchynlyth's heavy gloves and clapped it over it. He felt the insect thing buzzing under his hand. He carefully clapped his hand into the glove then pulled on the other one. It was all timing. He opened his trapping hand, and before the golden spider could flee, clapped the other hand over it.

Everett opened the latty door with teeth and a shoulder and clattered along the corridors to the galley to find a jar to secure it.

"Right you . . ."

At the table sat Mchynlyth, Sharkey, Captain Anastasia. In front of each on the table was a jar or a pot. Each container held a little golden spider.

"Join us, Mr. Singh," said Captain Anastasia.

Everett found a Kilner jar, shook the spider thing into it, and clapped shut the lid even as the creature made a leap for freedom. He locked the fastening. Wire-thin legs scrabbled at the smooth glass.

"What . . ."

Captain Anastasia raised a finger to her lips.

The yelling and hullabaloo could be heard in every part of *Everness*'s two-hundred-meter body. Fast footsteps clanging on metal mesh. Sen burst into the galley, hair mad and spiky, eyes wild and startled. One hand was clasped over the mouth of a glass.

"Full house," Captain Anastasia said. "Lady, gentlemen, we have intruders."

Sen deftly upturned her glass on the galley table. The thing inside rattled and spasmed.

"'The Day of the Lord will come like a thief in the night,'" Sharkey said.

"Mr. Singh, fetch Kax," Captain Anastasia said. "I would have words with her."

Captain Anastasia slapped the jar down on the cargo-deck floor. The things trapped inside jerked and scrabbled at the curving glass wall of their prison. She stood back, arms folded. Everett had seen her face this way before: when Mchynlyth had caught him stowing away on *Everness*. She'd been ready to throw him out the hatch as a saboteur of the Iddler.

"We found your bijou mates," Captain Anastasia said.

Kax crouched low, joints and muscles flexing in ways no human body ever could. She peered long and hard into the jar on the deck. Sharkey whipped out a shotgun and in a flash pressed the barrels to the back of Kax's neck. Her halo flashed red.

"Uh uh," Sharkey said. "'Behold, the day of the Lord cometh, cruel both with wrath and fierce anger.' Care to wager I can't blow the back clean off your head before you can lay a blade on me, lizard girl?"

Kax raised her hands, an eerily human gesture.

"If I could have a moment?"

The crew stood in a circle around Kax and the jar of golden spider things. She looked long and hard with her golden, vertically slitted eyes at each crew member: Everett the longest.

I'm not the traitor, he thought. *Is there still a trace of me in you, you in me; whatever those tiny machines orbiting behind your head did? If there is, you have to know I trust you.*

Everett had been sent down alone on the drop line, down into the dark, calling forest. He looked up to see light spilling from *Everness's* open cargo hatch. The faces of the crew looked down at him. Sharkey tipped the brim of his hat. Everett knew what that meant. Everett was the enemy again. A threat to the safety of the ship.

He called out into the forest, spinning slowly as he descended.

"Kax! Kakakakaxa!"

Shrieks, whoops, flutterings, and crashings as he spun lower.

"Kax!"

Then, far below, Everett saw a wisp of gold moving beneath the leaves like a trail of stardust.

"Everett Singh?" The words drifted up from far below.

"Kax! Captain Sixsmyth wants to see you. On the ship. There's a drop line coming down." He added the Airish warning for unpredictably moving overhead objects: "Tharbyloo!" There below!

"Coming up!"

And that's why I know you didn't send those little halobots crawling all over Everness, Everett thought as Kax turned her attention to the Kilner jar. *If you had, why would you agree to come up and have Sharkey stick his gun in the back of your head? And I don't think he's quick enough to beat you either. There are more things you can do with those halobots than throw missile knives at people.*

"They're not hers," Everett said, speaking the doubts in his heart. "Can't you see?"

"Your advocacy is admirable, Mr. Singh, but what has Kax to say for herself?" Captain Anastasia said. Kax lifted the jar and held it so close to her face that the breath from her flickering nostrils steamed the glass.

"These are not mine."

"Keep your weapon strictly trained, Mr. Sharkey. Explain."

"I know instantly but I could never explain to humans," Kax said. "It's like an aura, or a personal smell. Like the way we instantly know each other's Clade, where you would sense nothing. Like an extra color."

"She would say that," Sharkey said.

"Why?" Everett blurted out. "If Kax was spying on us, why would she come up here? She puts herself right into our hands."

"To get her wee spy beasties back," Mchynlyth said.

"If she can scan my brain, she can download straight from her bots."

Everett could see the Everness tarot hidden in Sen's hand. She cut the cards without thought, one-handed; a Hackney card-sharp's cut. Everett saw her flip up the top card. She pursed her lips. He caught a glimpse of the card before she flipped it back face down. A fat smiling woman on a throne, a rod in each hand, and a starburst at the tip of each rod. He couldn't catch the name.

"I can demonstrate," Kax said. Captain Anastasia looked at Sharkey, who gave a tiny shake of his head, at Mchynlyth, who tightened his lips. At Sen.

"Let her do it," Sen declared. "I believe her."

"Do it," Captain Anastasia ordered.

"Stand back," Kax announced. She drew herself up to her full height, which was a head taller than Sharkey, opened the Kilner jar and upended it. The crew leaped back as halo-bots fell to the floor and started to scurry. They were met by a shower of bots from Kax's halo that formed a circle around the spy-bots. The spy-bots halted. The encircling bots all took a step inward.

Everett held his breath.

In the blink of an eye the spy-bots formed into a wedge and tried to charge the encirclement. The siege wall bowed but held. Kax's bots replied instantly, reinforcing the weak point and closing in around the spy-bots. Tiny battle was joined on the floor of *Everness*'s cargo deck.

It's like a Napoleonic War battle, Everett thought. *All charges and close-in action. Only on the scale of insects. Claw to claw combat. Halobots! Thousands of 'em!*

The spy-bots fought hard but were overwhelmed by Kax's forces. They went down, legs flailing. Everett saw tiny machine mandibles take the spy-bots apart, hacking them finer and finer until no visible trace remained. They were only machines, but the death struggles of the spy-bots disturbed him.

Kax's halobots recombined, sprouted wings, and flew up to join her own halo. The crew waited as Kax's halo ran with rainbow colors. Her eyes were closed. Sharkey held the shotgun ready in his hands. Kax's eyes flashed open.

"It is as I feared, Anastasia Sixsmyth. The Genequeens know you are here."

"I still don't believe . . ." Sharkey began, but Captain Anastasia cut him off.

"The Genequeens?"

"The Worldwheel is ruled by six Clades. The Water-Born. The Stormsingers. The Genequeens. The Grain Queens. Strong-Against-Asteroids. The Sunlords. Each controls one vital function of the Worldwheel. Water, weather, biology, agriculture, space defense. The sun itself is the territory of my Clade, the Sunlords. The Worldwheel is arranged so that it can't function unless all of us work together. But there will always be . . . rivalries. This Crèchewood was designed by the Genequeens; their bots are all over it. They are aware of your ship, that it's from somewhere outside the Worldwheel, and they would claim it as their property."

"Mr. Mchynlyth, Sen, I don't care how much you're hurting, but all efforts to get us airworthy. Mr. Sharkey, Mr. Singh, as soon as it's light, you get down there and find that final engine. I want off this world quick smart. Kax, I apologize for doubting you. Please help my crew."

The Jiju riffled her crest.

"To work," Captain Anastasia commanded.

"Sen." Everett called her back as the crew went to their posts. "What was the card?"

"Dunno what you mean, Everett Singh."

Why did everything with Sen come down to a denial or a challenge or a game or a lie?

"I saw you playing with the tarot."

Everett could see no possible space to hide the Everness tarot in Sen's tiny clothing, but she produced the deck as if by magic and flipped up the top card: the fat jolly woman on the throne, holding stars on sticks. Everett could read the title now: *The Sun Empress*. He shivered. Coincidences, he was beginning to believe, were not coincidences, but subtle leaks and links between universes. Everything was connected.

"What does it mean?"

"A generous host. An unexpected visit or an invitation. 'Ware the powerful."

14

"Just two of you left?"

"Temporarily. Then two become one."

The engine hunters were ranging deep into unknown terrain. The number one impeller had sheared off first and so lay farthest from *Everness*'s crash site. Sharkey strode ahead, jaunty hat on his head and a shotgun cocked over his shoulder, but Everett knew that he had no idea where he was going. Finding pod one would be as much stumbling over it as jungle navigation. *We could be anywhere*, Everett thought. The forest looked different from every angle; they could be footsteps away from the drop point and never realize it. Kax assured them she would not let them get lost. Her halo was an external memory that logged every image, every footstep. Jiju sat-nav. It also contained a vast amount of forest lore. On every side were plants, bugs, miniature lizard birds and things that lurked in the permanent shadows on the far sides of the trees that could bite, sting, poison, blind, burn, trip out, infect, infest, and outright kill. Plus Sunlord hatchlings, hatchling hordes of other, hostile Clades, and Kax's rival for status as the Princess of the Sunlords. Poor old 'Appening Ed never stood a chance. If that same little geometry problem that crashed *Everness* hadn't dropped him from Earth 3 screaming into a kilometer of open air.

"If you don't mind me asking, how many of you were there originally?"

"Three or four thousand."

Everett's imagination reeled. This was death on an industrial scale.

"That's . . . That's horrible. That's mega-death."

Kax cocked her head at Everett in the way he had learned meant *you are so alien to me.*

"How can something die that isn't properly alive?"

"But, they're *you*." And there was a look that Everett gave Kax that said exactly the same thing.

"Do you worry about mega-death every time you masturbate?"

Everett tripped over a nonexistent root.

"Dah . . . wha . . . what?"

"It's a male ape thing, I understand."

"I . . . Don't . . . Never . . ."

"Really? From my understanding, that is almost unique."

"Kax, omis don't talk about that sort of thing."

"Why not? They should. But my point is, all those billions of sperm, do you worry about them dying? Of course not. You only worry about them when they become complex, living, thinking things. We're like that with hatchlings. Thousands come out of the hatching ponds, but only a very few become Jiju. All the stuff that you apes do inside you, we do out in the world. The fastest sperm, the toughest hatchling, it's no different."

Everett was still squirming inside. How deep inside had Kax's scanners reached? He felt as embarrassed as if she had examined his balls close up and very, very personal.

"So, how old are you?" Everett asked. Move the subject away. Move right away from teenage omi stuff.

"Almost six hundred days."

Everett relished the mental arithmetic. Diskworld days were about thirty hours. That made Kax about . . .

"Two years old!"

"Like I said, everything that happens inside for apes happens outside for Jiju. When the hatch is down to about a hundred, the first transformation occurs and we attract halos and become fully Jiju.

I'm still growing, but I have twelve kills." Everett was a beginner in reading Jiju emotions—they were not the same as human emotions, not the same at all—but he read the equivalent of pride in the display of colors on Kax's crest.

"You say that, but it's like so, so far away from anything I know. It's like . . . The nearest I can think of is like kids in Syria, or child soldiers in Africa. But I can't really know what that's like for them either—it's something I see on the television. I can't feel it. Life is so cheap with you."

"You are so, so wrong, Everett. Life is everything to us. Every moment is like a burning flame or a jewel or a flower to us, because we have so little of it. We have a word for it. It can't be translated." Kax gave a fluting, falling whistle. In that brief phrase was every musical turn, every chord change that had turned Everett's heart over. "Think of a storm, a great howling storm, bigger than any you have ever known before," Kax continued. "A storm so big it could tear the earth from the bones of the world. That storm has howled and raged forever. Then, for a moment, the wind drops and the clouds break and there is calm and sun. In the sun, in the stillness, a creature sings. Only for a moment: the song. Then the clouds close and wind returns and the storm roars on forever." Again, Kax spoke the ach-ingly beautiful tune. "That is the song in the heart of the storm. Life is precious to us because we don't live as long as you apes. By the time you are thirty, I will be dead. If my enemy doesn't kill me first. The world is a wheel of wonders." Everett had heard Kax use that expres-sion before, like a blessing, or an If-God-Wills-It. "We live our lives hard and fast and knowing that all this wonder will end. Everything I experience may be the one and only time I experience it, so I must suck every drop of nectar out of it. And it's the same for you. It's just that, because your lives are long, you think you will live forever. But no one lives forever, Everett. The storm will come and never end. I think our way is wiser."

A yipping rebel yell from ahead. Everett saw Sharkey's hat go up in the air on the end of his shotgun.

The impeller pod lay in a shaft of sunlight at the center of a clearing of snapped branches and smashed wood. Everett stared up the well the falling impeller had smashed through the trees. Up there, clear blue sky. The great forest of Crèchewood rang around him with voices; layer upon layer of sound, circling out farther and farther, creature calling to creature. It was dangerous here, but it was beautiful.

I'm trying to sense like a Jiju senses, Everett thought. *Each experience as if it were the first and last time.*

Nanocarbon was light and very strong—necessary qualities for airship engineering—and the forest canopy had broken the fall, but Sharkey still worked his way carefully and meticulously over the pod, feeling out every crack and break.

"I am still interested in your sperm," Kax said. She perched in a root buttress, grooming her crest with her thumb claw and examining what she found there. "Have you put any inside the girl Sen?"

Even Sharkey stopped his examination to stare at that.

"What?" Everett yelled. "What the f . . . God, no! She's only thirteen. Nearly fourteen. No!"

"Human females are fertile from that age?"

"Yes, but . . . we have rules. You have to be sixteen. I think."

Sen was as gobby and in-your-face about sex as the only child of a piratical Airish air freighter could be. Much more than Everett ever could be—she made him blush with her forwardness—but Everett knew it was just Big Talk. Sen was too proud, too self-possessed, too well brought up by Anastasia Sixsmyth to play around with sex. She was the captain's beautiful daughter: she was a princess.

"Silly rules. Jiju would not waste time."

"I don't . . . you can't say things like that. You can't talk about her like that."

"You don't? I thought you did. Maybe I was wrong about what I saw."

"You didn't see anything . . ."

"I did." Kax extended a fighting claw and gently touched the point to Everett's forehead.

"You had no right!" Everett yelled.

"This is my world. I have every right. So: what I saw, what did it mean?"

"I like her. She's a friend. A mate who's a girl. A special friend."

Kax blinked at Everett.

"I like being with her," Everett continued. "But she can be so annoying. Sometimes it's like she's the only one understands me, but then sometimes it's like she doesn't know anything, and I can't get anything through to her, and it's like she's being stupid on purpose. And then all those games she plays with me that I don't even know are games, let alone the rules. And she's so moody, like I'm scared to be near her half the time; and the other half of the time I don't know what I've done to make her be like that and she won't ever tell me and she gets on like she's so tough but she's not as tough as she thinks she is, no way. But she's always annoying, and stupid, but she's like always in my head and I can't get her out."

"Oh, man," Sharkey said. "You got it bad, omi."

"So do you or do you not want to put your sperm into her?" Kax asked Everett innocently. "I am confused."

"Let me tell you this, my reptile friend," Sharkey said, "you may have built this Diskworld, and that's a mighty work, but us apes, well, we done something greater: we created this funny little thing called love. Engine's good. Let's get back to the drop zone and get the hell off this terrible place—no offense, ma'am."

The plume of orange smoke from the distress flare rose straight up through the hole in the trees into the clear air. The final engine had fallen too far from the ship for brute-force, aching-muscle hauling to drag it through the forest. Captain Anastasia had a different plan. When the smoke went up, she would lay in a course, Mchynlyth would gingerly release what power remained in the batteries, and Sen would coax the creaking, groaning impellers into motion. She would fly her ship to the engine, haul it up, and make *Everness* a proper airship again, bona Hackney-fashion.

Everett shaded his eyes and peered up into the circle of bright sunlight.

"How long do you think?"

"Captain will take her own good time," Sharkey said. "You can't push the lady." But he, too, was scanning the sky, looking for the shadow of *Everness*'s hull.

The sound was small but unlike anything Everett had heard in the wheel of the world. A ringing, like high-pitched bells. It came from every side at once.

"What is that?" Sharkey said.

Kax reacted to the sound as if she had been electrocuted. She crouched, every muscle of her legs and arms, her tight belly, knotted like fists. Her eyes and nostril slits were wide; her pupils were black holes. Her halo was like a crown of blades, flashing silver-blue. Her thumb claws were out.

"Kax . . ."

"Arm yourselves, apes," she said. Her voice was like the edge of a blade along Everett's spine.

Sharkey threw Everett a shotgun. They scanned the edge of the clearing. Nothing to be seen, but again the ringing chime came from the tree shadows. And was answered. The blades of Kax's halo were striking each other, giving off beautiful, clear, tuned bell chimes.

"Oh. My. God," Everett whispered. It could only be one thing.

"My enemy has found me," Kax said. "The time has come. The final battle joined."

The adversary stepped out from the dark depths of Crèchewood into the light of the clearing. In every way she was Kax's double. At the sight of the humans she sank into a fighting crouch. Her halo flashed into a battery of hovering sword blades. Kax sang a long phrase at the adversary. The blades flicked back into the halo, blue-silver to Kax's silver-blue.

"Do not interfere," Kax said. "Whatever happens."

"At the same time, Mr. Singh, keep your safety catch off," Sharkey whispered.

"Kax!" Everett had not meant to say the word aloud, but the fear spoke out. Kax glanced at him. In the instant's distraction, the adversary attacked.

A storm of blades blazed across the clearing. Kax rolled, threw up a hand. Her halo reconfigured into a shield. The blades bounced. The adversary hissed, sent her blade storm high up into the air, turned them into spears, and brought them plunging down towards Kax. With a thought Kax dissolved her shield, flashed her halo into a swarm of dancing daggers. As one, each dagger targeted a spear and deflected it. Everett jumped back as a spear embedded itself in the leaf litter only a hand's breadth from his foot. Even as the adversary pulled her spears out of the ground, Kax threw the dagger swarm at her. The adversary shrieked in rage: daggers duelled with daggers in mid-air like a swarm of furious insects. The clearing rang to a rising, whistling whoop: Kax's war cry as she launched herself at her adversary, thumb claws extended. The adversary spun away, but Kax's left claw opened a line across her side.

The two Jiju rolled apart.

The shotgun twitched in Everett's hand.

"I've got a shot," he whispered.

Sharkey knocked the barrel away.

"And do you know which is which? This ain't our fight."

The Jiju had recalled their swarms of battling daggers and, in a blink, changed them into swords: long sword, short sword, swash-buckling back and forth in thrusts and cuts and parries while beneath them Kax and her adversary tangled in a blur of stabs, punches, slashes, bites. Blood sprayed as thumb claws opened up long gashes; Jiju feet slipped on the blood-soaked ground. The speed and savagery left Everett reeling; each blow, each rake of the claw tore across his own imagination. Sharkey was right, he could no longer be certain which was Kax and which was her adversary. Above them, the dancing swords cut and parried. Everett understood how this battle would end. Whoever lost concentration first died. The halo blades would make short and sure work of that.

The Jiju sprang apart with ringing cries that sent winged things surging up from the branches through the spire of orange smoke. They were hacked and bloodied. Everett could not look. His heart was hammering. His breath was pumping. There was a slow, steady beat behind his eyes. But he wanted to look. This was hideous and terrifying and the most exciting thing he had ever seen. This would end with bloody death, perhaps for a creature—a person—he had come to care about, and he could not take his eyes away. It was all he could do to stop himself from roaring as if he were in the North Stand at White Hart Lane. He hated himself.

A short sword parried a long sword and dived down to nick six quills from a Jiju crest. If the target hadn't seen it at the last moment, it would have cut her head in two.

This couldn't go on much longer. Not with this speed and savagery.

As if they both knew the battle was in the end game, each Jiju called back her halo weapons and bonded them to her hands. Spiked ball on a chain and a brutal stabbing sword against two sets of long curved claws. They clashed in flying sparks. Shrieks and piercing whistles tore the air. Everett had once heard a rabbit die in the jaws of a fox. It had squealed long and terrible, but never so filled with hate. The clearing rang with metal on metal. *Stop it, stop it*, Everett wanted to scream, but he could not speak, could not move, could do nothing but look in horror and wonder. Guys had fought at Bourne Green—Everett had not been one of them, but he had seen fights and he hated them: they made people—friends—into something he did not know and could not recognize. Ugly, harming things. He never looked at them the same way afterwards. They had seemed savage, those fights, but they were short and they had rules. This had no rules, and it would go on until only one survived. He cried out as a set of claws drew three bloody gashes across a belly. The one with the claws was the one with the cropped crest— that was Kax. Wasn't it? Wasn't it? But she also had the wound in her side. That was the other one. Wasn't it? Wasn't it? Then the other Jiju caught her feet in the chain of the morning star and tripped her over, then threw all her weight on top of the short, stabby, brutal blade, and the other Jiju tried to hold her off, but her strength was gone. She was bleeding from a dozen cuts and the blade was inching closer and she was trying to hold it off but her fingers were blood slippery and all of sudden it was the end and he could see it in both their eyes.

Suddenly his eyes were clear. Suddenly he knew what he had to do. There could be no mistake.

"Kax!"

He sent the shotgun sliding across the blood-slick earth.

As the tip of the short, killing blade pierced the skin of its throat, the Jiju on the bottom grabbed the shotgun, jammed it into the side of the killer on top and pulled the trigger. The blast sent the other Jiju into the air in an explosion of blood and meat and skin.

The spell was broken. Everett cried out. He fell to his knees. Retched. Threw up as the Jiju pulled herself up, went over to the twitching mass of shattered flesh, and plunged her claws into it, again and again and again and again.

"Kax . . ."

The Jiju looked up, darted her eyes towards him. Her face was a mask of blood. There was nothing in those eyes Everett could recognize.

"Oh God Oh God oh God oh God," Everett whispered. This was

death. Complete and bloody and vile. No argument, no coming back. In front of his eyes. Everett had never seen death before. It had not touched his family. When the alter Tejendra had died in the raid on Imperial College to get the Panopticon, Everett had been pushed away by Sharkey. He had heard death—two gunshots—but he had not seen it. He had now. He had seen it come painfully and without any hope of mercy or escape. He hated it. He hated that there was nothing he could do about it.

"'Now go and smite Amalek, and utterly destroy all that they have, and spare them not,'" Sharkey muttered quickly. "'But slay both man and woman, infant and suckling, ox and sheep, camel and ass.'"

The Jiju's claws came apart into their component bots and reformed a halo. The dead Jiju's weapons broke apart and rose up like a cloud of mosquitoes and joined with the living Jiju's halo. The halo burned brilliant. The Jiju staggered. She closed her eyes. Her thin lips moved, as if in pain or as if speaking new and strange words. Her eyes flew open.

"I know everything!" Kax cried. "I am . . . everyone!" She ran a hand over her face, groomed her maimed crest, stared in amazement at the blood and dirt. "Water! Water now!" Everett handed her a canteen. Kax poured the water over her head, scrubbed off the gore. No one looked at the dead thing at the other side of the clearing. "Everything! All the others—everything they saw and felt and knew and learned. All their memories, all their experiences. I have them all. I am the one and only. I am Kakakakaxa Harhavvad Exto Kadkaye, Princess of the Sunlords! Thank you, Everett Singh. The Sunburst Throne is in your debt." Again, Kax reeled. Everett imagined information downloading in her brain. "Come with me. You have to come with me. I will show you Palatakahapa, the palace of my mother. I've never been there—but I can see it all in my mind. It's so beautiful. I'll call a flyer. I can do that. A whole fleet of flyers! That would be cool. We'll go, yes, right now. Out of here! I hate this forest!"

"Hey now, hey now, that's all fine and dandy," Sharkey said, retrieving his shotgun and wiping it clean. "But before we go trolling off together, I've one question: where the hell is our ship?"

15

Charlotte Villiers tightened the waistband of her short battledress jacket and adjusted her beret to the correct angle. She snapped open the leather cover of the holster on her Sam Browne belt. There could be anything on the other side of the gate. Zaitsev strode three paces behind her. Out of those cheap, poorly tailored Earth 10 suits and in Royal Army battledress he looked almost respectable.

Ibrim Hoj Kerrim had been a man of his word. Advanced Earth 2 weaponry. Secure and exclusive access to a military Einstein Gate in the underground levels of the Tyrone Tower. The story was that the gate had been taken offline for routine maintenance. Her own Earth 10 private security force and Zaitsev, her henchman.

Two of her soldiers opened the double doors of the gate chamber. Her squad clicked to attention. Behind the banks of controls, her alter Charles and the Plenitude Gate Command tuned the gate. The great twenty-meter ring in the center of the chamber ran with flickers of lightning and cold blue Cerenkov radiation. The gate crew knew that the coordinates they had set were for a place outside the Ten Known Worlds of the Plenitude.

Charlotte Villiers turned to her alter and held up the relay strapped to her left forearm. Checks. Cross-checks. Charles Villiers nodded. The huge chamber hummed as the gate powered up. Charlotte Villiers admitted a flicker of apprehension at the thought of jumping out beyond the Known Worlds into the Panoply. A billion billion parallel Earths out there. More than all the stars in the sky. That would give anyone a chill of insignificance. How could you measure a human life against all those worlds? But the boy was out there. He jumped between worlds, Plenitude to Panoply, Panoply to

Plenitude, with the cheek and arrogance of a thief running across the rooftops of London. Last time she had sent soldiers out into the great unknown to catch him they never came back. It would be different this time.

"Ready whenever you are, Madam Villiers" The Gate Controller was a smart, groomed young woman. Charlotte Villiers approved of her makeup and the precise angle of her Gate Command forage cap. The controller could not hide the fear on her face that the things she saw and heard in this chamber would cost her for the rest of her life.

Charlotte Villiers faced her soldiers. A dozen of them in black Earth 10 fatigues. Inelegant, but practical. Squad leader Sorensen, a tough-faced blond woman, brought the squad to attention.

"At ease. You've been briefed but I have a few final notes. In a few moments we will be making an Einstein jump. My alter has set the coordinates to drop us precisely into the airship at the closest safe point to the tracking device. The gantries and walkways are narrow, so we will form up in two files. There are long drops inside the airship. Watch your step. Gravity is about two-thirds Plenitude normal. You may find the transition momentarily disorienting. The crew will be armed with standard nonlethal Airish self-defense weapons. They're painful and can incapacitate. My previous comments about heights inside the airship stand. If the crew offers any resistance, deadly force is authorized." Charlotte Villiers took a breath. "Concerning the Jiju. We do not anticipate encountering any, but on the minuscule chance that we do, do not engage. They are a civilization roughly sixty-five million years older than us. We do not want to anger them. Our mission is to obtain the Infundibulum by any means and return it to the extraction point, where I will activate the relay and return us to this world. Controller, we're ready now."

The Gate Controller pushed forward a lever and the chamber flooded with blinding white as the huge metal ring filled with light. *Ghost photons*, Charlotte Villiers thought. *A glimpse of the ultimate reality beyond both Plenitude and Panoply.* The light cleared. Beyond the gate was a long, spidery walkway overhung by the bulging curves of the lift cells.

"You are clear to jump, Madam Villiers," the Gate Controller said.

"With me," Charlotte Villiers ordered. She walked briskly and coolly up the ramp and into another universe.

Charlotte Villiers hit the deck of *Everness* and broke into a run. Behind her, her soldiers split off along the crosswalks and down the spiralling companionways. Airships were big, with many places to hide a small Earth 10 tablet computer. That was the briefing. The truth was that Charlotte Villiers knew it would not be anywhere other than the bridge. The hands that lifted the Infundibulum would be hers alone. She very much wanted to see how the Singh boy had made it work with the jumpgun. He was talented. Perhaps she should have abducted him rather than his father. Resourceful, too. Nevertheless, she would happily put three shots into him if he came between her and the prize. She might do it anyway. Deny his talents to the enemy.

Sirens blared, alarm bells rang. Too much to expect she would make it to the bridge undetected, but she had hoped for more of an advantage.

"Zaitsev!" Her lieutenant was at her shoulder, easily matching her pace. "The Confederate, the American with the mouth full of Bible quotes, he's the only real threat. He has real weapons. Find him, neutralize him." She jabbed a finger down the central access stair. From her close study of the schematics of commercial airships, she had learned that the weighmaster's station was in the cargo hold.

Alone now, and the gantries and spiral staircases and platforms of command, control, and crew zone were ahead of her. And a massive impact slammed Charlotte Villiers into the deck. Stunned, winded, she rolled. Something—someone—small and pale and very, very fierce dropped out of nowhere on top of her. The girl. The Sixsmyth kid. Charlotte Villiers punched hard, caught her in the stomach. The girl screamed and reeled back. You weren't expecting me to fight for real, Charlotte Villiers thought. Like an adult. Like it's life and death. Sen choked and puked. Charlotte Villiers grabbed her and threw her as hard as she could into a truss. Sen went down, broken, gasping, spasming like a crab on its back on the decking. Charlotte Villiers adjusted her beret.

"You've made me angry now," she said. "Vermin." She raised her boot to stamp the heel down through Sen's ribcage, snap it like a chicken's wishbone, burst her heart. A kick to the shoulder sent Charlotte Villiers staggering backwards.

"Not as angry as me." Captain Anastasia dropped from the kick into the *savate* fighting stance, coiled but open, charged but relaxed: deadly dangerous. Where had she come from? A harness, a zip-line. "So, you can beat up kids. Want to try it with momma?" She flicked her fingers: *come on if you think you're hard enough.*

"I do not have time for this," Charlotte Villiers said and drew the heavy revolver from her holster.

The whole two hundred meters of *Everness*'s hull shook. Charlotte Villiers staggered, the shot went wild. In the moment of distraction, Captain Anastasia scooped up her terribly damaged daughter, slapped the zip-line control, and was jerked up into the high vaults of *Everness*'s cathedral-like interior. Charlotte Villiers drew a bead. The airship jerked again, longer, harder. Debris snowed down from the high gantries. Charlotte Villiers grabbed the rail to steady herself and tapped the communications bar on her collar.

"What the hell is going on here?"

"There's something out there," Zaitsev shouted. "It's big. Christ it's big. Oh Jesus God!"

And now the voice of Sorensen, her lieutenant, filled with panic. Bursts of gunfire rang out from the lower levels of the airship over the clamor of alarms. "Jiju! Thousands of them!"

16

At the start of assembly the principle, Mrs. Abrahams, warned the whole school that she would extend the morning meeting for an extra five minutes. She had An Announcement. For the Whole School. She made it after the nondenominational hymn, the reading from Toni Morrison, and the regular announcements.

"The school has rats."

She waited for the laughter at the back of the assembly hall to die down.

"We have a small but stubborn infestation of rats. We have called in Pest Control to get rid of them, and they will be using poison. This will be clearly marked with a black and yellow checkerboard pattern. Do not touch the traps, do not investigate them, do not put them in your mouths. And do not touch, approach, or put in your mouths any rats, dead, or especially living. It is not cool, it is not cute. Rats have no bladders and so constantly leak urine. Rat urine is responsible for Weil's Disease, which attacks the kidneys and the brain and can be fatal."

Mass icks and ughs and whoas.

Rodent piss will do it every time, Everett M thought.

"Rats are vermin, and they will be exterminated from our school, so protests, Facebook campaigns, and petitions from PETA and any other animal welfare groups to save the cute furry animals will be ignored. Your energies would be better directed to your Key Stage SATS tests."

Mrs. Abrahams swept from the stage. The school drifted away in their Years and classes.

Noomi caught up with Everett M on the way to the lockers.

She'd done something manga with her hair.

"You've done something manga with your hair," Everett M said.

"Points for noticing," she said, flicking her fingers up her sculpt of gelled hair.

What Everett M was noticing was Gothy Emma and her emo friends hanging round at the end of the corridor. They looked self-conscious and uncomfortable and eager not to be noticed noticing. Everett M waved to them. They giggled but were unembarrassed.

"I like it," he said to Noomi.

"Trick with the car," she said. "Impressed. How?"

"It's about reflexes," Everett M said. "Timing." Her way of speaking was infectious. Noomi nodded as if he had handed her the key to all wisdom. She hurried along at Everett M's side, hugging her backpack to her chest. She was wearing over-the-knee socks again, Everett M noticed. He had always hoped he would be hot for a girl who wore over-the-knee socks. And that the girl with over-the-knee socks would be hot for him. Something went click in his heart. It was not a Thryn mechanism. It was an Everett thing. Noomi stopped suddenly. Everett M almost walked into her. She held out a Coke can.

"Could you?"

"No," he said and then saw her mouth open in disappointment, and the Everett thing in his chest died a little. "Not here."

They crossed the all-weather pitch and went behind the temporary classrooms. Gothy Emma and her cronies followed at a discreet distance.

"Give it here."

Noomi passed Everett M the Coke can.

"This will be quick."

"Can I?" Her phone was in her hand.

"No."

A flicker of Thryn enhancement, and he crushed the can, top to bottom, flat as a coin. Coke sprayed everywhere. Noomi leaped back but her eyes were wide.

"Oh, Everett."

Everett M felt a million miles tall. He could leap not just cars but whole continents, planets, galaxies. *I could get to like this feeling*, he thought.

"We're late for first class," he said.

"Oh, yeah yeah." Noomi seemed almost to be snapping out of a trance. "Shit. Damn. Stuff." She skipped away. "Impressed again, Everett." She joined her friends. They were in a stream that specialized in art, so their timetables never meshed with Everett M's. They were a wild crew, the Year Ten Art girls; wild and freethinking. They smelled of paint and modelling clay and art room. Noomi threw two words back over her shoulder. "Homework date."

"What?"

"Art plus science. I'll text you."

He was late to first-period maths. The teacher made small fun of him, but Everett M didn't feel belittled. In his mind, he was still striding over planets, world to world. Noomi used words like they were fifty pound notes, rare and precious. Everett M went back in his mind over every one of them. They were probably the most words a girl had ever said to him in one conversation.

But the big challenge that day was avoiding Ryun. School was not the place for difficult questions, otherwise Ryun would have asked them before now. But his manner had changed. He was tense, a bit standoffish, a bit wanting to be with Everett M, a bit spooked, a bit amazed. A bit like Noomi, Everett M thought. Starstruck. Except with Ryun, it's because I've been to a parallel universe and back.

Between Ryun and Noomi, the final bell could not come soon enough. Everett M's phone chimed on his first footstep outside the gates.

HOMEWORK DATE. The map linked to a coffee shop on Green Lanes. Everett M had noticed it. It had charity-shop sofas and desperate art on the walls, the kind that is beneath amateur but carries a ludicrously high price tag. The slacker dudes said you could buy skunk. Everett M had never noticed Noomi there. He had never really noticed Noomi at all until she started photographing his ass in goal.

She was waiting for him on a cracked brown-leather sofa. She had changed. Boots, knee socks over tights. Everett M loved her way with legwear. A tiny tartan kilt with straps that were just there for show. Jacket ditto. She had put on some makeup. Not too much. Everett didn't like too much makeup. It made girls look a little scary. But this was just right. It drew his eyes to her eyes, made them dark and mysterious.

"You look great," he said, crashing down onto the opposite sofa.

"Points for noticing," Noomi said. "No points for clothes."

Everett M felt self-conscious in his school uniform, but he slipped off the blazer, took off his tie, and untucked his shirt, and it looked a little more hip. Street-normal Everett M was hoodies and skinny jeans, which wouldn't have been that much less of a uniform. It was easier for girls to dress the way they wanted to be.

Noomi ordered Vietnamese coffee from the dreadlocked waiter. Everett M had never heard of Vietnamese coffee but it sounded cool and new and a bit sophisticated so he ordered one, too. It came in a tall glass and was very sweet, and there was a hint of cardamom off it. Noomi curled her legs under her.

"So far away, Everett." She patted the sofa beside her.

"Homework?" Everett M swiped open his tablet as he sat down beside her. Noomi swiped it shut.

"Later."

He could feel his heart beating. Every nerve and muscle in Everett M's body wanted to propel him out of that sofa, out of that coffee shop, down the road to Stoke Newington with every joule of Thryn energy.

"Relax." Noomi planted a hand on Everett's chest and pushed him back into the embrace of the sofa. "So tell me, are you a superhero?"

This time he almost did leap out of the sofa.

"Do you really want to know?"

Noomi leaned forward. She was wearing something that smelled very good.

"Say."

"I'm an alien cyborg double agent from a parallel universe. I've replaced the real Everett Singh."

"Lies!" Noomi punched Everett on the chest with enough weight for him to feel it.

"No, I work out."

"Teach me your workout. No. Seriously. I'd love to be really, really fit." She took Everett M's hand and placed it on her arm. "Chicken wings."

"It feels all right to me."

"Really?"

That makeup made her eyes very big.

"I think so."

Everett M had been kidnapped to the Moon, rebuilt by the Thryn Sentiency, turned into a secret agent, and thrown through gate after Heisenberg Gate; he'd been sent to face the Nahn on Earth 1, but he had never felt so completely out of his depth as he did here, on a leather sofa with Vietnamese coffees and Noomi Wong beside him. This was not a homework date. This was just a date.

"Little Lion Man" played on the café sound system.

"I know this one," Everett M said. Noomi had been nodding or tapping a foot along with every song.

"You like Mumford and Sons?"

"I said I know it, not like it."

"Points. So what do you like?"

"Oh, guy stuff," Everett M said and he told her all the bands he liked, some of which Noomi didn't know because those bands didn't exist in this universe, or had broken up a long time ago, and then he was talking about why he liked what he liked and how it made him feel and which bits he would play over and over just for that one moment when it all came together and lifted you and made you feel like a god, and how that was a thing you got in classical music, which some people thought was all meandering and no real tunes, but it was saving the real tune for just one moment of perfection, because if you did the real tune over and over again it would stop being special and be just like everything else, and the café sound system seemed to have hacked into his head because now it was playing all the things he was talking about (but not the classical—there were limits), and then he saw the dreadlocked guy slipping behind the bar every so often to press buttons and Everett M realized he was quietly DJing Everett M and Noomi, which in any other place at any other time Everett M would have found creepy but here in the warm with hot sweet Vietnamese coffee (where had the second one come from?) and the cold dark outside and the rain hard against the window it was wonderful, and Everett M was talking talking talking, the words just pouring out of him like he hadn't talked to anyone on this world, and he realized that Noomi hadn't really said anything at all, that she'd just sank deeper into the sofa and pulled her legs up closer to her, curled up and cozy, and he said *I'm sorry I'm doing all the talking*, and she nodded and said *yeah, you are, guy talk*.

The sudden yell broke everything apart. Dreadlock guy burst from the kitchen shouting, "Go on, get out of here!" and Everett M saw a rat run from under one of the sofas, making a break for the front door just as new customers opened it, escaping into the rain. "Bloody rats! Sorry about that. Coffees on the house."

Vietnamese coffee and the memory of Noomi's cute little cat-paw goodbye wave fueled Everett M home through the dreary rain. On Burma Road he stopped to check the Everett's Hot Ass page. Twelve hundred likes. Then he noticed the recent comments.

U LOOK GAY HA HA BATTY BOY

PAKI TWAT BNP ARE GOING TO BURN YOUR HOUSE AND FAMILY PAKI

SEE WHAT YOU THINK OF YOURSELF EVERETT SINGH WELL I'M HERE TO TELL YOU YOU'RE NOTHING SPECIAL I WOULDN'T GO OUT WITH YOU IF YOU WERE THE LAST BOY ON EARTH

SHIT GOALKEEPER.

GETS HIS KIT IN CASH CONVERTERS

HIS DAD RAN OFF BECAUSE HE'S LIVING WITH A BIG TURK GAYLORD IN DALSTON

Everett M felt like he had been hit in the stomach. The cold sickness was not fear but anger. Cold became heat, stronger than any Thryn technology. He drew back his hand to throw the phone at a shop shutter, smash it and stomp it and smash it. He held himself back. It was a good phone. It was only a phone. It was people who were poisonous. People hiding behind made-up names so they could be vile. Any of these people he could take in a straight fight; smash them open, make them weep with despair and then scream in fear for their lives. But his powers were powerless here. They hid behind pseudonyms and said whatever they wanted to say, knowing no one would ever touch them.

Like Facebook, like the world. With all the powers and weapons he had been given, he still couldn't touch any of the forces that directed his life. Charlotte Villiers and her creepy alter were whole universes away, but they still pulled the strings on his life. Charlotte Villiers had his family. His real family. Real power wasn't finger lasers and EM-pulse guns. Real power was controlling people.

He thought about Noomi. He thought about the furry animal-ear hat she had pulled on as she left the coffee shop. He thought about that little wave, fingers curled like tiny claws. Miaow miaow.

The world seemed a little warmer.

He heard the sound as he opened the front door. It cut off immediately, but there was no mistaking it. Crying. Adult crying. A terrible sound. Everett looked into the living room. His mum was sitting upright on the sofa. The television blared an early evening game show. Laura made a pretense of watching intently, but Everett M could see her chest tremble with each breath.

"Are you all right?"

She turned and pretended to be surprised to see him.

"Oh, Everett, I didn't hear you. I'm fine love."

Everett M turned up his Thryn hearing. He could not pick out Victory-Rose's from the soundscape of house noises.

"Where's Victory-Rose?"

"Nana Braiden took her out to feed ducks." Laura looked at Everett, then her face softened and she chewed back tears. "Oh I'm not fine, Evvie, I'm not at all."

"What is it?"

He had seen his mum like this, choking back from crying because she knew that if she started she would not stop. He had seen Mum break down helplessly. It had been at the funeral when Colette from the university read verses from the Bhagavad Gita. Everett M had stood beside her, not knowing what to do, whether it was right for a fourteen-year-old son to put an arm around his mother, afraid that if he did he would start crying too and not be able to stop, afraid that everyone would look and mutter and feel embarrassed for him if he did, afraid that everyone would look and mutter and feel embarrassed by him, if he did not. The boy who wouldn't hug his mother. He wished he had, more than anything. He wished he had as much as he wished his dad hadn't set out on the bike that morning.

"Oh, Everett, it's everything. Come and sit with me love."

Laura patted the sofa. Everett sat at the far end.

"I miss him, Everett. Oh, I miss him so much. Why? It's stupid isn't it. We're not even together any more, but knowing he's not there at all . . . Oh, I know you shouldn't ask why, but you can't help asking yourself, was there anything I did? I go over it again and again and again."

Everett M quietly reached for the remote control and turned off the television.

"You know, I don't think it would be so bad if he were dead. God forgive me for saying that, but at least I would know. But to be just gone—vanished—there one moment, away the next—well, you have to hope, don't you? And it's the hoping kills you, doesn't it?"

"I know he's alive," Everett M said.

"Oh, bless you love. I wish I could be as sure."

But he didn't know, not for sure. Charlotte Villiers had briefed him on everything about this world's Tejendra Singh, from the maths underlying the Infundibulum to the kidnapping on the Mall and corrupting the police to make it look as if his alter was a liar, to the moment in the Tyrone Tower on Earth 3 when Tejendra Singh had pushed his son out of the focus of the jumpgun only to be banished to a random parallel universe. The word *random* was the killer here. A million million differences could kill you—too hot, too cold, too high, too low, no Earth at all. But a billion billion similarities could save you, Everett M thought.

He shifted closer to Laura.

"And when you went away . . . oh, I'm sorry Evvie, I know they said you'd talk about it when you were good and ready. But no one's listened to me, no one's asked me how I felt. To lose two people you love, so soon, so quickly. You just went out to Ryun's house and didn't come back . . . you ask yourself, is it something I've done? You tell yourself, it has to be something I've done, because no one could be that unlucky."

"I came back," Everett M said.

Laura smiled.

"You came back."

She rested her arm on Everett M's arm. He moved close to her. Side by side. *But I didn't*, Everett M shouted inside. *I'm a fake. I'm a cuckoo in the nest. I'm not your son. I'm not even my mum's son now. The Thryn have made me into something I can't think about too much. But I know what it's like when an ordinary day turns into the worst day of all. There's no warning, no clues or signs. It just comes out of nowhere and happens.*

"It's a bloody horrible month, January," Laura said. "It never ends. All the dark stuff. You're a good boy, Everett."

I wish I could be, Everett M thought.

"When's Nana B bringing Vee-Ar back?" he said.

"She said they might go to McD's."

"Do you want me to fix you something, food wise? You just stay there, you don't have to do anything."

"Would you? You're a better cook than me, Everett."

My alter is, Everett M thought.

"You stay there."

As he hunted through the kitchen for things he could cook, Everett M heard the crying start again. *You're not my enemy now*, he thought. *Not you, not Victory-Rose. Not even him. The alter. Everett.*

Everett M jumped as he looked up from the fridge to see the rat on the window ledge. Its black eyes fixed on his. Everett rapped the glass. The rat looked at him.

"Cheeky . . ."

Everett opened the back door and lunged at the rat. It leaped down from the window ledge and ran a few meters down the garden. It stopped in the path and looked long and hard at Everett M. He chased it; it retreated another few meters. And again.

"This is stupid," Everett M said, then ran with a yell at the rat. It fled and dived out through the cat hole in the rear gate. Everett followed it out into the back alley. And stopped.

Rats. On the trash bins. On the walls. On the discarded washing machines and rotting sofas and old kiddie trikes that the people of

Roding Road had left out for collection. On the cracked flower pots and planters. On the scabby concrete. Rats. Dozens of black eyes, watching Everett M. The eyes . . . Everett M thought power into his Thryn weapons. He felt the seals in his skin unbind, a sick sensation of coming apart he knew he would never get used to. He clenched his fists. In a blink, the rats vanished, as only rats can.

17

He waited beneath the diplodocus. The Central Hall was huge and cold draughts blew in from odd directions. Ten minutes to closing and the hall was still thronged with visitors. Schoolchildren with enormous backpacks snaked towards the gift shop, looking up at the wonderful things over their heads. Bones and dead stuff. Long-armed skeletons swung from the roof beams: gibbons or some other tree-swinging monkey, he reckoned. Looking up and round eventually brought you to the diplodocus, the center and heart of the hall. Its head was really, really small, he decided. He checked the time. Five minutes since he'd last checked. The public address announced that the museum would be closing in five minutes.

It had taken all his courage to make the call. Picking up the phone, cold-calling the university, asking to be put through to Doctor Colette Harte. Her phone had rung and rung and rung. He had ditched the introduction he had prepared and worked out a new one for the message service, but then a real, live human voice had answered and both the new script and the old one went out of his head. He stammered. He jabbered.

"Who is this?" Colette Harte sounded fierce.

"Ryun Spinetti. I'm a friend of Everett's. Everett Singh. Like you were. Are."

A long pause.

"What's this about?"

"I need to see you. There's things that don't make sense."

A longer pause.

"All right. Central Hall at the Natural History Museum. Closing time."

"Where?" he had asked but Colette had disconnected.

When he got there, the answer to the question was obvious.

"It's not real, you know." The sudden voice startled Ryun, gazing up at the tiny head on the elegant curved neck. "There are at least a dozen other replicas in museums around the world."

Colette Harte. Taller and younger than he had imagined, but his imagination could not have predicted the purple hair. New Rock boots. She offered a hand and an introduction. Her grip was strong.

"Okay, Ryun, we're going to go somewhere else. This is a bit déjà vu because I met Everett right here, just before Christmas."

"I know. You went for sushi. You gave him a memory stick."

"You like sushi?"

"I like sushi a lot."

In the taxi she asked him testing and detailed questions about Everett, the kind that only a best friend would know. She asked for a booth at the sushi place while Ryun left his shoes by the sliding door. He wriggled his feet around to hide the hole in his sock, right over the big toe. The booth was warm but small and Ryun felt self-conscious so close to this woman who was only one step away from being a stranger. She ordered tea and a round of smoked eel nigiri. Ryun went for the crab roll.

"Did you see what was on the memory stick?" Colette asked.

"Everett showed me it, yes."

"I wish he hadn't done that."

"Parallel universes exist."

"They do. They're real. You didn't take a copy of the files on that memory stick, did you?"

"No."

"That's good. That's about the only thing that is good."

Ryun took some tea from the bowl. His heart was fluttering; he could hardly breathe, hardly lift the tea bowl to his lips. His hands shook. He had been scared making the call, scared when Colette had agreed to meet him, scared when he told his mum and dad a lie about where he was going after school, scared all the way down on the train and the tube, scared going up the steps to the imposing front of the Natural History Museum, scared in the taxi, and scared in this paper booth. He had thought that maybe there was a place beyond scared, like the eye of a hurricane where there was calm and cool and peace. There wasn't. Beyond scared was only more scared.

"When Everett disappeared, he went to one of those parallel universes."

"Where did you get that idea from?"

"He told me."

"What did he say?"

"He said his dad was heading up some interuniverse defense force, protecting the Ten Worlds of the Plenitude. He said like his dad was in some kind of witness protection scheme, and that he—Everett—he'd been assigned like a special protection team—like Navy SEALS but with an airship. If he opened an app on his phone, they'd jump in from some other universe. But . . ."

"But."

"But I don't believe it."

Colette Harte closed her eyes and let out a shallow sigh.

"From the curiosity of teenage males, good Lord deliver us. Ryun, why did you call me?"

"Because you worked with Everett's dad. I thought you might know the truth."

"Do you think Everett's not telling you the truth?"

"I don't think so."

"If I knew the truth, do you think I would tell you?"

"Maybe. Maybe not."

"What if I said everything he said is true?"

"Well, then, that's good. But . . ."

"Your 'buts' are spooking me, Ryun."

"But then there's the text message."

He held out his phone.

"Get this 2 Mum: am OK. Dad OK. See u soon," Colette read.

"Yes, but . . ."

"But . . ."

Another round of sushi arrived, and fresh tea and Kombucha for Ryun.

"First thing: why would Everett send that to me, when he was coming back the very next day?"

"There's a second thing?"

"The second thing is: when I showed it to Everett, he said he hadn't sent it. Then he said he didn't remember sending it. Then he said he'd lost his phone. Why would he send that text and then say he'd lost his phone? Doesn't make sense. But there's a third thing. Well, third and a fourth. Third thing is: in the showers? At the school? In the changing room? Well, he never used to go into the showers with everyone else because he was shy that way, but he did, and he had all these scars, like lines along his arms and legs. I never saw those before. They made me feel weird. And that's also the fourth thing, because since he came back, well, there's things he does he never did before, and things he doesn't do that he used to. Sometimes I don't know him at all. He's like a totally different person."

"What do you think I can do, Ryun?" Colette asked.

"Well, I think you know what's happening."

"Ryun, do you think you can trust me? You've met a complete stranger and she's taken you for sushi, and you've gone with her, without checking, without asking, without thinking. You know nothing about me, Ryun, who I am, what I do, who I work for? I could be a very dangerous person. I might be about to have you abducted or killed. Have you told anyone where you are?"

Suddenly Colette was the fierce voice he had heard on the phone and Ryun realized that he had lived his life among people who were basically good and true and honest and reliable—even in school—and had assumed that everyone else was like that too. The world didn't have to be like that.

"Everett trusted you, and you trusted him, so I will."

"Then I will tell the truth. The truth is that if I told you the truth, the whole truth, you would be in danger. Very great danger. Me and Everett's dad were members of a research group exploring the possibility of the existence of parallel worlds, and communicating with them. We first made contact with a plane we call Earth 2."

"That was the one you sent the drone to?"

"Earth 2 is a member of a federation of parallel universes called the Plenitude of Known Worlds. There are nine alternative earths. We are in the process of becoming number ten. I've become involved in the accession process—it's long and it's complicated and it's politics and stuff I don't get and I don't like. But it involves me in a lot of jumping around between parallel universes. You've dropped your sushi, Ryun."

He hadn't noticed it slip from his chopsticks. Colette smiled.

"Yes, me. This morning I had breakfast in a café on Earth 7. The Plenitude is moving its headquarters from Earth 3 . . ."

"That's where Everett was!" Ryun exclaimed. "The one with no oil."

"And airships," Colette continued. "Wonderful airships. The Plenitude is moving offices from Earth 3 to Earth 7. I only got back on this world at lunchtime. I was just back in my office when you called. The Plenitude is big and it's powerful, but it's just a handful of worlds among the billions and billions of the Panoply. That's the multiverse, Ryun, the whole shebang. All the parallel worlds. And there are worlds—forces, powers, species—that are a threat to the Plenitude, and our world as well. But the Plenitude has its factions and groups and parties, and they don't always work together. And some of them are powerful and dangerous. And some of them want what Everett's dad has."

"The map of all the worlds."

"The Infundibulum. It's a very powerful weapon in the wrong hands. We have to keep it safe. Everett is in danger, his dad is in danger, I'm in danger. If I told you everything, you'd be in danger too. The fewer people who know, the better, Ryun. Ignorance is safety."

This wasn't right. Wasn't *right*. Maybe it was a stupid, naïve thing, to go asking big questions without thinking about whether he could take the answers. Maybe he trusted people too much and assumed everyone was a white hat. But her answers had answered precisely nothing. Colette had just turned his questions back on him. *Trust me, it's for your own good* was never an answer.

"But he's a mate. He's my friend."

Colette laid her hand gently on his.

"Be a mate." She gripped his hand firmly but gently. "Be there with him. Don't push him. All those 'buts' you have—don't say them to him. Keep them to yourself. But look out for him. Be a friend."

The bill arrived, immaculately folded. Colette slipped a card onto the little lacquered tray.

"Are you a friend, Colette?"

Ryun looked her in the eyes. He never felt comfortable doing that, but what he saw in her eyes, he could believe.

"He doesn't know it yet, but I am. I always have been. Ryun, you can call me. If you see anything strange, if you get worried about him, call me. Be my eyes, would you?"

Ryun nodded. Colette tapped the screen of her phone.

"I'll get you a taxi home. It's a long way back to Stokie."

"Thank you for the sushi."

"You're welcome."

Ryun slipped on his shoes and waited on the bench seat by the door for the minicab to arrive. Colette slipped out into the night. He watched her purple hair blend into the crowd of muffled-up winter pedestrians. She had told him nothing, but he had learned something anyway. He had been concerned before. Now he was afraid. Terribly afraid.

She didn't hear him. She didn't see him. A cold wind, gusting sprays of piercing rain, had blown up in the Georgian streets and squares of Fitzrovia. Colette pulled up her collar and put her head down and so she did not see the man get up from his table in the window of the Cypriot café opposite and step out into the street. He kept six pedestrians between him and her. He was careful to look as cold and angry with the weather as everyone else but she did not look behind her. She was an amateur at this and he was a professional. She turned onto Tottenham Court Road. He kept his distance but did not let her out of his sight. She swiped her Oyster card through the gate of Warren Street tube station and she didn't see, didn't hear, didn't suspect the follower six bodies behind her. He passed his hand over the scanner and the clever little chip embedded in his fingertip fooled the computer and let him through.

Cold winds were also blowing sleet through the alleys and canals of the elegant city of Heiden, on Earth 7, where a man sat back in his comfortable leather chair by a coal fire, closed his eyes, and watched his twin a universe away stalk Colette Harte across London.

18

Charlotte Villiers snapped the revolver on to the figures flying up into the folds of *Everness*'s gas cells. Snapped it away. The bridge lay before her, and the prize. She had a finer revenge in mind for Anastasia Sixsmyth; it could wait until her squad armed the demolition charges and blew Captain Anastasia's ludicrous gasbag to rags and scraps of ship skin around her.

The Jiju. They had not been part of the plan. That they were here could only mean one thing: they sought the same prize she was chasing. Ibrim Hoj Kerrim's nightmare: the Jiju, a trillion of them, with a sixty-five-million-year head start on humanity and a million open doors into the Plenitude. Worlds would burn.

Beams of light slashed across the airship's gloomy interior; from above, left and right, stabbing up from below. The Jiju were opening holes in the hull. Cries. Screams. Human voices. Her squad was engaging the Jiju and losing. The Infundibulum was everything. Revolver in hand, Charlotte Villiers ran for the head of the ship. Would no one shut those alarms off?

"Ma'am, ma'am, they're coming through the walls!" Sorensen's panicked voice in the earpiece. "They're everywhere!" A stutter of automatic fire, on the radio and from deep down in the belly of the ship. A cry, quickly cut off. In the edges of her vision, Charlotte Villiers saw the darting, dancing movement of Jiju warriors. The Dear, they were fast. Again, the ship lurched and threw her against the railing, almost toppling her over. A falling object hit the walkway with a hard crunch. A head. A human head. Charlotte Villiers fought down the reflex gag. The headless body lay on the edge of the topmost catwalk. Blood dripped through the mesh. No time for horror. Only a few meters more to the companionway down to the bridge.

"Sorensen!" Dead air on the radio. "Zaitsev! Report!"

"I'm on my own. They're cutting us apart."

"McClelland, Akauola, Chambers?"

"Gone."

Four left. Four left. For the first time, Charlotte Villiers knew the cold helplessness of panic. She did not know what to do. No. Command is command: give an order. It doesn't matter whether it is right or wrong, good or bad. Do something. Then she thumbed the communicator bar on her collar.

"Everyone to the forward companionway. We will rendezvous, take the Infundibulum, and get the hell out of here."

"I've got you, I've got you."

Flashes. Flying: lift cells like big full moons above her. Arms locked around her. Loud noises, bangs, shots. A hard landing that made her cry out.

"Come on, Sen. Come on my love."

Holes opening the skin. Light pouring in: and more than light. Flashes. That crying sound: it was her own voice. But over under inside more than everything: hurt. Hurt outside: every inch of skin and muscle a wall of pain. Hurt inside: things broken there. Hurt in the heart: the Villiers polone had smashed her like a cockroach. Hurt everywhere, so big the only way to get away from it would be to die.

Flashing in and out of black. A voice: "Come on, my love, my dilly, my dorcas. We're almost there."

World shaking. Nothing to hold. Tumbling down stairs: hurt on hurt. Crying with pain. Black is good. Black is warm. Black is no pain.

"Come on my love stay with me! Sen, stay with me!"

Black/no black. Black/no black. Don't go to the black. Don't go. Don't go!

Door banging open. "Mchynlyth! Mchynlyth! First aid!"

And silence. So sudden, so sharp she forced herself up out of black. Forced eyes open. Great window. Out there. *Out there*. Tentacles. Living/machine. Twisting/twining. The ship in its grasp.

Black.

And out. She hurt, so she was alive. On her back on the deck. Looking up into Mchynlyth's brown face. Hiss, spray. Cool . . . and *no pain*.

"Easy easy. Jesus Krishna; that bitch, if I ever catch her . . ."

The ship shook again. Behind Mchynlyth, the tentacles opened. At the center, a steel squid.

"What . . ."

"Sssh." Shots. Figures running along the tentacles. "This'll hurt a wee bit." Mchynlyth's hands on her shoulder, then a wrench and more pain than the universe could hold. Black.

Into Ma's black face.

"Sun. Gun. Sungun."

"Sen, don't say anything. You're hurt bad."

"Sungun. Earth 1. The black things . . ."

"Captain." Mchynlyth's voice. "That thing Everett did. It could get those bastards away from the ship. Sen, polone, can you work it?"

"Saw what he did."

"Sen, no. Mchynlyth, help her."

"It's the ship!" Mchynlyth's voice blazed with anger.

"Mr. Mchynlyth, control your anger." Captain Anastasia's voice was as cold as Mchynlyth's was hot. "It's *my* ship. And I will save my ship. But right now, my daughter needs me more. Help her, Mr. Mchynlyth."

A pause, a hiss of defeated rage.

"Aye, ma'am."

A crash so huge it jolted her out of the warm black. The bridge door was down, smoking. Jiju on the bridge. The deck beneath her lurched. The ship was moving. Mchynlyth was shouting. Ma was shouting. The Jiju were singing. But loudest of all was the black, and she answered it, and went deep down into it and let it cover her over.

Charlotte Villiers saw the soldier die in front of her. He clattered down the companionway to arrive breathless on the platform at the end of the main spine, gun covering the angles. Then the air between him and her curdled like heat haze, and three Jiju were there. Each held a staff in her hand. One spread her long fingers wide and stabbed them towards the soldier. The globe at the tip of the staff dissolved into a dozen flying metal shafts that ran the solider through and through. The Jiju curled her hand and the shafts vanished and reappeared on her staff.

The Jiju turned towards Charlotte Villiers.

She held the gun steady. She was the Empire Games Small Arms gold medalist, but even she could never take all of them.

Time slowed to crawl. Every moment was frozen. This was what death was like, time frozen, one final moment that lasted forever.

A Jiju extended her staff towards Charlotte Villiers.

Behind the Jiju, Zaitsev pounded up the companionway.

It was all over.

"Forgive me," Charlotte Villiers said. She held Zaitsev's eyes as she hit the relay on her arm. The Einstein Gate opened. She could still see the look on his face—betrayed, abandoned, left to die—as she dived into the white light.

19

The Sunlord ship turned in the air over the slash in Crèchewood. There was no mistaking *Everness*'s crash landing—she had torn a path of snapped wood, torn branches, headless trees through over a kilometer of forest canopy. *Everness* herself: not a sign. She had vanished.

Looking down from the observation bubble in the left hull of the Sunlord sky catamaran into the empty space, Everett was gripped by a terrible fear. *Everness* gone cleanly, completely, without a trace or a mark: exactly how it would look if she had made a Heisenberg jump.

Sen had watched everything he did. She was observant, smart, a clever copycat. She didn't need to understand how to calculate jump points for the Infundibulum; all she had to do was pull them out of the memory and hit the jump button. Marooned on Diskworld. She would never do that. Not Sen. Captain Anastasia would never order it. Unless the ship was faced with something so terrible, so total, that the only option was to make a Heisenberg jump. *Unless*: such a sneaky, mean little word.

Crèchewood had shaken to a boom high in the air. Sharkey reached by instinct for his guns. *That's a sonic boom*, Everett thought, *but you won't ever have heard that*. Sharkey's world had no jets, no rockets, no missiles. Moments later the Sunlord skymaran arrived over the clearing. It was as nimble as a dragonfly. Everett could not tell what made it fly. Nothing as ordinary as lift gas or wings or jet engines. *There's some physical principle at work here*, Everett thought. *It's not scifi magic keeping it up. And it's not antigravity either.* That was just another kind of magic, one pretending to be science. Like time machines and transporter beams. But it was impressive, the way the machine folded up like an origami bird to descend down the shaft between the trees.

Kax's halo was rippling silver-green: excitement, Everett guessed. The skymaran touched down light as a kiss. Two Jiju descended the ramp between the twin hulls. At the sight of the humans their crests rose and their halos snapped into a ring of spikes. Kax sang a short song; the Jiju folded their hands together in a gesture that, to human eyes, looked half prayer, half worry: to Kax, then to Everett and Sharkey. Sharkey stowed his guns and returned the greeting with a bow. Everett had never learned any lessons in reptile etiquette.

"We will go and find out what has happened to your ship," Kax said. The Jiju stood aside to let her and the humans board the skymaran.

These are the first adult Jiju you've ever seen, Everett thought as Kax stalked proudly past. This is as new to you as it is to me. But it's all in your halo: the wisdom of all of your Hatch, and the wisdom of all the Jiju.

"This is some bona kit," Sharkey whispered as the flyer lifted. Through the portside viewing blister Everett could see shy scavengers sneak out of the forest to pick and tear at the carcass of the dead Jiju. So end princesses, he thought. Above the trees the skymaran unfolded into flight mode. Kax took a proud position in the transparent bubble at the front of the starboard hull. At the center of the craft, where the hulls joined, the Jiju crew moved their hands over a hovering projection of Crèchewood. A gesture sent the skymaran over the forest canopy. It came to a halt over the *Everness* crash site without any discernible shift in acceleration.

"'Thou art a stranger, and also an exile,'" Sharkey whispered. Everett stared at the empty space where the airship had lain. He did not know what to do. He was out of ideas. His cleverness had come to an end.

The Jiju pilot sang something. Kax was in the other hull but her voice came clear to Everett and Sharkey.

"We've picked up four contacts on our scanners. Three skyqueens of the Genequeens, and one human airship."

"*Everness*," Everett whispered. He hadn't been abandoned. He wasn't alone, marooned. The ship was still here, and all the people he cared about. It had been taken by the Genequeens, but that was a solvable problem. He would think of something. He felt sick with relief. In the opposite pod Kax heard him whisper and glanced over. Everett hardly recognized her. Physically she was the same Kax, minus a few centimeters of crest, plus a few cuts and scars, but everything was different. It had been the same for the guys who had fights at school. Before the fight, they had been his friends, his schoolmates; after it, it was as if the fighting had stained their skins. There was violence on them. They seemed less human to Everett.

"Well, let's get after them and visit some righteous wrath on their reptile asses, begging your pardon, ma'am," Sharkey said. "I mean, your Highness."

"This is a Sunlord Royal Yacht," Kax said. "Those are three well-armed skyqueens. They would cut the bones out of our bodies."

"We can't leave them!" Everett shouted. The Jiju pilots' crests shot up.

"I won't," Kax said. "I owe you, Everett. But for you, I would be dead in the Crèchewood. Instead, I am a princess." Kax held out her hands. The deck opened, machine arms reached out, unfolded, draped Kax's body in a richly worked tunic and a heavy jewelled collar. "Clothes do make the woman," Kax said, admiring herself. "One needs to be properly dressed to visit my mother."

Jiju faces. Nostrils flickering, eye membranes blinking. Close enough to feel their breath against her cheek, and taste its sweet, musky smell on her tongue. Sen cried out and surged up, hands slapping, beating them away. The Jiju reeled back, fluting in alarm.

"Easy, easy." Hands on her shoulders. Jolting pain. She remembered Mchynlyth taking the shoulder in his hands. He swore constantly, softly, deeply, angry beyond any anger at what Charlotte Villiers had done. "This will hurt." He did something to her shoulder so painful it had been bliss to drop back into unconsciousness. She had put it out, broken it, done something. No, she'd done nothing. That polone, that Villiers, she had done it to her. Sen felt dirty, abused, violated. Someone else's hands had worked their will on her body.

The middle one of the three Jiju lowered her staff towards Sen's face.

"You get your witchy shite away from that wee polone!" Mchynlyth yelled. His face was tight with rage, the spit flying from his mouth.

"Easy, easy." Ma's voice.

The staff ended in an amber sphere the size of a fist. The sphere touched her forehead. And Sen saw . . .

Cities woven from forests. Skyscrapers made from living trees. Vehicles, factories, flying machines that weren't completely machine, but half living. Wooden temples pouring out torrents of water and Jiju hatchlings. Prairies grazed by rainbow-colored bird dinosaurs the size of houses. Huge ocean waves that were sea creatures. Living clouds. The images danced to a million voices singing and piping in her head.

"Ah!" Sen gasped. "Oh!"

Then the amber globe was lifted away from her forehead. The visions died. The song ended.

"Are you well?" the central Jiju said.

"Aye, she's only got cracked ribs, internal bruising, and a dislocated shoulder," Mchynlyth growled. "And concussion. She's as right as ninepence." The Jiju ignored him.

"You stole my language!" Sen said. "Like . . ." *Like Kax*, she had almost said. Sen shut herself up.

"Like?" The three Jiju cocked their heads to one side. Also like Kax.

"Like magic," Sen said. Out of the corner of her eye she saw her ma smile.

"I'm Jekajek Rasteem Besheshkek," the middle Jiju said. It had her voice, her accent, her way of speaking. "This is Deddeshren Seveyamat Besheshkek." The Jiju on her right pursed fingers together and dipped its head. "And Kelakavaka Hinreyu Besheshkek." The Jiju on her left repeated the gesture. "You are under the protection of Her Exaltation the Marquis of Harhada. Hold still, polone."

The three Jiju passed their staffs over Sen's body. Their voices were like a conversation of birds.

"The DNA is alien to us," Jekajek said. "There are limits to what we can do."

"Ma?" Sen whimpered.

"What are you doing?" Captain Anastasia said.

"Why, making her better," Jekajek said, blinking her eye membranes. The staff tips unwound into steamers of golden dust that twined over Sen's face, settling lower and lower until they flowed over her features like rivulets of liquid light.

"What? No . . ." They were up her nose, in her ears. Sen blinked as they wormed into her tear ducts. A gasp, and they were down her throat. She choked and sucked them into her lungs, gagged, and they slipped into her stomach. After the moment of panic, of the horror of being invaded, there was no pain. Waves of warm pleasure pulsed out through her body like the ripples of many stones dropped into clear water meeting. "Ooh," she said. "Ah. Uh! Oh! Oh! Oh!" From her lungs down through her body, her kiki, down her thighs and out through her toes. Up through her heart, each valve pulsing glowing heat, like a steam engine, into her throat like the warm warm rakia Sharkey gave her from his hip flask on the cold Baltic runs. Down her arms, like strength in every muscle. Her fingers tingled. She felt like she could play a piano.

"Oh the Dear oh my word oh . . ."

Spasms of warmth inside. The Jiju stood upright and the streamers of gold snaked out of the orifices of her body and wound around the staff heads to once again form amber spheres.

Sen felt drunk. There was no pain. No pain at all.

"Oh, wow." She tried to get to her feet, wobbled. Captain Anastasia caught her.

"Are you all right?"

"Yes." Sen was still woozy from the treatment. Then, "no!" The cough came up from the very bottom of her lungs, a wracking, retching heave that dragged up all the clogged buried stuff deep down and wrapped it into a ball of vile phlegm. "It's black!" Sen yelped at the gob that came up from her lungs onto the deck.

"I'm not cleaning that up," Mchynlyth protested. "Just so as you know."

"Your respiratory system was badly congested with carbon soot," Jekajek said. Years of flying through the Smoke Ring, the circle of coal-fired power plants that fed London's burning addiction for electricity. Smogs and soots and smokes and vapors. Sen gulped, once, twice.

"I can taste the air!" She licked her lips. "It's like . . . douce, bona, clean. Now I knows what Everett Singh was cackling on about."

"We also found a congenital deformity in one of your heart valves," Jekajek said, "It could have limited your life in later years. We repaired it. However, there was a sickness we did not heal—an imbalance in dopamine, norepinephrine, and serotonin levels in your brain that was causing irrational behavior. We believe it was connected with human emotions of attraction and attachment to the young male, Everett Singh. If you want, we can remove them."

What were they saying about her heart, and Everett? Didn't matter: beyond the great window was something amazing: steel tentacles. Sen rested her hands on the glass. *Everness* was clasped in the embrace of three large flying devices—her mind went first to the word *machine*, but no machine ever moved so gracefully, with so much life. Armored tentacles studded with suckers held the hull firm. Jiju images flashed through Sen's brain of lashing tentacles in a vast vat of dark, oily liquid: the Genequeens built machines that were half alive and living creatures that were half machine. But in her head, cries rang out: those tentacles thrashed in pain. *It hurts, don't it?* Sen thought, looking out at the huge armored body of the flying machine/ creature. *Every day, every hour, every minute. It never stops.*

And she hurt in a place Jiju medical technology could never touch. But Charlotte Villiers touched it; Charlotte Villiers stabbed a fist into the heart of it. Her violence had told Sen: you are nothing, no one, you have no value, you are just a thing, and I crush you under my foot. Sen knew she would hurt there, every day, every hour, every minute. It would never stop. *Until I cut your heart out*, Sen whispered under her breath. And that's an amriya, polone.

20

The cities went on forever.

Everett had lost all sense of distance and time, leaning against the observation bubble at the front of the flyer's left hull, hypnotized by the view unrolling beneath him. From the vantage of *Everness*, caught in the high branches, Everett had not been able to see any end to Crèchewood, but now he saw that it was only a park—a city square, even—in endless farmlands punctured by mile-high towers of glass and metal and monstrous stepped pyramids the size of entire Earth cities, so tall their summits reached outside Diskworld's atmosphere. Aircraft by the hundreds darted like swarms of flies. The Alderson Disk could hold a billion such cities and still be mostly wilderness and empty space. The Sunlord royal yacht had accelerated smoothly to supersonic speed, but the dull sameness of the farm, pyramid city, farm, pyramid city made Everett feel like he was moving but standing still at the same time.

He had never felt so far from home.

"That was fun. Not as much fun as having a rectal boil lanced, but close."

Everett had not heard Sharkey come up behind him. For a tall man, Sharkey was light on his feet. He had been engaged in the corner of the yacht that the crew used as their toilet facilities. The Jiju did not share human ickiness about bodily functions. As long as it was hygienic, it did not matter that it was in full view of the pilots' station. Everett worried about that. Everett worried also about what they would get to eat. Everett worried every second about everything.

"I think they must do it with electromagnetic forces," Everett said. "I mean, this thing is like as aerodynamic as a brick, but what speed is it doing? Well over supersonic, but you don't feel a thing. There must be something around us, making us more streamlined, that we can't see. Some kind of force-field thing, and if they can do that maybe they can also use it to fly with, or maybe like magnets; if they had room-temperature superconducting magnets, they could do almost anything with that: magnetic levitation and everything; and if they can draw power through the ground—if there's like a super-conducting network through the whole Diskworld . . ." Everett broke off. "I'm talking really fast, aren't I?"

"Yup," Sharkey said. "And a lot."

You don't have to try to explain everything, Captain Anastasia had told him when he came upon her repairing the wreckage of the High Mess. He knew his mouth got fast and full of ideas when he was scared. It was the one thing he could control, the science.

"I'm sorry, it's just, everything. Everyone. The captain, and Sen . . . and Dad. I feel like . . . I should be doing something, and I don't know what. I don't know what to do Sharkey."

"Maybe you don't have to do anything, Everett," Sharkey said. "Maybe this time all you have to do is trust that other people can get themselves out of trouble without you. Sen, Mchynlyth, the captain—the Jiju have got themselves a passel of trouble there. They'll be fine and dandy, Everett. The captain looks after her own. Let me tell you a yarn.

"I believe I've intimated to you that I am a no-good sixth son of a sixth son—it's a Southern superstition: seventh sons of seventh sons have an angel in them, but sixth sons of sixth sons are marked for hell. The sixth son of a sixth son of a sixth son, should such a being ever exist, well, he'd be the anti-Christ himself."

"The Number of the Beast," Everett said.

"Correct, Mr. Singh. 'Let him that hath understanding count the number of the beast: for it is the number of a man; and his number is six hundred threescore and six.' You do well to heed the word of the Dear. Me, I quote it but I don't practice it. Don't even much believe it, truth be told. I was in Stamboul when the captain found me, down and out in Eminonu with five thousand Ottoman Lira on my head. It's a fine city, Stamboul, a true navel of the world, but it's no place to be when every hand has a knife in it. I'd been carrying out contract work for the Sublime Porte. The kind best done by foreigners who can be got out of the country discreetly. Except that my employer decided that it was cheaper just to issue another contract—on me. They came close, in an alley in Sultanahmet. I saw the knife in time. I sent that one to the bottom of the Golden Horn. God is great, but I knew I wouldn't get a second chance. And I was tired . . . I shipped over to Haydarpasha—you'll never have seen the airships over the hills on the Asian side of the Bosporus kindling shimmer and gold in the dawn light. There is no sight like it. From the little I've seen of your world, Everett, it seems a poor place. Flavorless. Pastel colored. Passionless. No offense.

"The captain knew what I was the moment I walked into the bar, but she never said a word. Never raised an eyebrow. I'd heard she was looking for a weighmaster and I worked enough on the Atlanta-Mejico lines to convince her I knew what I was doing. She took me in and weighed me, just like I weighed you up, sir. Worth my weight in ballast water. And do you know, we cast off and ran out over the Bosporus and the minarets of the mosques with the winter light on them and Asia at my back and my face set to Europe, and I cried, Mr. Singh. I cried like an infant. And I cried like a man—and that's some deep crying, like something tearing inside you—because I realized I had been sick, heart sick, of all the things I had done, and the man I had become. Sick of myself. Sick for a long long time. Cried like a little tiny child, Everett. The ship gave me a new family.

"But those Ottomans take their contracts serious and collect their dues. I had made the Baltic run a dozen times, sailed the Atlantic to the three Americas; Iceland, St Petersburg, Old High Deutschland, and I got used to the work, I got comfortable in my latty and down in the Knights of the Air. I got lazy. I didn't see them. I never thought . . . The knife was within an inch of my kidneys when the captain jumped them. She fought like a lion, sir, a lion. Four of them, and me down and bloody, but she beat them down. She put them to the dirt and ground them in. The fight was all but over by the time Mchynlyth arrived—he is quite insane; sometimes that works for us, sometimes it works against us."

"He seems very angry," Everett said. "He has what we call anger-management issues."

"He has reason," Sharkey said. "But this is the point. I picked myself up and wiped off the blood and the captain never said a word. Not a question about who these people were and why they wanted to extract my liver with a hooked Ottoman blade. She knew. She'd known from the moment I'd arrived in the Hezarfen Celebi Bar spinning her my little lies. Maybe that's why she took me in—she's always had a soft spot for waifs and vagabonds. She took you in."

Everett shivered, remembering how poorly he had repaid that trust.

"Sen, Mchynlyth—he'd been her chief engineer long before I trolled along . . . me."

"Mchynlyth was in the navy, right? I remember him saying he was an engineer on the *Royal Oak*. Why did he leave?"

"Love," Sharkey said. "Why else does anyone leave? But it was love His Majesty's Air Navy didn't recognize. Nor the Word of the Dear, for that matter. They gave him a choice, give up the person he loved or be cashiered. He chose love."

"Why would the Navy . . ."

"Think about it, Everett."

"Oh," Everett said. And "Ah."

"We're a ship of lost souls," Sharkey said. "Every omi and polone of us an orphan of some kind. And I'm including the captain. She saw a ship die, burn up right there in the sky."

"She told me about the *Fairchild*."

"She never stops seeing that. No, the captain has an amriya with herself, and that's never give up on anyone who needs her. Which is me saying; she didn't give up on me, and I'm the vilest of sinners; a liar and an assassin. And she won't give up on you. You don't need to make everything right to look good to her."

"Mchynlyth," Everett said. "Wow, I never thought he was, you know . . ."

"You're still saying too much, Everett," Sharkey said. "You don't need to talk. 'A time to rend, and a time to sew; a time to keep silence, and a time to speak.'"

But silence is scary, Everett thought. Things get in where the words aren't. Memories fountained up. Throwing the shotgun to Kax. The suddenness with which the battle of the Princesses turned to killing. Real killing. *Everness* ploughing into the forest, pierced again and again. The Brigadier hitting him hard in the stomach, hitting him like an adult. Opening up the sun gun on Imperial University, feeling power and joy so dark it hurt. The look on the face of that other Tejendra as the Nahn tentacle punched through him and he knew he was worse than dead. His enemy, his alter, the Anti-Everett coming towards him through the snow of Abney Park Cemetery. His dad, pushing him out of the way of the jumpgun. The look on his face—a moment then gone. Thing upon thing upon thing. One hammer blow after another. No time to recover, to be able to do anything but react. No end to it. Thing after thing after thing. Hurt after hurt after hurt. Pain after pain after pain.

"I hate this!" And this was the time to speak. The Jiju at the helm looked up, blinked their eyelids. Kax in her princess finery glanced over from the opposite hull. "I want my dad back! I want Sen here. I want the captain safe, I want the ship back, I want my mum and Victory-Rose. I want home. I didn't ask for any of this. All I did was look for my dad. I didn't ask him to give me the Infundibulum. I didn't ask him to build a Heisenberg Gate and discover all . . . you. I could have lived my life without you, any of you. I didn't ask for any of this. I'm tired and I don't know what to do and I'm scared all the time. All the time. Every second every day. I wake up in the morning and there's two seconds when I'm warm and I think I'm home and then it crashes down on me and I'm so scared it's like being sick. I am so tired of being scared."

"Me too, Everett," Sharkey said. "Me too."

And for a moment there was silence, where no one needed to say anything. Then Everett saw Sharkey's mouth twitch and his eyes harden and Everett knew Sharkey had seen the next thing they would have to cope with. He followed the weighmaster's gaze and his heart sank. Their resources would be used to the very last drop.

A huge oval of darkness lay over the endless city of the Jiju. The skymaran raced at full speed towards it. The narrow oval shape was foreshortening; as it drew closer it opened into a circle: a hole in the world. Everett made a grid out of his fingers and held them to the glass. It must be twenty, twenty-five kilometers across.

No, not a hole *in* the world, Everett realized. A hole *through* the world, from one side of the Alderson disk to the other.

The skymaran dropped to weave between the pyramid cities. The hole was like a storm front, a storm from beneath, coming up out of the world. Then the skymaran flashed over the edge and plunged into the hole. Everett braced himself against the glass. The speed was thrilling, terrifying. Beneath his feet the walls flashed past, studded with balconies and terraces, walkways and windows, lit by a long arc of sunlight that Everett could see visibly moving up the wall as the distant sun dropped through the hole at the center of the world. In front of him, darkness. He was seeing the night sky of the other side of the world. Down in the darkness, at the center of the cylinder was a stationary thunderstorm, four bolts of lightning arcing from the wall, meeting in a blazing knot around something at the center of the hole. Something huge. Something like a floating mountain, with another mountain turned upside down fused to its base. A floating double mountain from the dreams of some mad Gothic architect: by the flickering lightning Everett saw fantastical turrets and spires, soaring vaults and arches and buttresses, pinnacles and minarets and orioles thrust out over the bottomless drop. A Gothic castle, kilometers across, floating at the center of a neverending lightning storm.

"That's so Warhammer 40K," Everett breathed. Whistling in the dark. Somewhere, guys were painting armies of orcs and space marines, and that comforted him. He saw Sharkey nod, though he could not possibly have understood the reference. Sharing in the wonder and the fear. Looking at Sharkey, his face lit by lighting flickers far below, Everett understood that it was the same for the American. It was the same for everyone on the ship. Scared all the time, with every breath. It made him feel . . . not better, but equal. Brothers in scared. The skymaran screamed into the bottomless pit. Everett felt off center, disconnected, as if gravity was weaker here. *Of course.* The center of the pit was like the center of the earth; the masses above and below balanced each other. Gravitational attractions canceled each other out. The dark castle floated in free fall. The skymaran swooped in around filigree tower tops, spires that looked spun from the finest ebony spider silk, and Everett felt his feet leave the floor. He glanced over at Kax. The lightning cast her face in shadows and angles he had not seen before. *This is as new to you as it is to me*, Everett thought. Her halo flickered with reflected lightning. It gives you the knowledge, but that's not experience. This is you finding a new home.

Narrow bridges, thin as knife blades, bound the city mountain to the wall of the cylinder. The skymaran looped under and around the bridges; Everett saw Jiju bustling along them, crowding and pushing and quite oblivious of the fact that there were no safety railings. But if you fell, you wouldn't fall very far. Gravity would pull you one way, then the other. You would bob up and down, in the same way that the sun bobbed up and down through the hole at the center of Diskworld, until you came to rest beside the same bridge from which you had fallen.

The Sunlord pilots brought the skymaran up and folded it into landing configuration. It dropped lightly onto the end of the slender stone buttress that arced out from the main body of the castle over the void. Everett made the mistake of glancing down as he stepped from the aircraft. Down, down, way down, the bottom of the world was filled with stars. He felt Sharkey's hand firm on his arm.

"Steady there, Mr. Singh." A troop of Jiju palace guards, crests red and halos all displaying the same pattern of colors, opened ranks to admit Princess Kakakakaxa. Kax turned and beckoned for Everett and Sharkey to follow, a human gesture.

"What was that worldly song you quoted me, when we went down in the pits of the Nahn?" Sharkey said.

It took Everett a moment to recall the song and the occasion.

"'You'll Never Walk Alone,'" Everett said. The escort fell in on either side of them. The stairway down to the glowing gateway in the tower was steep and precipitous.

"Remind me how it goes again."

Sen took a sip from the mug but could not hide the wince.

"Too much chilli," Captain Anastasia said. "Isn't there?"

"It's good, Ma," Sen said.

"No it's not," Captain Anastasia said. "Only Everett can do Everett's chocolate."

Sen was perched on the flip-down seat in the captain's latty. It had been a long time since Captain Anastasia had heard her daughter's tap-de-la-tap at her latty door but she had known the code at once. *Can I talk?*

"No!" Sen raised a finger. "Rule one!" Rule one was rule only. Girls talk. No men, no boys. Just girls talking together. Sen slid the chocolate cup away from her across the small fold-down table. "It's not that bad," Captain Anastasia said.

"Yes. No. Maybe. I don't know!" Sen flared suddenly. She fidg-
eted on the narrow seat. "Why are we sitting here drinking hot chocolate when those lizard polones have the ship and they've cut all those
holes in the hull and they're taking us the Dear knows where and
okay, I know it's omis, but Everett and Sharkey, they don't even know
what's happened to us, and we need to do something about it right
now. It's the ship."

Captain Anastasia took a sip of her chocolate.

"Like what?"

"Like I don't know. Like something. You're the captain. You
think of something. You always think of something. Like that time
at Tromso."

A sudden blizzard driving down out of Svalbard and Tsar Alex-
ander Land had pinned down half of Europe's Scandia liners from
Narvik to Helsinger. At the same time, St. Petersburg had moved
against one of the frequent, regular, and doomed Scandic uprisings.
The crew of *Everness*—Sen a rambunctious and lippy ten-year-old—
anchored down, battened in, and drank hot toddy while the sound
of automatic weapons firing rattled among the wooden houses of
Tromso. Five days, and then out of the storm came a ragged group of
refugees and revolutionaries; Norgic separatists, beaten and bloody.
They had begged for passage to England. They had gold. Roberto
Henninger had been weighmaster then; he and Mchynlyth had
argued fiercely against giving the Norgic haven but Captain Anastasia knew the savagery of the Tsar's Kazaks. On the sixth day, the
blizzard swirled off over High Deutschland; *Everness* lifted and was
immediately hailed by a flotilla of Imperial frigates. They searched
the ship. They searched every span and spar, every sheet and square
foot of her. They didn't search the ballast tanks, where Captain Anastasia had submerged her stowaways, breathing through air hoses.

"Yes, it's hypothermic," she said. "You want to be hypothermic
in my ballast tanks or hypothermic in a Siberian Penitence Camp?"

It took the entire flight to England for the refugees to get warm again. Captain Anastasia left them on the coast of Old Anglia, far from the eyes of Customs Inspectors, and took their gold.

"I had the luck of the Airish. It the Kazak captain had looked down instead of up . . ."

"So why can't we do something like that? We need to, I don't know, fight back. There are only those three."

"And three whole shiploads just out there." The latty's porthole was dark as night, the light shut out by a metal tentacle. The three Marquis sky squids had *Everness* tightly wrapped in a web of claspers and tendrils. Captain Anastasia winced in pain every time she heard tentacle rasping over the skin of her beautiful airship. "Maybe you didn't see what the Jiju did to those ground-pounder soldiers, but I did. We wouldn't last two seconds." The Jiju had carefully removed every last body part of Charlotte Villiers's strike squad. Captain Anastasia imagined vile explorations of human anatomy. The ship still smelled of blood. It would for a long time.

"Well, we need to do *something*," Sen declared.

"We are doing something. We're drinking hot chocolate and having a talk," Captain Anastasia said. Once again Sen twisted uncomfortably on the fold-down seat.

"I cannot sabi this: Captain Anastasia Sixsmyth, my *ma* . . ."

"Sen." Captain Anastasia's voice was sharp now. "I am captain."

"Sorry. It's just . . ."

"It's not the ship, is it?" Captain Anastasia knew that with her adopted daughter truth was like buried water. Drill right, drill deep, and the true feelings would fountain out of her.

"It is. But . . . Ma, them Jiju, you know that took the palari out of me. Well, when they did that, they like put something in."

"They did what?" Captain Anastasia's eye bulged in anger. Her rage filled the tiny wooden latty. Sen shrank back. She had seen her mother's fury like this only three times before and it awed her as much as scared her. It was a force of nature. The lioness roused.

"Sorry, sorry, that didn't come out right. Didn't mean to scare you."

"If they've hurt you there are not enough Jiju in this entire universe to keep them safe from me . . ."

"No, they didn't hurt me, honest, bona. No codding. It's more like, a two-way flow. They get some of me, I get some of them. Ma, I saw . . . stuff."

"What sort of stuff?"

"Fighting. Always fighting. Everywhere, everywhen. They fights from the moment they hatches out. Millions of them, and only one or two make it through. Oh, I saw it and heard it. But there's more. They fight each other. Like Kax said, there are big families run everything? Like the Bromleys back in Hackney? 'Cept there's six of them. What did Kax call them?" Sen closed her eyes. "Nah, I can't remember the words. But I can see them." She touched fingers to her forehead. "In here. There's seas so big no one's ever sailed across them. The ones what weave weather into storms. Living cities. Fields of crops that go on and on and on. There's the ones what throw space rocks around and blow up planets. Then there's the ones who control the sun. If you controls the sun, you controls everything. I saw them all, in here, and I seen them all fighting, forever. I seen them living cities blasted to ash by tame lightning storms. I seen all those fields of crops turn brown and die from drought. I seen like tidal waves a thousand feet high. I seen them turn off rivers and whole oceans disappear like someone pulled a plug. I seen them throwing rocks down out of space . . . the size of cities, the size of countries. I heard the whole Diskworld ringing like a bell—like a cymbal on a drum kit. The sun . . . I seen the sun stop on one side of the world—like night for a hundred years. Ma, they've fought thousands of wars—millions of wars."

Sen broke off. Her face was ghost pale.

"Are you all right?" Captain Anastasia asked.

"Yeah. Bona. It's just kind of . . . intense. I see it, and I feel it. Ma, I's been thinking. Like, on our world, when did the dinosaurs die out?"

"I think it's about sixty, seventy million years," Captain Anastasia said. "I can look it up. I think Mchynlyth has the comptator system up and running again."

"Sixty, seventy, whatever," Sen said." Here's the thing. That's like . . . *mad* time. Like, if the lizards had that much of a head start on us, there wouldn't just be one Diskworld, there'd be hundreds of them. It'd be Jiju all the way up and all the way. They'd be all over the Nine— Ten Worlds. We wouldn't be *here*. What did Kax call us? Apes. I don't think she meant that as a joke. I don't think Jiju even know what jokes are. The Jiju'd be like gods. But they ain't. So: why ain't they?"

Sen looked long and hard at her mum, asking her to arrive at the same conclusion she had.

"The wars keep knocking them back," Captain Anastasia said.

"They build it all up, and then along comes another war and bangs it all flat again. Thing is, Diskworld's so big, they can't get everyone, so someone always survives, and they creep out of their holes and start all over again. Thing is, they're kind of overdue for another one. I got the idea that it was Kax's people . . ."

"The Sunlords," Captain Anastasia interrupted.

"The Sunlords versus everyone else. I got the feeling that the last time, the Sunlords almost killed everyone else—the only thing that stopped them was that it would have killed all of them too. And I think it's all built up and up and wound in and in and it's balanced so fine and delicate that the weight of a fly might tip it over to one side or the other."

"Or the weight of an airship," Captain Anastasia said.

Sen nodded.

"We do not want to be in the middle of a barney between coves can throw asteroid around and shut the sun down," Captain Anastasia said. "But on the other hand . . ."

"It's like an opportunity," Sen said.

"The Sunlords adversity may be the Airish opportunity . . . We'll show them what apes can do."

"Everett's not the only one can do the big thinking," Sen said and then clapped her hands over her mouth. "Rule one!"

The hall was Sunlords all the way in and all the way out. Sunlords rustling and twittering like a cave of birds. Sunlords, their halos shimmering, taking a thousand different shapes and colors. Heads turned as Kax led her guests into the Presence Hall. The ripple of attention fanned out across the vast chamber; halos flashed as they turned to scan the strange new thing among them. The birdsong fell silent. At the far end of the aisle, miles away it seemed, something moved in the light radiating from the Sunburst Throne.

Everett felt every eye on him. He straightened himself up, drew his stomach muscles in, pulled his shoulder back, clenched his ass cheeks. He might be smudged and smeared with Crèchewood dirt, wearing a badly cut-off T-shirt and rugby socks, but he could make the most of it. He saw Sharkey spruce himself up, take a deep, chest-filling breath. It was all about making an entrance.

"Approach," said a voice from everywhere. In the radiance of the throne, a clawed hand beckoned.

"She's learnt our palari already," Sharkey said quietly. "Stay sharp."

Everett and Sharkey fell into step behind Kax. Solemn procession was tricky in the microgravity, but Everett kept in step with Sharkey. The Presence Hall was a cavernous half egg that would be impossible to construct under any greater gravity. Stars and constellations moved across the vaulted roof, so high it almost seemed a sky. The Sunburst Throne of the Empress of the Sun occupied the smaller end of the half egg. It was well named. It blazed so bright that Everett had to squint to make out details: spines and spikes like crystal thistledown. Light streamed from between the rays. It didn't seem entirely connected to the ground. The dark silhouette at its heart seemed larger and differently shaped than the Jiju that pressed into the body of the hall.

"Luke Skywalker and Han Solo," Everett whispered to Sharkey. They were halfway to the throne. Everett's confidence grew with every step. "Getting the medals after they blow up the Death Star."

"Wish I knew what you were cackling on about," Sharkey whispered back. "But if it makes you feel better . . ."

Hissing whispers rippled out through the Jiju on either side as the procession passed.

"My sisters are jealous," Kax threw back. "There has been nothing like this in the Worldwheel for ten thousand days."

"Sure are a lot of princesses," Everett whispered to Sharkey.

"There's always a lot of princesses," Sharkey said. "It's one of the problems of monarchy. I can tell you, I've known a few princesses. Known in the Old Testament sense of the word, sabi? Never any of the ones who might inherit anything. Funny that."

"Hey, where are the boys?" Everett said. "Have you seen any?"

"See those tiny little mini Jiju, scuttling around?"

Everett had noticed miniature Jiju creatures, thin and finely featured, knee height and furtive, darting between legs, hiding behind patterned skirts, blinking wide eyes at the aliens.

"I thought those were pets."

"I reckon those are the omis. You don't need that many if all they have to do is squirt some boy juice onto a pile of eggs. It's a woman's world up here."

The glare from the Sunburst Throne dimmed with every step Everett took towards it. Now he could see details of who sat on it. The Empress of the Sun was impressive. Half again as tall as Kax, she was heavily built and massively muscled. The minute scales on her biceps and thighs and abdominals rippled with oil sheen as the muscles moved. Her crest was long and fell on either side of her head to her waist, like rainbow colored dreadlocks. The fighting claws on her thumbs were long and curved and worked with exquisite silver filigree. Her forehead was studded with jewels and gold wires inlaid into the skin. Everett could see no halo. Then he realized: the throne on which the Empress of the Sun sat was her halo. Kax's halo had absorbed that of her dead rival; it must be like that for each successive Empress of the Sun. Kax had said that her people did not live very long, but Diskworld and the line of the Sunlords was very old. Halo upon halo, memory upon memory, life upon life: there must be millions of them. Tens of millions of them. The true throne must be enormous, the size of this castle. Maybe it *was* this castle.

"Heads up, Mr. Singh." Sharkey must have noticed that, step by step, the bravery was leaking out of Everett. The Empress of the Sun leaned forward in the heart of her floating sunray throne, flared her nostrils. Everett took a deep breath, felt it carry oxygen to every muscle and nerve, igniting them, filling them with energy. It was a trick he used in big football games, on the walk out from the dressing rooms to the goal line. It was always a long walk. But this was longer.

"Mother and Mary and sweet Saint Pio," Everett whispered; the old Sharkey family battle cry and private oath.

"Fine sentiment, sir, fine sentiment." Sharkey straightened the feather in his hat. "Leave the talking to me. This is my bailiwick. A little old-school Atlanta chivalry can sweeten the sourest of social situations."

"You ever been to a Punjabi wedding?" Everett asked.

"You have me at a disadvantage there, sir."

"Let's just say, you're not the only guy can do old-school chivalry."

Everett stopped before the hovering throne. From the heart of a dazzle of light rays, the Empress of the Sun looked down at him. His pride, his little tricks to make himself confident, all evaporated in the searing light. The sense of power and presence made him want to turn and run. This creature made the sun dance for her amusement. He had never felt more like a mammal, more like a small, scuttling, 'fraidy male. Everett pulled himself upright, pressed his hands together in a Namaste, and dipped his head in a brief bow. Sharkey whipped off his hand and bent a leg in a theatrical bow.

"Miles O'Rahilly Lafayette Sharkey at your service, your Majesty," he declaimed.

"Everett Singh; goalkeeper, mathematician, traveller, Planesrunner," Everett said. The same formula he had recited when he had first been introduced to Sharkey, right after Sharkey had tried to throw Everett off *Everness*.

The Empress of the Sun sat motionless. Not a movement. Not a word. For a long time. *I know what you're doing*, Everett thought. *You're making us feel like little squeaking apes. It's working. We are.*

The great Hall of the Presence was silent. Not a claw clicked on the polished floor.

The Empress of the Sun blinked her eye membranes.

"Welcome Planesrunner. I am Gapata Hehenrekke Exto Kadkaye, Empress of the Sun, Clade-Mother of Sunlords, Chatelaine of Palatakahapa. Welcome to my lands, demesnes, and cities." The Empress of the Sun's voice was soft and light and maddeningly familiar to Everett. "You've come a long way. Please enjoy the hospitality of the Sunlords." He had it now. The Empress of the Sun spoke in his mum's voice. Everett wasn't sure what shocked him more, that Kax had dragged a memory of his mother out of his head and given it to her own mother or that he hadn't immediately recognized Laura's voice. Either way, it was one of the creepiest things he had ever heard. "My daughter has told me so much about you. What a thrill!" Kax's skin flushed a delicate turquoise; her crest turned crimson. "When the probe from your universe came through to the Worldwheel, we knew it would only be a matter of time before you returned. And you have come with a gift that none of us could have imagined. We are a people who enjoy gifts. In the exchange of objects—gifts, ideas, hostages, family members—we show ourselves to be civilized beings, don't you think? It shows willingness and appreciation."

Everett's voice was as cold as the lump of dread in his heart. "I know what you want." He saw Sharkey glance at him, a tiny nod of the head: do it. It's the only way. "You want the Infundibulum."

"Want is such a cold word," the Empress of the Sun said, and Everett felt sick inside because she used the same tone Laura used when she was very, very angry, but all she wanted to show was her deep, deep disappointment. Hurt was crueler than anger. "We would appreciate a token from you in return for what we're doing for you. A consideration. The Genequeens are an uncouth, rough people, with no manners and less culture, but they do respect protocol. They claim you and your ship by right of it having landed in Crèchewood, which they stubbornly and against the sense of all the other Clades believe to be their territory. By the Treaty of Hedrehedd Larsweel the Crèchewoods were established as common grounds eight thousand years ago—things may be different on the Outward Rings, but they are cold and barbarous creatures out there, far from the light of the sun. Barely sentient at all. My esteemed daughter Kakakakaxa has filed a claim that you enjoy the protection of my Clade as our honored guests." Kax's shade of turquoise deepened. Pride, Everett guessed. The newest princess in this hall of a thousand princesses had outshone all the others. What were the colors for jealousy and resentment? Everett suspected that Kax's battles to the death were not over yet. "Our lawyers have formed a case. The High Magisterium is weighing it. We expect judgement within the hour. The High Magisterium's judgements are always honored, but we'll send a detachment of skyqueens. An escort, an honor guard. The Genequeens can be sullen, petty creatures. Your friends and ship will be returned to you by sunrise."

"And in return . . ." Everett said.

"We only want to study the Infundibulum," said the Empress of the Sun. Everett knew that mild, reasonable tone too well. His mum had always used it just before she asked him something he did not want to do.

"If they can learn our language before they even meet us, that's as good as giving it to them," Sharkey muttered.

"What do we do?" Everett whispered back. He could feel the weight of every eye in the Presence Hall on him. "

"Everett, that's not my decision."

"You're the officer in charge here. The adult."

"The Infundibulum is yours."

"You were the one who would have given it to Charlotte Villiers to save the ship."

"Yes, I would have. I would always act for the good of the ship. And it's clear to me what the good of the ship is. But the Infundibulum is yours. You must decide. 'Choose this day whom ye shall serve.'"

"But if I give them the Infundibulum . . ."

"No one said it would be easy. Decide Everett. The Empress is waiting."

There was a way of standing, a way of walking off the pitch after you had lost a game, a way of holding yourself that Everett had learned. You are small and shriveled inside, but you focus on every muscle to make you tall and proud. The hall was vast and filled with powerful and dangerous aliens; he was far beyond the edge of all Known Worlds, stranded on the biggest engineering construct in the multiverse, before the shining throne of a ruler who could make the sun itself dance for her amusement. But by the Dear, he was not going to walk the Walk of Shame.

"Your Majesty," Everett said in his loudest, clearest voice, "I am honored to share the Infundibulum with you."

21

The knock on the antechamber door was sharp and clear. Three raps.

"Enter." Charlotte Villiers applied the last precise touches to her makeup. Her eyes widened in surprise at the figure that came through the open door. A flicker, no more. The mask of cosmetic perfection betrayed nothing.

"Well, I certainly wasn't expecting you," Charlotte Villiers said. "Have you come to gloat? Schadenfreude is such a grubby little emotion."

"A dozen deaths are not a thing to gloat about," Ibrim Hoj Kerrim said. He was dressed for the Heiden winter; heavy gloves, comforter knotted tight around his throat, the collar of his brocaded coat turned up. In his right hand was a heavy cane. Its heavy silver knob had produced the sharp knock on the anteroom door. From the solidity of the knob and the obvious weight of the cane, Charlotte Villiers guessed a hidden purpose.

"Sword stick?" Charlotte Villiers said. She turned to Ibrim Hoj Kerrim. "Do you think I'm that much of a threat to you?"

"We all face a greater threat," Ibrim Hoj Kerrim said. "I come to offer you my support. A full session of the Praesidium must be an intimidating prospect."

"It's nothing compared to the Jiju," Charlotte Villiers said. She straightened her attire, adjusted the set of her hat. "Veil up or down? Up I think. It shows openness. Your support is welcome, Ibrim."

"I will back up whatever you tell the Praesidium."

"I shall tell the Praesidium the truth."

"Will you tell them how you alone of your entire squad came back from the Worldwheel?"

"Are you accusing me of abandoning my soldiers? Cowardice, Ibrim?"

"That would be dishonorable. You do, however, have a keen sense of self-preservation. I will say that I sanctioned the operation. I will also swear before the Praesidium that the soldiers were an Al Buraqi unit and not your private Earth 10 army. You have informed the next of kin?"

"McCabe is looking after that," Charlotte Villiers said. "What's your price?"

"My price is the vigilance and security of the Plenitude of Known Worlds, nothing more."

"Oh, come on man!" Charlotte Villiers flared with anger. "Say it; you want my resignation from the Plenipotentiate and the Security Council."

"The Praesidium had already suggested that," Ibrim Hoj Kerrim said. "I persuaded them that you had been a good and faithful servant of the Plenitude. Special threats call for special circumstances. Personally, I want to keep you where I can see you." His grip tightened on the sword stick. "God's mercy on you, Charlotte." Ibrim Hoj Kerrim tipped the ferrule of his cane against the jewel of his turban, a farewell gesture. The door closed heavily behind him.

Do not imagine that pretty sword will save you, Charlotte Villiers thought. Cowardice. She shook with rage. The Villiers did not forgive such insults. How dare that smooth, oily Buraqi suggest that she had abandoned her squad to their deaths to save her own skin. She had made a terrible but correct decision. Someone had to bring the information back. Someone had to warn the Plenitude. How the Plenitude might defend itself was not her concern—her alter Charles was already consulting the Thryn Sentiency on the far side of Earth 4's Moon. Even the Thryn might not be able to withstand a full Jiju invasion of the Ten Worlds. If only she had the Infundibulum. For if it was everything she suspected, even the Jiju were chaff in the wind before its power. *Her* power. Again she trembled with rage at Ibrim Hoj Kerrim's presumption. Accusing her of cowardice.

I will deal with your insult in time. And it will be direct, and it will be personal.

Another knock at the door, this one discreet and polite.

"Madam Villiers . . ." a male voice began.

". . . the Praesidium is waiting," a second, almost identical male voice finished.

"I am ready."

Veil down, she decided. For her entrance at least.

The twin ushers swung open the double doors. Charlotte Villiers walked between them and up the short flight of wooden steps into the council room. She stood at the center of a horseshoe of box pews, banked up tier upon tier like a vertigo-inducing lecture theatre. Every pew was occupied; the twins of Earth 7 pressing close together, the periwigs and quizzing glasses on sticks of Earth 5's delegates, Earth 2 turbans and lace headpieces, Earth 6 silks and elaborate hairstyles.

"Charlotte Villiers . . ." a woman's voice announced.

"Earth 3 Plenipotentiary to Accession Applicant Earth 10," her twin concluded.

Charlotte Villiers surveyed the amphitheatre as the last Praesidium members took their places. Yes, the veil was a good idea. She could watch without being watched. She saw Ibrim Hoj Kerrim sit down among his Earth 2 colleagues, slip off his coat, and unwind his scarf. He gave her the briefest of nods. Paul McCabe was high up in the Sojourners' Gallery, among the carved cherubs that squabbled on the ceiling. No sign of the Harte woman. Charlotte Villiers waited until all eyes were on her. *This is a theatre not of dreams, but of nightmares, and I shall give you such drama as you never imagined.*

The silence was total.

Charlotte Villiers lifted her net veil. She looked up at the rows of faces.

"I come with the worst possible news," she said.

22

The Rentokil van had sat outside the school for two days before anyone noticed. Then Mr. Culshaw had peered through the windows and within half an hour another van had arrived from the pest control company, and shortly after it, a police car. By now it was break time, and a small crowd had gathered.

"He's dead," Noomi declared. "Drank his own rat poison. In the back. He was starting to smell. That's my theory."

Everett M had fought Nahn shape shifters and Victorian zombies, but Noomi's taste for dark weird stuff still surprised him. They were on their third Homework Date. No homework had been done or would ever be done, Everett M suspected, but he was allowed to walk home with Noomi, as long as he wasn't in school uniform. Or wearing anything else she might be embarrassed by. She had given him a couple of websites to check for fashion if he was too wimpy to go into a real clothes shop. No snog yet. It would come.

"Right you lot, back to your classes," Mr. Culshaw shouted. "The bell's gone. Nothing to see here."

The Rentokil people had forced open the back of the van. Noomi tried to get a look inside before going back to the art room. Ryun and Everett M went to biology.

"Um," Ryun said. Everett M had noticed that Ryun had started saying that at the start of every sentence he said to him, as if Ryun was uncertain, or about to apologize, or had bad news to break. Since the night Everett M told him the lie that was a truth, Ryun had been different with him. It was as if Ryun was watching himself—he was still friendly with Everett M, made jokes, talked about games and movies and comics and football, but it was as if he was checking everything he said, guarding everything he thought. Every word, deed, thought had an *um* in front of it. "Um, Ev, is this something to do with you?"

"I didn't kill a Rentokil man."

"I know that, just, um . . . those rats."

I have a theory about those rats, Everett M thought. *But I don't want to tell you, and you don't want to know it.*

"Not every piece of weird shit is connected to me," Everett M said. But this one was. He had been certain of it since the night the rats fled from the alley behind his home at the mere flicker of his Thryn power. The Battle of Abney Park 2 had been just that—a battle. The war against the Nahn was not over.

"Um, are you dating with Noomi again after school?" Ryun asked.

"It's homework."

"It's so not."

"Well, I am."

"Have you, um?"

"Snogged her yet?"

"Yeah."

"This afternoon."

"Okay."

He wouldn't. There wouldn't be a homework date either, though the thought of not seeing her curled up on a coffee-shop sofa, comfortable and casual in a way he never could be, cutely weird, her hands dancing as she told him things things things, made him feel sick with wanting. This afternoon he would once again become Everett M. Singh, cyborg agent of the Plenitude of Known Worlds, and go in search of a missing pest-control man.

The police were winching the pest-control van onto the back of a tow truck.

Everett M had a word now for all those ums and hesitations and uncertainties he saw in Ryun.

Scared.

Scared.

It had taken Ryun a sleepless night to identify how his feelings had changed toward his friend.

Scared.

The taxi had dropped him home. His mum had believed the lie about going to a friends and eating there. Stacey was on the Kinect again with her friends in pink, and Dad was out at his Tuesday night D&D game, which, to Ryun, had always been a geek too far. He hadn't heard a word anyone had spoken to him, his Facebook page was a jumble of random posts and pictures of people taken at odd angles, the television and radio jabbering with stuff that made no sense. His head was full full full of what Colette Harte had told him. Or rather, what she hadn't told him. Every one of his *buts*, she had cleverly turned back on him.

She was scared, too.

Stay away. Here be dragons. Things humanity was never meant to know. Who could resist a Keep Out sign?

All that night thoughts and imaginings rattled around his head. Each time he reached the edge of sleep, a fresh, darker thought would wake him up with a start. *Sometimes I don't know him at all* he had said to Colette. *He's like a totally different person.*

What if he was?

The thought jolted Ryun wide awake. His phone read twenty past three.

Once brought to mind, the idea would not go away. Parallel universes, parallel yous. Everett had gone to a parallel universe, yes, but someone else had come back. An alternative Everett. A cuckoo in the nest. The perfect secret agent. Identical in every way. Not quite every way. The stories didn't match up. The scars that weren't there before. The little differences in personality.

At three thirty in the morning it was the only thing that made sense.

Another thought jolted him like an electric shock. *What had happened to the real Everett?*

Had Colette Harte been trying to warn him that this Everett was a parallel-universe double, an alternative Everett? Feed him enough doubt to make the guess? There was danger here. If the cuckoo Everett ever suspected that Ryun knew he was not the real Everett Singh, he was in terrible danger indeed.

He had to know.

Scared, and tired. He had never been any good at acting and now, with Everett/not-Everett, Ryun had to pull off the trick of acting on two audiences. Ryun had always hated acting. It had always been obvious to him that it was just some ordinary person dressed up and pretending. He couldn't suspend his disbelief. Now he had to make someone else believe his act, as if his life depended on it. The first audience was everyone, including his family. He had to pretend that he didn't know Everett had been to a parallel universe for Christmas and could summon up an interdimensional magical airship. The second was everyone and Everett. Everyone and no one. No one could ever see that he suspected this Everett was a parallel universe doppelganger and a secret agent of one of the Dark Forces that Colette Harte had hinted at. All the time, everything he did, everything he said, acting. It was dishonest and it was neverending and it was the most exhausting thing Ryun had ever done. And he wasn't sure he was doing it very well.

There was a third audience. That was Everett, if he really was Everett, his oldest and best friend—not in a BFF way, understand, guys didn't do that: the real Everett would be puzzled and hurt by his BFF going weird and cold and distant on him when he needed Ryun most.

Ryun hated acting all the more. His world was simple and honest and open.

Scared, tired, vigilant. He had decided that night that he would watch Everett. Watch without being watched. It was not so hard now that Everett had been distracted by Noomi Wong. She was quite a distraction. Ryun had always thought of girls theoretically: theoretically you were supposed to fancy them, theoretically they fancied you, theoretically you dated them, but in Ryun's life they had remained just theories—distant, impressive, but unattainable, like amazing super planets around distant stars. In any other situation he would have been hurt that Everett had so easily dumped him to see Noomi, talk to Noomi, do little dates that weren't really dates with Noomi, meet up with Noomi, drink Vietnamese coffee, whatever that was— sounded disgusting—with Noomi. But it drew his attention, and, ignored, Ryun could go about his mission, finding out the truth about his best friend.

23

SO DSPOINTD, EV.

The text beeped in on Everett M's phone and he felt ten kinds of guilty. Guilty that Noomi was so excited about meeting him that afternoon. Guilty texting her that it would be really good seeing her. Guilty hiding himself away at the end of school so Noomi would not find him. Guilty imagining her waiting and waiting at the Turkish minimarket where they met. Guilty about the excuse he texted her: SRRY FAMILY THNG CUM UP CANT MKE IT. Guilty at her disappointment. Guilty seeing her and Gothy Emma cross the end of the lane where he was hiding and go off together. Guilty at having to lie to her so early in the relationship—if it even was a relationship. Whatever it was, it was not the kind of thing between two people where they could and should lie. Guilty at having to lie to her at all.

That was only nine kinds of guilty.

Ten. Guilty at keeping secrets from her, from Ryun, from Laura, from everyone.

He lingered in the lane that led to the old bike sheds that no one used any more—everyone came on the school run now, apart from Weird Kid Jasper. The name was enough of a clue. There was a corner that the smokers used. He stood among cigarette ends and opened up his Thryn senses. Once again, he dived down between the electromagnetic jabber of Stoke Newington, identifying and screening out the minicab radios and the wireless networks and the police and the dubstep pirates and the delivery trucks. The individual Nahn nanomachines must communicate by radio waves, Everett M had deduced: the buzz he picked up on his Thryn senses was them relaying instructions and information. And there it was: subtle, but there could be no mistaking, the sound of the Nahn thinking.

Everett M shivered: a sudden stab of fear. The Nahn scared him. Scared him deep, scared him true. Even as he gleefully blasted them to black slime and rotting Victorian bone in Abney Park, he had been afraid. The Nahn took everything you had and everything you were and made it theirs. He couldn't imagine what would be worse, to know that, or not to know it, to be just a mindless drone with a bulb of throbbing black Nahn stuff for a brain. And they were clever. Scary clever. Of course his Nahn double on Earth 1 had known he would break his promise to them. The possessed dog, the zombies of Abney Park, they had been Big Obvious Shoot-Me Enemies. The real Nahn invasion was happening somewhere else, in creatures that were everywhere, went everywhere, small and smart and nimble. The rats. "You're never more than ten feet from a rat," his dad had said one day when they were all out for a walk on the Regent's Canal and a very young Everett M had seen a rat swim across the canal, climb out onto the towpath, look at them while it cleaned its whiskers, and then vanish into the long grass. If you're never more than ten feet from a rat, you're never more than ten feet from the Nahn.

He'd though he was smart. Stupid. Stupid.

He should tell Charlotte Villiers. She could bring the technological might of the Plenitude down on the Nahn. But that would mean confessing to her the deal he had made to bring the Nahn to this Earth. It would mean her revealing that she had sent him to quarantined Earth 1. She would agree, she must agree, there were bigger issues here than her plans and schemes. The whole Plenitude was in danger. It was what she might do afterwards, to him, to his family, that scared him more than the Nahn.

"Gives you cancer," a voice said behind him.

Everett M felt his implanted weaponry leap into action at the surprise. He struggled to keep the ports in his arms and hands closed.

"Smoking." Mr. Myszkowski the groundsman stood behind him.
"I'm not . . ."

"Of course. I have to lock these gates."

Nothing for it then, and no one else to do it. To battle. Heroes
with girlfriends . . .

The signal was very faint and indirect. A hint here, an echo there, a
confusion of signals bouncing from metal garage doors. He had to
stand on the spot and turn several slow circles before he got a fix on
that one. He hoped no one had seen him. A pattern emerged: rat runs
all over this part of Stoke Newington, all converging in one place. Take
out the Central Node: wasn't that how they did it in action movies?

How many action movies had the Nahn seen?

Everett M followed invisible lines of radio chatter along Stoke
Newington Church Street. The web seemed to focus around Green
Lanes. He had an instant flash of Noomi, curled up in her great
legwear on her sofa at the Mermaid Café. His imagination put another
guy, another homework date, at the other end of the sofa, with a
Vietnamese coffee and the dreadlocked DJ—his name was Aidan—
playing all the tunes of his life. The stab of jealousy was so sharp that
Everett almost vomited. It took him a moment to get his breathing
back to easy and comfortable. Concentrate.

Aden Terrace was a narrow alley at the rear of a row of Victorian
terrace houses on Clissold Crescent. Behind the padlocked chain-link
fence local gardeners had created a secret urban farm of allotment
plots. The gardens were grey and wet and sludgy in damp, dark
January, but the chatter of Nahn activity was deafening. *Go*, Everett
M thought at his implant weapons; he shivered at the surge of power
as they armed and readied.

A few paces up and down the lane established the focus of the
signal: the shed in the fifth allotment down. The shed was the usual
allotment mash up of door and pallets and old windows raided from

dumpsters and house clearances. A wheelbarrow leaned up against the door. The raised beds were black with the rotting remains of the growing season. A few Brussels sprouts stood proud and green. Garden ornaments and cheap concrete Buddhas leaned at odd angles. Rusty wind chimes and Tibetan prayer banners hung in the still air.

The shed.

Everett M realized he hadn't seen a rat all day.

The flicker of a finger laser dealt with the padlock. The one on the shed door would pose no more difficulty. Hit hard, hit fast, take out everything. If only he had some of those sweet little Thryn EM-warhead nano-missiles. He had used them all in his battle of Hyde Park on Earth 1, when he drove back wave after wave of Nahn. But the Nahn always had one more wave.

Battles. Too many battles.

Pulser muzzles emerged from the palms of his hands.

"WTF. Everett Singh?"

Everett M reeled forward with shock and banged his head painfully against a hanging watering can.

"Okay: your family lives in a garden shed?"

Noomi. Standing in the open gate, arms folded, head cocked to one side, eyes wide and nostrils flared and angry in that will-someone-please-explain-to-me-what-is-going-on-here way that is more aggressive than any shouting. At the end of Aden Terrace was one of her friends/spies, arms also folded, head also cocked to one side, showing that she was as disgusted as her friend.

"No points for lying, Everett Singh."

"Noomi . . ." His hands. The pulsers were still in his palms. Concentrate. Concentrate. He willed his weapon ports shut.

"I had hopes," Noomi said. "Minimum standards: truth, honesty, caring." She never looked more fabulous to Everett M. Singh than the moment he knew he had lost her. "What is this, some kind of boys club? No girls? You got porn in there?" She held up a mittened hand.

"No. Don't want to know. Disappointed."

Nahn buzz sang as loud in Everett M's head as Noomi. Too much. He thought his Thryn systems down into standby.

"I can explain!" Everett M said. She was already walking away. And he couldn't. The only way he could explain was to show her what was inside him, what he feared hid inside the shed.

His phone pinged as Noomi reached the end of Aden Terrace.

YR DMPD.

She didn't even look back.

"I'll get back to you later," Everett M said to the allotment shed. "And you are dead. That's a promise."

He turned on Thryn speed. Heads turned on Green Lanes as Everett M ran past, backpack flapping, faster than any jogger or runner or cyclist. He arrived at the door of Mermaid Café and was waiting as Noomi and her friend arrived.

Noomi's brow furrowed. "How?"

"I'm sorry," Everett M said.

Noomi nodded her head at her spy friend. She went and looked around a Boots local across the road in a sniffy bad temper.

"My life is weird," Everett M said. "But, how I got here ahead of you, that's the same as how I did that thing with the Coke can, and jumping over the car. There's other stuff I can do, and that shed back there, that's part of it too."

Noomi's silence was killing him.

"I can do things that no one else can," Everett M said. "But that means I can't be like everyone else."

"Stop doing those things," Noomi said.

"I can't. They're part of me. It's a physical thing. There's stuff I can't even tell my mum."

"It's okay if you're gay. That's cute."

"I'm not gay!" Everett said, then, again, gently, "I'm not gay."

"Oh, sad. I could have dressed you. Are you a werewolf?"

"What? No! Yes. Sort of. No. Werewolves don't exist. This is what I mean. Maybe I'm just not the type of person who should have a girlfriend."

"Who said I was your girlfriend?" Noomi said.

She was tying him in knots. He had said too much already.

"Well, we meet up, and we talk, and it's . . ."

"It's what?"

"I really like you! I want to be back with you again, like the way it was."

Noomi looked at him a long time.

"Hm," she said, then turned and crossed Green Lanes to join her friend shopping for cosmetics.

What? Everett M wanted to shout. *So, are we on or off, are we okay or not okay? What?*

Everett M's phone pinged again. A new SMS.

YR BACK ON.

Nahn, you almost broke me and Noomi up, Everett M thought at the buzzing node of communication channels behind the rooftops and aerials and satellite dishes of Green Lanes and Statham Green. *You're double dead now.*

24

"Madam Villiers, do you think . . ."

"Madam Villiers, what can we . . ."

"Madam Villiers, help us . . ."

Madam Villiers . . . Madam Villiers . . .

Charlotte Villiers flipped down her veil and pushed through the press of clamoring Plenipotentiaries. *Madam Villiers, help us.* Help yourselves. You are the leaders of the Ten Worlds. You are the power. Zaitsev would have made this easy. He would have cleared a path through the frightened, bleating politicians. He would have made sure she got the respect she deserved. She had not respected him. She had seen that in his eyes, as the Jiju blades came in and she operated the relay that bounced her back to the jump room deep in the undercroft of the Tyrone Tower. The gate crew would have seen it, too, in that moment of clarity as the gate opened. They would have seen the Jiju, and the blood.

I treated you shamefully, Zaitsev, Charlotte Villiers thought. *I hope at the end you understood the necessity.*

An Earth 5 symbiont stepped into her path. The tayve's long, bejewelled arms and legs wrapped around its hrant host's body; its feeding finger tapped into an artery in the neck.

"Madam Villiers!" the tayve announced in a thin, fluting voice. Charlotte Villiers swept past. "Our world may not enjoy your technical arts, but Earth 5 will not shirk its part in apprehending this criminal Everett Singh!" the hrant cried. Charlotte Villiers said nothing, but she smiled behind her veil. If she had made Everett Singh the most hunted boy in the multiverse, she had won a great victory.

25

Palari was a tongue rich in swearing and Sen employed it joyfully, inventively, and horribly. Captain Anastasia had heard every race abused and sexual practice accused and deity offended in the docks and warehouses of Old Hackney but even she looked up at Sen's outburst.

Sen sucked the burn on her forearm.

"Dorcas, if you covered up a bit more," Captain Anastasia said.

Sen scowled and pushed her goggles up onto her head. Her face was greasy and smudged with smoke. Her hair smelled of burned insulation. The two women were at work on the power linkage to the number two impeller. It was cramped, intricate, high-voltage work. It involved power tools and welding guns. Sen usually loved working on the ship, wielding electrical tools like Sharkey did his shotguns—with bravado and serious purpose—but today the work felt like emergency surgery on a sick and dying creature. The ship had been wounded again and again and could never be whole again: the number three impeller was gone. Lost. The impeller, and the ship's weighmaster and planesrunner. Sharkey and Everett.

Sen did not like to stop too long to think about Sharkey and Everett, or the great wound to the ship, like a missing foot. It made her feel as if the bottom of her world had opened beneath her feet, and below her was an endless drop through tinkling darkness. The ship—her home, her safe place, her heart—might never be whole again. Sharkey and Everett might never come back. She might never leave this hideous, hideous world. Sen patched, Sen cabled, Sen welded.

"Tharbyloo!" Sen looked up. High above, tiny in the fingernail-sized patch of brightness, Mchynlyth's face looked down through one of the gashes the Genequeens had cut in the skin. If there was one thing Sen loved more than digging into *Everness*'s innards, it was working with the chief engineer out on the hull, the two of them whooping and yoo-hooing with insane glee as they leaped and swung on drop lines across the hull. But more than the missing impeller and the piercings and the gashings of the shipwreck and the Jiju hijacking, Sen hated to see *Everness* bound and captive in the steel tentacles of the Genequeen squidships. The ship looked like a picture she had once seen in a Cyclopeeja of a deer caught in the coils of a constricting snake; the loops drawing tighter and tighter, squeezing the life out of it. The deer's eyes had been so calm. It was the calm of surrender to inevitable death. Sen shuddered at the thought of those filthy half-living, half-machine tentacles closing around the hull. It was as if the ship's skin was her own. "Come on oot. I've a wee dilly-dandy you need to see."

"That's a nasty enough wee burn you got there," Mchynlyth commented as Sen and Captain Anastasia stepped out onto the balcony on *Everness*'s midline. He belayed down off the tentacle that coiled up over the top of the hull and dropped lightly to the metal grating. Sen found herself looking down along the tentacles onto the bridge of the Genequeen squidship. There were graspers and cutters and a clatter of mechanical manipulators at the center of the knots of tentacles, and half a dozen goldfish-bowl eyes. Behind each transparent bubble, a Genequeen. Over the curve of the hull, a second squidship grasped *Everness*'s starboard side. The third ship held *Everness* by the head. Looking down through the metal mesh, Sen saw treetops move lazily far below her feet. They were not out of Crèchewood yet. *Everness* was a big fish, to be landed carefully.

"Hates it," Sen whispered for her own ears only. She hugged herself and gave a yelp as she set off her still-seeping burn.

"You've something for us," Captain Anastasia said. Sen could see that she was also sickened by the sight of her beloved ship trussed and helpless, like a great and noble whale hunted and harpooned by tiny, jabbering humans.

"Aye." Mchynlyth pulled a fist-sized device from one of the many pockets of his orange coveralls and held it out. A white egg, flattened on one side.

"What is it?" Captain Anastasia asked.

"I dinnae sabi, but it was down at the tail end, stuck to the skin, and sure as eggs is eggs, it's nae part of the general schematics of a cargo airship."

"Someone put it there?" Captain Anastasia asked. Sen picked the thing up, dropped it as if it had been lava.

"Plastic!"

"Oh ho," said Captain Anastasia.

"Ah hah," said Mchynlyth. Earth 3 possessed no usable reserves of crude oil. No oil age, no plastic age. This device could only come from a plane other than Earth 3. "How do you think yon Villiers woman dropped her wee toy soldiers right onto our main catwalk?"

"Give it to me, Sen," Captain Anastasia ordered. The captain held the device up in front of her face. Her large eyes narrowed. "Evil thing. How did it get . . . Never mind." She dropped it to the mesh and brought her heel down sharply. Plastic splintered.

"What are you doing?" Sen shrieked. "Everett could . . ."

Captain Anastasia stamped it into shards then kicked the shards through the mesh. They snowed down on the crimson treetops.

"Everett could, I have no doubt. But Everett's not here. And this is my ship. And she's suffered enough."

"Don't say that, Everett's not—" Sen began, then cut herself off before the word took root in her mind. To say *dead* meant that he might be. But Everett was the planesrunner: he was too smart, too quick, too important to let something as slow and stupid as death catch him. But no, death is quick and smart and catches everyone.

You learned that early among the Airish. Friends had fallen, ships had burned, captains had been lost in storms. Death was a frequent visitor to the Airish.

"Ooohhh the Dear," Mchynlyth said suddenly in a voice that snapped Sen and Captain Anastasia's attention away from the fragments of the plastic tracking device. He was looking to stern, body tight as a hunting dog. "Our wee ship's no done suffering yet. Not by a long chalk." Sen looked where he pointed. Far astern, half hidden by tail fins, was a swarm of black specks. Sen knew at once that they were large and far away, not small and close. And they were moving fast. In the few seconds she had been observing them they had gained shape and definition.

Captain Anastasia pulled her monocular from the holster on her belt and focused on the objects. Sen saw her bare her teeth, hiss an intake of breath.

"Ma, can I?"

Captain Anastasia handed her the monocular without a word. Sen adjusted the focus. The objects came into resolution. Three-hulled aircraft; two hulls above, one below, mean as daggers. Ten, eleven, twelve . . . twenty-three twenty-four twenty-five of them. Big. Half the length of *Everness*. No obvious lift cells, or even wings like the airoplans she had seen on other Earths, but they moved like they owned the sky. Air shivered around them like heat haze; light glinted from dozens of windows. Sen clicked the monocular up a notch. The pursuing aircraft leapt in magnification and she saw that the heat shiver was a cloud of much smaller flying objects. Nanobots: swarms of them. Even their aircraft had halos.

The Genequeens were already aware of the closing fleet. Jiju moved in frenzied action behind the eye ports. *Everness* lurched under Sen's feet as the tentacles shifted their grip. She grabbed the railing. The entire two hundred meters of hull gave a terrible straining creak. Sen felt her center of gravity move as the ship accelerated.

"You'll tear my ship apart!" Captain Anastasia shouted. "You're killing her!"

"Who are they?" Sen asked.

"Kax's people," the captain said. "There's only one possibility . . ."

"The Sunlords know about the Infundibulum," Mchynlyth said. Again, *Everness* shifted and groaned as the Genequeens struggled to press the ungainly flying circus to greater speed.

"Everett!" Sen exclaimed. "That's how they know. Everett told them about it. Everett's all right."

"And Sharkey," Mchynlyth said. Captain Anastasia took the monocular from Sen and shifted the focus from Sunlords to squid-ships, Sunlords to squidships. Sunlords to squidships.

"Miss Sixsmyth, you know Everett better than any of us." Sen was always suspicious when Captain Anastasia addressed her by her crew name. Ship stuff coming. "You remember I told him to hide the Infundibulum—where would he have hidden it?"

"That's easy! He's so naff at hiding things. I mean, I know where he's put everything."

"Well, bring me the Infundibulum. I will get the jumpgun. Mr. Mchynlyth!"

"Yes, ma'am!" Mchynlyth too knew the tone and words of command.

"Prepare the escape pod."

"Captain, due respect and all that, but I'm no likin' what you're implying," Mchynlyth said.

"In a very few minutes, we may find ourselves in a fight between the Sunlords and the Genequeens that will make our barney with the Bromleys look like a Sunday-School picnic. I fear that the Genequeens will destroy the Infundibulum rather than let it fall into the hands of the Sunlords."

Sen's mouth fell open, her eyes went hollow, her breath faltered with horror.

"They wouldn't do that!" she said.

"Polone, people do it all the time," Mchynlyth said. His jaw was tight, his face was grim.

"And they're not even people, but yes, they would," Captain Anastasia. "I am captain of this ship and I love it with all my heart and my hope and my dear life, but my duty is to its crew. Prepare to abandon ship."

"No!" Sen shouted. "No! You can't! The ship . . ."

"And I am its captain. You have your orders Miss Sixsmyth. Mr. Mchynlyth?"

"Aye, ma'am."

"Quick's the word, sharp's the action."

26

The Jiju skyqueens were big, fast, powerful, and absolutely thrilling to fly aboard. From the moment the royal flagship led the fleet from its docks in the wall of the hole in the world, Everett had not moved from the observation deck. Like the royal yacht, the skyqueens of the Sunlord Navy were catamarans: twin hulls joined at the rear; but the warships carried a third hull beneath the main booms, at an angle that suggested the open claw of some hunting raptor, ready to strike. Everett reckoned that was entirely the idea. There was a clue in the ship's name: *Death Falls from an Azure Sky*. The observation deck was in the lower part of the portside hull; Everett was surrounded by glass, even beneath his feet. Below the third hull, the red roof of Crèchewood moved at a speed that made Everett dizzy if he looked at it too long. Sunlord pilots liked to fly low and very, very fast.

"In your world, Mr. Singh, do you have anything to compare with this?" Captain Anastasia had asked when *Everness* had flown out through the Smoke Ring to join in *kris*, the duel of honor, with the Bromley flagship *Arthur P.* "No," he had answered. It had been true then. This was something beyond. On *Everness* he had been amazed by the sensation of being lighter than air, drifting silent and unseen over the winter world . . . *floating*. But aboard *Death Falls from an Azure Sky*—or just *Death Falls*, Everett had decided—with its crystal-clear glass beneath him, in front of him, and on either side of him, the sensation of flight was more intense. Flying free and fast. Breathtakingly fast. Sharkey had been less impressed. "Who puts windows in warships?" he had sneered before curling up on an oddly shaped Jiju couch and going to sleep.

That's nice for you, you have a good sleep, Everett scowled. He was still furious with *Everness*'s weighmaster. Sharkey had thrown the decision of whether to surrender the Infundibulum onto Everett. Yes, the Infundibulum was his; yes, no one else had the right to make that decision; but Sharkey was an officer and an adult. Responsibility was his job, and guilt should be the price of *his* decisions. You don't load that onto a teenager, no matter what your Down-South Daddy taught you about standing on your own two feet and shooting your own food. There was no other decision that Everett could have made, but that didn't mean that he was the right person to make it. What hurt him the most was the deep needle of guilt in his heart. He was the bad guy. He had no other choice but to be the bad guy, but he still felt dirty and dark inside: darkness walking. Everett Singh: betrayer of worlds. Was this the lesson Sharkey had wanted to pass down to Everett: that sometimes all adults have is a choice between darknesses?

Everett was still feeling guilty and dark and very, very angry. And that made him all the more helpless, because he knew that when the Sunlord fleet found *Everness*, he and Sharkey would need to work like family.

The birdsong chorus of Jiju voices throughout the cruiser shifted tone and rhythm. Something had changed. There. Everett pressed his hands against the glass. Ahead: a dark knot on the horizon, the apparent size of an insect. Such was the speed of the Sunlord fleet that in an instant it had leapt into focus: *Everness* entangled with three alien aircraft. *Insect* was the right image: the ship looked like something from a particularly savage David Attenborough wildlife documentary: a beautiful caterpillar paralyzed, trapped, and digested by three grasping predators. Closer, and now Everett could make out details of the capturing craft: they were like airborne steel squids, elegantly patterned in tiger stripes that constantly shifted color: red and blue, purple and green, red and white.

Everett shook Sharkey. He woke with a yell and Everett found himself looking down the barrels of a shotgun.

"Sorry, brother." Sharkey flicked the gun away. "Bad conscience."

"We've found *Everness*."

Kax came down the staircase from the upper deck and joined Everett and Sharkey at the observation bubble. The Genequeen skysquids were trying to escape at best speed with their prize but *Everness*'s sheer size and ungainliness meant they could not possibly outrun the Sunlord Navy.

"We're hailing them and informing the Princess Jekajek Rasteem Besheshkek of the judgement of the High Magisterium."

"What is that judgement?" Sharkey asked. He slept as lightly as a cat; in the few seconds since Everett had surprised him awake, he was fully alert and aware.

"That your ship and all its crew are honored guests of the Empress of the Sun and enjoy the status of diplomats from your universe to the Worldwheel."

"'For we are strangers before thee, and sojourners: our days on the earth are as a shadow, and there is none abiding,'" Sharkey said darkly.

The Sunlord ships were slowing, opening their formation into a horseshoe around the lumbering Genequeen flotilla. The skysquids maintained heading, speed, and their grasp on *Everness*. The skyqueens held position and velocity.

"What's happening?" Everett asked.

"Princess Jekajek Rasteem Besheshkek is considering our judgement," Kax said.

A movement beneath his feet made Everett look down. The lower hull was opening dozens of small hatches like the individual flowers of a bluebell. The air buzzed with motion: nanobots. Each of the ships in the Sunlord fleet was following suit, sowing thousands of nanobot seeds.

"Okay," Everett said. "What's happening now?"

"Princess Jekajek Rasteem Besheshkek has rejected our judgement," Kax said. "We are exercising our legal right to enforce compliance."

"You can't! They'll kill them all!" Everett shouted. The swarms of nanobots dived on the skysquids. At the final instant, they reshaped themselves into spear points, each the size of a family car, aimed squarely at the tentacles. Those tentacles sprouted smaller tentacles. They met the Sunlord blade missiles in a storm of flashes and sparks. The Sunlord strike hit hard: two severed tentacles released their grasp on *Everness*'s hull, slipped, and fell to the forest canopy. The Sunlord spears dissolved into their component nanobots and reformed into super-speed sword missiles. The Genequeen close-into defenses detached from the main grasping tentacles, reformed into sword missiles, and streaked out to meet the attackers in a mid-air flying sword battle. Cut, stab, parry; thrust and dodge; a hundred sword missiles duelled back and forth in the airspace between the two fleets.

"'And there was war in heaven: Michael and his angels fought against the dragon; and the dragon fought and his angels,'" Sharkey said with reverence. His eyes were wide: he was in awe. But Everett had seen another thing, beyond the flashing blades. Those tentacles that remained were tightening their grip on *Everness*. Everett could see the ship's skin bulge and strain around the constricting coils.

"They're going to destroy the ship!" The observation deck gave Everett a front-row view of the death of his friends. A flash, a sharp fast shadow out there in the sky, then Sharkey threw himself at Everett, hit him hard, smashed him up against the rear of the observation bubble. His ears popped, wind and noise hammered him. Everett scraped his hair out of his eyes. The front of the glass blister was gone, neatly sheared off. The sword missile that had cleaved it in two looped away.

"Whoa. Thank you."

The wind was brutal, a lashing hurricane, whipping tears from

Everett's eyes. Everett struggled to his feet against the shrieking gale.

"Come on, here, here." From halfway up the staircase to the upper level, Kax offered a hand. The crew gave respect and moved out of Kax's way as she brought Everett and Sharkey to the upper bridge. From the gallery Everett could see the entire battle spread out across the sky. Swords missiles and nanobot swarms clashed and slashed. A Sunlord skyqueen spiraled slowly downwards, unravelling a thread of smoke from it starboard hull. One of the skysquids that had held *Everness* was gone, but the other two held on with a death grip. Swords missiles dashed and parried, steel flashed, another severed tentacle spun away from the airship. It was thrilling, it was terrifying, and Everett knew how it would end: with the total destruction of the loser. He had seen it when Kax fought her rival to the death to become a Princess of the Sunburst Throne. It was the Jiju way.

Everett had ended that fight. He had thrown Kax the shotgun. There had been no other way. She would have died. He had done right, but he did not feel right. He never would feel right about it. There had to be a better decision than death, between a choice of darknesses. There had to be a better way, a cleverer way.

"Sharkey, you're the weighmaster, is there a way of opening the cargo hatch from the outside?"

"There's an external switch. But it's on the bottom of the ship, underneath the hull."

That was the first part.

"Kax, you're in command here?"

"As a member of the Royal Family, yes, I am the highest ranking officer."

"Can you bring us in underneath *Everness*? Like real close? Close enough to hit a switch underneath the ship?"

Kax exchanged a flurry of song with the bridge officers.

"It can be done."

"I can get you the Infundibulum."

Omis were so predictable. Sen went straight to the hammock, tipped the sheets onto the floor, and took the T-shirt-wrapped object hidden under the bedding. Clever about some things, Everett Singh, not so clever about others. The T-shirts, the hammock, the latty smelled of him. Slightly sweet, slightly like honey, with a slightly stomach-lifting undertone of sock and jock. Sen tucked the Infundibulum under her arm like a rugby ball to her chest. *Everness* shook again, sending her reeling into a bulkhead. Sen felt every creak and strain, every grate of the squidship tentacles across the hull, as if they were on her own skin. They would crush it like an egg, like the skull of old Gadger Ree, The Knights of the Air's legendary drinker, who had fallen asleep on the railway line.

Another ship was going to die.

Sen froze as memory, strong as a blow, took her back to that first escape pod, falling free from the burning hulk of the *Fairchild*, hanging there against the storm clouds, burning burning until the parachutes opened and hid the terrible sight.

She was cursed; she drew misfortune to her like the spire of Christchurch Spitalfields, the patron church of the Airish, drew lightning. She was Dona Darkside, the Airish Saint of Scapegoats, Fortune, and the Weather. She was Sen Shipkiller.

Sen stopped to take a last look into her latty. The clobber, the mess, the makeup and smelly stuff, the magazines, and the little box where she kept the ideas and clippings and bits of shiny things for cards. Almost, she took the box. Rugby players looked down from the walls of the latty; imaginary boyfriends, muscled sports gods. *Save yourself, Sen.* A last look, but not the last thing. Sen stopped a moment at the head of the main companionway. She could still smell the blood. The Genequeens had healed her body but it still remembered the pain Charlotte Villiers had worked so easily on it. Sen slapped open the armory cabinet and took a thumper. No one would hit her like that ever again. A slap on the red button armed it. Sen clattered down the main companionway. *Everness* rang to a barrage of booms. The ship's spine groaned and twisted: debris rained down on her from the high gantries.

Everness was dying. Sen froze, helpless with horror and grief. This was how it would end: three humans in a tiny pod swinging over an alien artificial world.

"No!"

With her one free hand, Sen tried to wipe away the tears. They would not stop.

"Sen!" Captain Anastasia stood in the hatch to the escape-pod, a brass egg held in a drop cradle over empty space. Mchynlyth had opened the emergency hatch in the ship's belly. All they needed was her. She could defy them. She could refuse to leave. They wouldn't abandon her. The ship would make it. The ship always did.

"Sen!"

"Ma! I's here! I's here!"

Down the companionway she ran, across the cargo deck, the batteries still half repaired under her feet. Past Mchynlyth's engineering cubby. The latches that held the cargo containers. All those runs to the cold north, the impellers at full thrust, driving into the wind from the pole. All those warm nights when she slept down in her special place on the cargo door and let the warm night wind of Amexica lull her in scents of juniper and sage.

Emotion stopped her in her tracks.

A Jiju figure appeared from a stairwell, tall and lithe and oddly jointed, pointing a globe-topped staff at her head. Between her and the escape pod.

"Sen, give me the Infundibulum," the Genequeen said in Sen's own voice. Jekajek Rasteem Besheshkek: the Jiju who had healed her, the Jiju who had taken her voice and language, the Jiju who had put the whole terrible history of her people into Sen's head.

"No, I won't. You shall not have it."

"Sen, the Sunlords will kill us all. Every last one of us. It's what they want. It's what they's always wanted. They rule the *sun*. You's *seen* it."

The images, the endless wars, the cycles of building and destruction; they had not been an accident, a leakage from brain to brain. Jekajek had placed them there for this moment. Sen could see and understand the Sunlords and their plan over millions of years to be the sole rulers of the Worldwheel. Sen had seen. Sen understood. Sen understood much, much more.

"I don't care. You get that? I don't care! You can all burn. All of you. This is mine. I's keeping it."

Jekajek hissed and stabbed her staff at Sen. Sen's fingers were quicker than the Jiju's will. While the nanorobots took the shape of Jekajek's will, Sen's finger had pulled the thumper's trigger. The soft, heavy stun bag hit the Jiju hard in the center of her narrow chest. The staff flew up in the air and fell with a clatter to the deck. Jekajek went reeling back toward the open emergency hatch. Her arms flailed, her crest rose, her eyes went wide. Then, with a long piercing whistle, she went over.

Sen stared at the open hatch. With a wordless cry she threw the thumper away from her. It skidded across the deck and followed Jekajek down through the hole.

"Sen!" Captain Anastasia held out a hand. "You're all right. You're all right. Come to me."

"Ma, I . . ."

"Come to me."

Everness groaned and shook, but Captain Anastasia's hand was firm. Sen gave another cry and ran to the hatch. At the very last minute she grabbed the Jiju staff then dived into the soft padded nest of the escape hatch. Captain Anastasia sealed the door behind her and armed the launch button.

"What are you doing with that unholy thing?" Mchynlyth

nodded at the Jiju staff. Its amber head rippled with swirls of gold and chocolate.

"I don't know," Sen said. "I kinda heard something in my head. Like it was talking to me." When she picked up the staff Sen had felt a warm glow flow up her arm, over her heart, into her head like a spray of Christmas bells. The things Jekajek had put in her head, the staff heard them. The staff was calling to them. "Ma, Jekajek, I shot her, she's . . ."

"You did what you had to do Sen. You're safe."

The launch button glowed red under Captain Anastasia's hand. The escape pod rang like a bell to a barrage of distant booms. Sen pulled the Everness Tarot from the zipped pocket on her shorts and turned the deck over and over and over in her hands. The pod shook savagely; Captain Anastasia looked up at the sound of a series of terrible wrenching groans, as if the bones of the ship were being pulled out one by one. Still she held her hand over the launch button.

"What are ye waiting for?" Mchynlyth shouted. "If the ship goes down, she takes us with her!"

Sen pulled her knees close to her chest and tried to push herself down into the impact padding. It was happening again. The soft leather, the safety gel, the smell of leather and brass and grease, the shaking and the shocks and the not knowing what was going on out there. It was happening again and she could not do a thing about it.

"Speak to me," Sen whispered. She turned over the top card of her deck. *Two Bad Cats*: cut-out cats with hypodermic syringes for claws in the back of an open-topped car. "What?" *Two Bad Cats* meant fun that could backfire on you; enjoy now, pay later. Pleasure with a sharp edge. Meant nothing. The cards had stopped speaking to her. She was losing the trick. It was all the stuff Jekajek had put in her head, the stuff that sent chords of electric music through her brain every time she looked at the Jiju staff.

The pod lurched, metal screeched and tore. Sen, her mother,

and Mchynlyth all looked at each other at the sound of a long, slow scraping from the top of the ship's hull all the way to the bottom.

"What was that?" Mchynlyth snapped. "What. The hell. Was that?" His eyes were wide and wild. His breath came in short, shallow gasps. He leaped for the door, tried to wrestle Captain Anastasia away from the lock. "My pipes! My pipes are out there! I cannae leave my pipes!" Sen grabbed Mchynlyth's legs and dragged him from the hatch. His skin was grey with pallor. His hands shook. "I'm sorry. I'm sorry. It's just . . . I'm a wee bit . . . *claustrophobic*."

The pod—the entire ship—trembled to the longest, hardest shaking yet. Still Captain Anastasia held her hand over the red launch button. A terrible, shrieking rip, like every soul in the world being torn in half. Booms. Thuds. Another long shredding screech. Then silence.

"Ma . . ."

Captain Anastasia held up a finger. She looked up at lights.

Silence.

Sen was holding her breath. Mchynlyth was holding his breath. Captain Anastasia was holding her breath. Sen strained for sound, any sound.

A clunk. A whine. Mchynlyth looked flabbergasted.

"That's the . . ." Captain Anastasia shushed him. He mouthed the words *cargo hoist*. A pause. A second whine. A clunk. *Closing*, Sen thought. Even her heart was too loud. What was that? Did she hear? Footsteps. Two sets.

Footsteps.

Captain Anastasia threw all her weight on the release lever. The hatch locks hissed open. Sen seized the Jiju battlestaff. The idea for how to use it formed in her head; the nanobots turned the idea into physical shapes. Captain Anastasia swung open the door. Shafts of light beamed through a dozen rips in the ship's skin, like a cathedral hit by a tornado. Standing in the light before the emergency pod hatch were Everett and Sharkey.

27

C harles was waiting in Charlotte Villiers's room, perched on the deep windowsill overlooking the snow-flecked dark water of the Oudeshaans Canal. He applauded her entrance.

"You played the Praesidium like a piano, cora."

Again, her alter's use of the term of endearment grated on Charlotte Villiers.

"We've shown our hand. The eyes of the Plenitude are on us. It will be much more difficult for the Order to operate now."

And for me to gain control of the Infundibulum, Charlotte Villiers did not say. Charles Villiers raised an eyebrow. Sometimes her alter was too like her. She peeled off her gloves.

"Any success with the Thryn?"

"The Thryn are hard to motivate. Human needs and emotions are quite alien to them. They may well regard this as a biological versus biological spat." Charles Villiers reached lazily for an orange from the fruit bowl on the table beside him. He thrust thumbnails into the rind, releasing a tiny spritz of zest into the air. "And even if we can persuade them that our concern is their concern, that concern may extend no further than Earth 4. They have no reason to aid the rest of the Plenitude. The Thryn Sentiency has never shown any interest in the rest of the Known Worlds."

"Then we shall all have to take refuge on Earth 4," Charlotte Villiers said.

Charles Villiers peeled the orange and split it deftly into segments.

"Oh. Yes. And another thing. That tracking device. It's not transmitting anymore."

"The Jiju . . ."

"Or the crew. But I suspect the Jiju. In which case, they have a direct quantum link back to us. To us personally." Charles Villiers popped a piece of orange into his mouth.

A knock at the door. A man dressed in Heiden fashion—brocade waistcoat and tailcoat—entered and gave a small bow.

"Ebben Heer, so good to see you." He was a member of the Order, a junior staffer far below the politicians who formed the heart of the Order, and all the more valuable for his lesser rank. He—or his twin—could go places no Plenipotentiary or Security Council member could. "You have something?"

"My twin has been following the people you specified." Ebben Heer opened a leather briefcase and laid a picture on the table beside the fruit bowl. It showed Paul McCabe, lost in his own thoughts, waiting at a crossing on Exhibition Road. He looked small and scruffy and completely unaware he was being watched. Charlotte Villiers had heard that the people of Earth 7 had developed quantum scanning technology that could tap the entangled state between twins and draw information from it. In this case, images. She was seeing what Ebben Heer's twin on Earth 10 had seen, what Ebben Heer saw in his own head when he fully opened his mind to the two-in-oneness.

Charlotte Villiers found the idea hideous. Nothing private, nothing sacred, nothing secret. Ebben Heer laid out more images: Paul McCabe taking a taxi. Paul McCabe crossing the college court-yard. Paul McCabe with students. Paul McCabe, dull Paul McCabe, boring Paul McCabe, unexceptional and average in every way.

"These are more interesting," Ebben Heer said. Colette Harte: looking over her shoulder as she went up the steps at the front of the Natural History Museum, as if she expected someone to be behind her. Colette Harte in the Central Hall among the bones of long-dead dinosaurs. Colette Harte shaking the hand of a teenage boy.

"Who is the boy?" Charlotte Villiers asked.

"I don't know. I have another image that shows him more clearly."

Colette Harte and the same boy entering a bright and cheerful Japanese restaurant, glimpsed from a few meters distance.

Charlotte tapped the picture with a manicured nail.

"I know this school uniform. I don't know the boy, but I know the school. Bourne Green School. Everett Singh's school. Now, why would Ms. Harte be interested in a Bourne Green schoolboy? She wouldn't be so foolish as to be indiscreet about my agent, would she?"

Charles Villiers had left his comfortable seat and pored over the photographs.

"It seems Ms. Harte is not staunch."

"Ms. Harte is very far from staunch. Disloyalty is a vile crime. It will have to be dealt with most harshly. Thank you, Ebben Heer. This is excellent information."

The Earth 7er touched forefinger to forelock.

"By your leave, Fro, do you think my twin might be returned to me? I'm feeling the Separation Sickness—I can't sleep at night and I'm getting these terrible anxiety attacks and bouts of dizziness when I don't know what world I'm on; and it's as bad for him. And that world . . . I know you're Plenipotentiary there, but I don't like what I see of it. No, I don't like it at all."

"In a while, Ebben, in a while. I need you—sorry, your twin—to complete one more task for me. This boy, I want to know who he is. Bourne Green School in Stoke Newington—let your twin know. One more task and you are done."

Ebben Heer closed his eyes. His lips moved, and Charlotte Villiers knew that even as he shaped the thought, the same words and images appeared in the mind of his twin, across universes. She shivered. Every world in the Plenitude came to the Heisenberg Gate in a different way: Earth 3 through research, Earth 5 through its naturally occurring zones where planes overlapped, Earth 7 through the inherent quantum nature of its citizens.

"I'll do it." An earth 7 *I*, meaning *we'll do it*.

"Thank you. Now, Charles. I need to arrange a full meeting of the inner circle of the Order to brief them on the changed nature of things. Not on this world—if you'll excuse me, Ebben Heer. At my apartment. At your convenience. But first, I want to have some words with Everett M. Singh."

28

Ryun Spinetti liked being a detective. He liked knowing things about people they didn't know he knew. He liked watching them and following them and them not knowing he was watching and following. He liked the skill in trailing someone and not being noticed. He had learned how to trail people on a website called "Be Your Own Detective". Never let them see you looking at them, the site said. Use reflective surfaces: shop windows, car glass, even puddles. Follow their reflections. He stayed up late reading the chapter about how to go through people's trash to find useful information—latex gloves, a large empty garage, and chopsticks were the keys here. He hoped it wouldn't have to come to the Trash Thing with Everett.

The girl who was following Everett, Noomi's mate Becs, she was a rubbish detective. She would never get a job on a Sunday tabloid newspaper. First rule: blend in with the crowd. In her white Boy London leggings and Nicky Minaj boots, she could not have been more obvious if she had been a Dalek. Terrible at following but easy to follow. If she caught him following her, there were creepy, stalkery consequences he didn't want to think about. He'd end up with his face on some super creep name-and-shame site.

Noomi's mate Becs, was she going out with anyone?

He watched Becs watch Everett at the allotment. How long had they had that? He'd never mentioned it. Maybe it was his Grandpa Singh's. What have you got in there? Ryun wondered, zooming in the telephoto lens on the family SLR. "Be Your Own Detective" said it was a lot less suspicious than a pair of binoculars. Becs had a great ass but she chewed gum constantly. Ryun thought that made people look stupid. Then Noomi arrived and it got crowded.

His dad was playing World of Tanks when Ryun got in.

"Dad, can I get some money?"

"How much?"

"Forty quid."

"Forty quid! Hell's teeth, Ryun!"

"I want to get night-vision goggles."

"Night-vision goggles?"

His dad explored several ways to ask *what do you want those for* without actually asking *what are you up to?*

"Proper night-vision goggles," Ryun said. "They're on the Rampage Airsoft website."

"Actually, for proper, forty quid's not bad . . ."

Ryun whispered a victorious *yes* to himself. His dad wanted second play with them. Now the finisher: "They've got a place on Highbury Road. Can you take me over there?"

"What, now?"

"They're open until seven."

And Mum didn't ask *what are you up to* when he slipped out after dinner with the new night-vision goggles pushed up on his beanie. On the street there was too much light to use the goggles. Ryun found the bent bar in the railings around Clissold Park and squeezed through. After dark the park was a bad place of drinkers and drug dealers. Ryun could clearly see them, spooky ghost figures at the bandstand and the tennis courts. He could see them. They couldn't see him.

"Cool," he said to himself. The park was a glowing plane, like a phantom zone. The street lights were exploding stars, car headlights swords of light so bright he could almost hear them in his head like lightsabers.

He slipped the goggles on again at the end of Aden Terrace. House windows were white squares, the allotments a confusing weave of plots and paths, fences and sheds, water butts and bamboo poles. A cat stared glowing eyed at him.

The padlock hadn't been opened. It had been cut off. That was good. He wouldn't have to use the bolt cutters in his backpack. There were cooled drips of melted metal on the hasp.

"Weird," Ryun said. He stepped into the allotment. Dead tomato plants and rotting courgette leaves were treacherous under his feet. The shed padlock had been cut off as well. "What you got in there?"

Is it your interdimensional portal/stargate? Ryun thought. Had to be. If Dr. Who could put a Tardis inside a police telephone box, the Plenitude of Known Worlds could put a jump-gate inside a garden shed.

Ryun reached out to open the bolt. Hesitated. More buts. More questions. If Everett—or the pseudo-Everett's secret jump-gate was in there, why did he need to cut the locks off? Why was the metal melted? He could hear his heart. He had never been so apprehensive in his life. Ryun swallowed. You have to know. You have to know.

He pulled back the bolt and threw the door wide.

The night-vision goggles showed every detail of the horror within.

The body was naked, pierced through and through with pulsing black tubes. Spread-eagled against the wall, it hung like a huge, pale spider at the center of a web of black strands that covered every centimeter of the inside of the shed. Thick black fluid dripped from the web to the floor and was absorbed silently and completely. A cluster of black tendrils burst from the body's mouth, opened in a frozen scream. The tendrils waved slowly, dripping black, oily slime from their tips. The chest was open, split throat to navel, ribs cracked and held open by struts of the same black substance that infested the shed. Inside, where the heart should have been, something stirred. A rat, a rat made from five rats melted and fused together. The night-vision goggles spared him nothing. The rat that was five rats turned its five heads towards Ryun. Five mouths opened in a hiss. Glittering eyes opened all over the inside of the shed. Hundreds of rats—half rats—were melted into the black web. They echoed the heart rat's hiss. And at the sound the body opened its eyes. Its eyes. Its eyes—they were insect eyes. Strands of black web stuff, like frozen dark lightning, sprouted from the eyes, reached towards Ryun.

"Ah!" Ryun said. He was beyond words, cries, even screams. Nothing but paralyzed, animal grunts came from his brain. "Uh." He backed away, slipped on a treacherous mulched courgette leaf. The black eye tendrils loomed over him, fused together, formed into a face. The face of the thing that had been a man melted into the living ooze. The face. Some part of Ryun's brain, which would not, even at the very end, stop asking questions, realized it was the face of the missing Rentokil man. The oily black face looked into his.

Then a hand grabbed the hood of his parka and pulled him away. Ryun cried out as he came down rib-cracking hard on the edge of a raised bed. Another ghostly face in his night-vision goggles. Everett.

"If you want to live, don't touch the black stuff."

"Everett?"

His hands. What was wrong with his hands?

The black face lunged. Everett stabbed out his right hand, palm forward. The face exploded into a smear like burst fruit, froze, and shattered like glass. The hut was a shrieking, hissing, thrash of rats and black tentacles. Two hands now. Ryun's night vision flashed painful white. The hissing and shrieking stopped. Everett grabbed him by the hood again and dragged him out into Aden Terrace.

"You okay?"

"Uh. Ah. What? That . . . He . . . You."

"Can you walk?"

"Think so."

Everything hurt. Ryun's mind was still numb from what had happened. It hadn't been real. Couldn't have been real.

"We'll need to get out fast. There's one more thing I need to do."

Through night vision, Ryun saw round metal and plastic objects melt into the palms of Everett's hands. The skin closed over them. The tips of each of Everett's forefingers peeled back. Metal emerged, unfolded. Everett advanced down the allotment patch of badly laid concrete paving slabs. White-hot beams lanced across Ryun's night vision, again and again, like swords of light. He pushed up his goggles to see Everett walk back to him, silhouetted against the blazing garden shed. He held out a hand to Ryun. His fingers were whole again. But unnatural strength pulled Ryun to his feet.

"The fire brigade'll be here soon."

"Everett . . ."

"Later. Why did you . . . No. No time."

It hurt to walk, hurt so bad Ryun wanted to cry out with every step. He had never been hurt in his life, Ryun realized. Not really hurt, body-harming hurt. He froze at the end of the terrace where it opened onto Clissold Close.

"CCTV cameras," Ryun said. "They'll have filmed . . ."

"I took them out on the way in," Everett said. "I've been doing this a while. Come on. Let's get you back to your place. You're still kind of shocky. And there's things you need to know."

One thing Ryun did know. He didn't like being a detective anymore.

29

"Can I see them?" Ryun asked.

The room was warm and dimly lit, and the familiar things on walls, shelves, screens made the thing in the shed seem unreal and distant, but Ryun was still shaky and shocky. So much, too much, too soon, too fast. Start with Everett. Start with the thing you know. Even if, as Ryun realized, he didn't.

"It's kind of private," Everett M said. "It's like the inside of my body."

"You didn't mind back there." Ryun said.

"I was saving your ass back there. You want to end up like Rat Killer guy, with Nahn for brains?"

Everett M had explained the Nahn, but there was so much rattling around inside Ryun's head; hard, gritty things, like stone-washing jeans. The Nahn had taken over one parallel world and wanted to take over another. This world. The Nahn were The Bad.

"Okay," Everett M said.

He took off his top and sat bare-chested beside Ryun on the bed. He turned his forearms upwards. The lines Ryun has noticed in the showers darkened and split along the seams. Skin panels folded and retracted. Ryun glimpsed spidery white devices inside the cavities. They unfolded from Everett M's arms, unfolded again; racks and clips.

"They're usually fitted with nanomissiles, but I used them all up on Earth 1. I'd have to go back to Earth 4 to resupply."

To Ryun the weapons that unfolded from Everett M's body were the most beautiful and at the same time the most repulsive things he had ever seen. He wanted to choke and hurl. He wanted to touch them. He extended a hand towards the white machinery. Everett M slapped it away. Ryun gasped and nursed wounded fingers.

"You almost broke my fingers!"

"Sorry. . . No, I'm not. Don't touch me there."

"Does it hurt?" Ryun asked. His face was a picture of wonder and horror, equally colored.

"Every time," Everett M said. "Every. Single. Time. The really clever stuff isn't the weapon systems, it's the stuff you can't see. I'm faster than you, I'm stronger than you, I can go on for longer, and I can hear and see things you can't. I'm faster and stronger and better than anyone on this world."

"See things? Can you, like, undress people like Superman's x-ray vision?"

"No," Everett M said. "I've tried. There's other senses as well. I can hear radio. That's how I tracked the Nahn down."

Footsteps on the landing. The two boys froze. The feet could go two ways, to the bathroom or to the bedrooms. They were coming to the bedroom. Everett M snapped his ports shut and was wriggling into the T-shirt as Ryun's dad knocked and opened the door. He did a quick double take at Everett pulling his T-shirt down over the waistband of his jeans.

"Are you guys okay?"

"We're okay," Ryun said.

"Good. Excellent. Um, Ryun. Those, um, night-vision goggles? Are you using them? Could I have a go on them?"

"One thing I've noticed," Everett M said when Ryun's dad had gone back down the stairs, goggles in hand. "You've stopped saying *um*."

I have, Ryun thought, and he knew exactly when he had and why. When: the moment he had seen the alien tech retract into the palms of Everett's hands. Why: he knew now. There was no doubt. His suspicions were confirmed. This Everett was not his best-friend Everett. He was the double from a parallel universe. Everything Ryun had feared was true, and more. This Everett was not just a double, but an alien-re-engineered cyborg agent. Working for the bad guys. Planted with the real Everett's mum and kid sister. Who had tried to kill the real Everett. Who had sneaked brain-devouring alien nanotech from Earth 1 to this world and then accidentally let it loose.

"Colette was right," Ryun whispered.

"What?"

He hadn't realized he had spoken aloud.

"Colette. Your dad's friend. I mean, your alter's dad's friend . . ." It would always be an easy mistake, confusing alter for original. Especially when the question of who was alter and who was original depended on who you were and in what universe.

"You saw Colette? Man, I wish you hadn't done that."

"She didn't tell me anything. She said it would be dangerous."

"It is. I am."

"I know." Everett M had explained the politics of the Plenitude and the Order and Charlotte Villiers and her alter Charles and who their agents were on this world and who could be trusted and who couldn't, but it wouldn't all fit in Ryun's head. He reckoned Everett M didn't fully understand it himself.

"I don't know what I'm going to do," Everett M said suddenly.

"You got the Nahn," Ryun said.

"Yes. No. Maybe. Not the Nahn. Yes the Nahn. Do I tell Charlotte Villiers? If I do, what happens? She's got my mum—my real mum, back there. And what about my mum here? What about Noomi? You. Us. I don't know what to do!"

For all his powers, Everett M was powerless to know how to use them, Ryun realized. It's the superhero problem. You can blast the energy of the sun from your hands but that doesn't battle starvation. You can throw skyscrapers into orbit but that won't beat creeping corruption. You can read the innermost feelings and desires but that's no good against homophobia. Superpowers make everything personal. Batman versus Joker. Fantastic Four versus Galactus. The Big G might be the Devourer of Worlds, but in the end he's just a dude. Beat him and the problem goes away. But the real problems aren't like that. You can't solve them by hitting them. The real supervillains were the ones who had smashed Everett apart and rebuilt him and taken him away from everyone he knew and loved and sent him here and expected him to be their warrior. He had no power against them. They were people in suits who met in rooms and decided things. Destroy one and another would take her place.

"I want it to stop!" Everett M shouted.

"Sh, Ev, keep it down, my folks . . ."

"I don't want all these things inside me," Everett M whispered. "I look at them and I hate them. They make me want to throw up. They filled me up with . . . dirt. I never feel clean. I never feel warm. I never feel safe. I want *me* back. I want this all to end and I want to go home!"

"Everett, Ev . . . it's all right."

"I don't have anyone. Do you understand that? There's not anyone knows, understands. I hate him, that other me, your friend. I'm here, I'm all this, because of him. But I can't hate him . . . he's me. I don't have anyone. Every day, I'm alone. I can't do anything, I can't tell anyone."

"Everett, I know."

"No you don't. No one knows. No one can know."

"I know about you. I know *you*."

When he had suspected this Everett was an alter, Ryun had looked for every possible difference from his Everett. Now that he knew the truth, Ryun saw the similarities. They were both clever but kept it hidden, both shy around other people, both brave when they had to be. But knowing that his Thryn tech gave him the power to do almost anything he wanted gave, this Everett displayed a flicker of arrogance and confidence. Ryun liked that. The other Everett would never have had the balls to take Noomi up on her Homework Date. The other Everett would have found a way to hack the Everett's Hot Ass page and take it down rather than endure everyone rating his cute butt. The other Everett went home after football rather than sharing the shower with the other guys. And the flipside of that confidence and arrogance was anger. Anger was the fuel that powered this Everett. Every time he opened those alien hatches in his body, every time he used his weapons, that anger boiled out of him.

Ryun knew what he had to do. He had never done it before. It scared him. But now that the thought was in his head, it was the only thing to do. He put his arms around his friend. Everett M's body was hard and tight and cold, and Ryun felt him stiffen and tighten further, then relax. Cold. So cold. The room was stifling but Ryun shivered. He felt Everett M shake.

"It's okay," Ryun said. "It's okay."

3 0

Charlotte Villiers had made herself comfortable in a chair in Mrs. Abrahams's office. Her bag was on the principle's desk, her hands folded in her lap, her legs crossed demurely at the ankles.

"Ms. Villiers is taking you out of school," Mrs. Abrahams said in the tone of someone whose authority has been simply and efficiently overruled, in her own office, at her own desk.

"I'll return him as soon as my business is done," Charlotte Villiers said. "Everett?"

"Can I go to the bathroom first?"

"I'd prefer if he used yours," Charlotte Villiers said to Mrs. Abrahams with a small smile. "Security." The final victory. Abuse of the executive washroom.

Everett M locked the door and whipped out his phone. Message: contacts. NOOMI: CANT DO CAFE—MSSNG DAD STUFF. COPS. Truth, honesty, caring: he hit all of Noomi's points. Sort of.

Message: contacts: RYUN: CV GOT ME. GPS ME. FOLLOW. His thumb hovered over the send button. What if Charlotte Villiers was monitoring his phone. She could do that. She should do that. If she was, then she knew about Ryun anyway. It got complicated when other people were involved: Ryun, Noomi. Laura, Victory-Rose. What did she want with him? Was it another off-world mission? He needed a witness, someone to notice, someone who knew.

Send.

A taxi waited at the school gate.

"Where's the Merc?" Everett asked.

"I lost my driver," Charlotte Villiers said. She studied her face in the mirror of her makeup compact. Everett M noticed the wicked little gun in her handbag. He was meant to.

"I thought some lunch," Charlotte Villiers continued. "Are you hungry? A decent lunch puts the day in proper order." The taxi driver negotiated the lunchtime traffic of Stoke Newington Church Road down onto Albion Road. Everett M glanced up at the front of Noomi's house. "At least I no longer have to drag myself all the way up from that dank hole in the ground in Kent every time I need a chat with you. We've built a new gate, a little closer to the centers of power."

This world was Charlotte Villiers's first First Contact, but she had heard from the Accession Team that had brought Earth 9 into the Plenitude that politicians were surprisingly easy to manipulate. Bring them to the Heisenberg Gate and let them look through to what lay beyond. The realization that their concerns and ambitions were less than an atom of relevance in the vastness of the multiverse gave them a proper sense of perspective—and their own importance.

Charlotte Villiers snapped her compact shut.

"The Plenitude is in peril."

That made Everett M stop slouching.

She knows about the Nahn.

"Your alter has betrayed us all," Charlotte Villiers said.

Everett M's heart started again. *Your alter.* Not him. Not *him.*

Charlotte Villiers went on: "Your own world, my world—even this world. Every soul in the Ten Worlds is in clear and present danger. You're intelligent, so I don't need to spell out much more than the bare bones. In our worlds, the dinosaurs became extinct tens of millions of years ago. Imagine a universe where that didn't happen. Now imagine sixty-five million years of evolution. What are the implications of that?"

Everett M's head was reeling from the realization that it wasn't the Nahn. Thought was difficult. There was another threat out there? Bigger than the Nahn. What was she saying? Super evolved dinosaurs? "They have a sixty-five million year head start on us."

"Correct. Twenty times the entire existence of humanity as a species. This is Big Time."

Traffic was stop-start, stop-start down Essex Road.

"Wait a moment though," Everett M said. "If they're that advanced, why aren't they here already?"

"Good boy. Because they are aggressive and vicious. They are factional and warlike. Every time one of their factions gains an advantage, the others band together to destroy them before they are destroyed. Jiju civilization has been built up and knocked down again thousands of times. Tens of thousands of times."

"Jiju?"

"I need to tell you a bit of secret Plenitude history. In the early days of the Plenitude—before there was a formal Plenitude and before the great quarantine—when there was only Earth 1 and Earth 2, Earth 1 sent probes on a series of random exploration jumps. They mapped several hundred planes. One of them was the plane of the Jiju. We had to destroy that probe before the Jiju learned too much from it, but we got enough information back to know that we should never go near that plane again. You alter's search for his father took him there. And he has let the Infundibulum fall into the hands of the Jiju."

"He wouldn't do that if he had a choice," Everett M said.

"Where has this sympathy for your alter come from?" Charlotte Villiers asked.

"He is my alter. I'm him, he's me. I would never do that. Not unless it's life and death."

"As you say, you are his alter."

On to Pentonville Road, through heavy traffic. A cyclist in yellow hi-viz came up on the taxi's inside as the traffic lights at King's Cross turned red.

"Where are we going?"

"For lunch. The Praesidium is on high alert, though what we could do should the Jiju decide to invade, I don't know."

"The Thryn." As he said the word, the implants inside him felt strange and alien, separate from his own flesh. "Madam Moon could stop them."

"We're investigating that."

The full implication hit Everett M. Madam Moon, Earth 4, his home: "My mum, Vicky-Rose . . . Bebe Singh, Gramma Braiden!"

"We will protect them as best we can Everett. Have no fears about that."

Everett M would have jumped out of the cab in an instant, in a burn of fear and anger; run somewhere, anywhere, nowhere; shouted aloud what he felt to no one. But the little red door lights were on. The doors were sealed. He was locked in with Charlotte Villiers.

"It's imperative you stay here, Everett. If the Jiju invade, the real . . ." Charlotte Villiers caught her slip. "The other Everett will come for his family. We need you to be ready for that."

"Mum, Vicky-Rose," Everett M said again.

"The Order will do its best."

The cyclist pulled up onto the pavement and dodged pedestrians down to Gray's Inn Road. A fleet of buses pulled in at the stop outside King's Cross Station. After days of snow and sleet, the sky was clear, a brisk wind drying the streets and sidewalks. Light glinted from the glass annex to King's Cross and the gaudy plastic signs of cheap Bangladeshi restaurants. St. Pancras was like a little bit of Gotham dropped into northeast London. Everett M tried to imagine that blue sky filled with invaders: airships, starships, motherships, second moons, Death Stars, millions of shooty space fighters, tripod fighting machines, giant city-stomping Godzillas. What did superintelligent dinosaurs drive?

"This isn't real."

"It's the most real thing there is, Everett. He will come. Whatever happens, be ready for him. No mistakes this time."

The taxi lurched onto Euston Road, turned left onto Tottenham Court Road.

"Where are you taking me?"

"Do you like Japanese food?" Charlotte Villiers said. "Your friend Ryun does." The taxi pulled up outside a small Japanese restaurant. A Maneki Neko cat waved from a small window beside the door. "In fact, he should . . . ah, there he is."

The door opened. Ryun stepped out. He was in his school uniform. He looked small and pale and frightened. A man stepped into the doorway behind Ryun. He was short, a little chubby, his hair slicked down. He did not look comfortable in his clothes.

"What's going on?" Everett M asked.

"We're having lunch," Charlotte Villiers said. "With friends. We need to get a few things straightened out. Your friend Ryun is very loyal, but he's let his curiosity get the better of him. He's not very good at following people. He never thinks that someone might be following him. Not much of a detective. Pandora's box can't ever be closed again. That's a pity. At least you've been discreet with your girl-friend—Noomi's not her real name, surely—that says a lot about boys and who they trust, don't you think? You see, I need to know that I can trust the people I work with. You, your friend Ryun, even your girl-friend, Colette Harte—he's been talking to Colette Harte. I'd advise against that. You see, we can offer protection, or we can withdraw it."

"You go near Noomi, I'll kill you."

"You won't, Everett. Don't bluster. Do you see my colleague Heer Daude? He is an Earth 7 twin. I'm sure you learned about them in school. Everything he sees and hears, everything he feels and thinks, is shared by his Earth 7 twin, Ebben Heer. Except Ebben Heer isn't on Earth 7. Ebben Heer is now on Earth 4, in northeast London. Roding Road, Stoke Newington. Number 43. You're fast, Everett, but you're not faster than quantum entanglement. Now that we know where we stand . . . Sushi?"

31

The Sunlords turned Everett and Sen into superstars.

WELCOME OUR GUESTS FROM ANOTHER UNIVERSE!

They rode in a gossamer howdah on the back of a huge, ambling sauropod down the ten-kilometer royal road that spiraled down the inside of one of the enormous black ziggurats Everett had seen from the flight in to Palatakahapa on the Sunlord royal yacht. Hundreds of thousands of Jiju lined the way, raising their crests in a synchronized Mexican wave of purple flashing into red into orange. Kax rode an ornately jewelled saddle far up the sauropod's long neck, just behind the head. She raised a hand and her crest to the adoring thousands. It took hours to make the procession. Everett and Sen fell asleep against each other, curled up like kittens.

OUR PLANESRUNNING ALIEN FRIENDS CELEBRATE MATCH DAY!

They were given the royal box at the arena for some sporting event that played like basketball with ten hoops all around the court. Everett threw in the ball. A dozen hands rose to meet it. Body slammed and crunched against Jiju body. Kax went through a dozen changes of skin color and sang an entire opera in twittering Jiju in her excitement but Everett could not understand what was going on. He thought about the family seats in the North Stand at White Hart Lane and talking about the game with Dad on his way back to the flat to try something new for Cuisine Night.

THE MASTER OF THE MULTIVERSE AND HIS FEMALE COMPANION ENJOY CULTURAL ACTIVITIES OF GREAT SUNLORD PEOPLE!

Ten thousand Jiju performed a long, elegant, intricate dance involving multicolored fans, massive puppets on sticks, and glowing auras of light among the great trees of a park at the base of the ziggurat city of Palapahedra. Each pyramid was a single building that was also an entire city—and they extended much farther beneath the ground than they did above. Self-contained, self-maintained, and self-powering, each housed one hundred million Sunlord Jiju. On the slow flight to Palatakahapa in the heavily damaged *Everness*, Everett had lost count of the number of black pyramid cities in the horizonless landscape. "Female companion, huh!" Sen complained.

APE-PEOPLE GO SAFARI!

They went out on wave-skimming sky sleds over a sea that was wider than any ocean on any Earth. Sen pinned her great hair back and wore her welding goggles and clung to the edge of the little raft with wild glee. *Lower, faster, closer!* She urged on the pilot. The pilot spoke no English but understood her excitement. This small landlocked sea—by Worldwheel standards—was a reserve for a rare species of marine wildlife. Everett had seen computer simulations of sea creatures from the age of the dinosaurs—snapping jaws, long snake necks, powerful flippers—but these dwarfed any of those monsters, dwarfed even the great whales of Earth, the largest creatures that had ever lived on those worlds. Flying animals—half bird, half pterodactyl—circled, hunting fish, when Everett saw dark shadows rise up below the surface. The water exploded in white foam; monster heads on long necks burst from the waves and snatched mouthfuls of pterobird. The pilot sent the sky sled weaving in and out of the necks. Sen shrieked in delight.

ALIENS MARVEL AT POWER OF SUNLORDS!

They were in a chamber in a chamber in a chamber at the very heart of the palace of the Empress of the Sun. Everett and Sen were guided along corridors and through locks and doors, but each room they entered seemed larger than the one that contained it. *Infundib-*

ular, Everett thought. *Like a Tardis.* In the center chamber, at the very heart of the place, which seemed the biggest chamber of all, was a model of the Jiju universe. They stepped out onto a floating disk—gravity was so weak here that every step took Everett a dozen meters—at the center of which blazed a model sun. Around the edge of the disk stood Sunlord technicians at floating consoles. The technicians dialed down the sun blaze until the humans could see the other objects at the hollow center of the ring: a circle of hovering rectangular plates—each in reality must have been the size of Earth, Everett calculated—upright to the sun; and over the sun's north and south pole, complex mechanisms in ghostly silver. Nothing physical could have existed more than an instant so close to the boiling surface of the sun: Everett reckoned they must use the same force-field technology that made their aircraft and palaces fly. The jets that move the sun, Kax explained, and Everett sensed her pride and power. This was her inheritance: the ability to make a star dance to her will. *But I've done that, too*, Everett thought. He had punched a Heisenberg Gate into the heart of a sun and emptied its energy onto the Nahn nest in Imperial University in Earth 1's London. He knew that what he was seeing was more than a model; it was a control system. A touch on one of those control pads could fire the star jets and make the sun itself move. Geek Everett should have been thrilled to the roots of each hair on his head. In that head was the knowledge that the Jiju were reverse engineering the Infundibulum—his Infundibulum, the Infundibulum his Dad had entrusted to him. Him alone. *For you only, Everett.* I'm sorry Dad. I had to give it to them.

Kax led them back out through the doors in the nested chambers along the corridors. Everett moved close to Sen and whispered, "Can we stop this? I hate this."

"Me too," Sen whispered. "I's had enough being a princess. Princesses are naff."

Tippy-tap. Scrit-scratch.

"Uh?"

Rap-rappety-rap-rap.

"I's coming."

The door opened. Sen's eyes went wide in surprise. She gave a cry, covered her small breasts with her hands. She was wearing only panties.

"Everett Singh! Go way go way go way! I thought you were . . . someone else."

"Sorry sorry sorry." Everett's face burned in embarrassment. The latty door slammed in his face. "Sen, can I come in?"

The door opened again. Sen had pulled on a rugby shirt.

"It's kind of messy."

Kax had offered the crew apartments of staggering luxury and opulence in Palatakahapa's Sojourners' Tower. Everett, Sen, Captain Anastasia, Mchynlyth, and Sharkey had each on their own decided they preferred to sleep on the ship. The ship was the one place you couldn't see the ship. *Everness* was a terrible, tragic ruin of an airship. Her spine was warped, her catwalks and companionways twisted. Ceilings were bowed in, latty doors jammed. Her skin still gaped in a dozen places from the crash and the Genequeen assault, and it was ripped and torn where squidship tentacles had resisted giving up their grip. Of the three engines that had been sheared away in the crash landing, only one had been replaced. The second was still in engineering. The third was lost forever. Everett could not look at the ship without pain. But sleeping in her was more than just not having to look at the wreckage: it was an act of loyalty. It was an act of love.

Sen's porthole was cracked and the wooden roof paneling was splintered, but her hammock hung level, her overstuffed drawers spilled clothing, there was dusty makeup strewn over every surface, and her rugby players looked down from the walls. Everett moved a short wooden staff to sit down on the pull-down door seat. The amber globe on top of the staff rippled like jelly. Everett dropped the staff with a yelp. Sen picked it up quickly. The gel flowed with gold, cinnamon, shades of yellow and orange, and settled back into a sphere.

"Oh wow, that's it," Everett said. "Can I touch it?"

"It doesn't like anyone else touching it," Sen said. She leaned the staff carefully in a corner. "Anyone but me."

"Can you make it work?" Everett asked.

Sen nodded. "But I don't like it. It's like it's in my head."

"I got stuff in my head, too," Everett said.

"I know."

"I don't want it there. I don't want any of this. I don't want to be here. Sen, I gave them the Infundibulum."

"You had to, Everett. You couldn't have done anything. I would've done the same. Any of us would."

"But that doesn't make it right."

"I'll tell you you're all right if you tell me I'm all right," Sen said.

"You had to shoot that Jiju. The captain—Annie said you had to do it."

"It was just so fast," Sen said. "Like it happened before I had time to think about it. I pulls the trigger and the thumper shoots and it's gone and it was like all so slow but so fast at the same time and you think you can go back and make it not happen but you can't. No one can. I's killed someone, Everett Singh. I'm not clean. I feels dirty. I'll always feel dirty, in here."

Everness moved at her moorings, buffeted by the winds that blew forever up or down this shaft through the world.

"I killed someone, too," Everett said. "Not directly. But I gave Kax the gun. She killed the other princess."

"If you hadn't Kax would've died. Do you think that other Jiju would've said *thank you oh so much Everett Singh and Mr. Miles O'Rahilly Lafayette Sharkey*? She'd have thought something meese onto that dolly riah of hers and cut you and Sharkey up into mince. You done right. We done right. 'Cept."

"It doesn't feel like it."

"It don't."

"And Kax is taking us around like we're . . . gods or something, and all I'm thinking is I wish my dad had never given me the Infundibulum. I should have just deleted it. I could have. I thought about it. There was a moment . . . just a swipe of the finger, and it would have been gone. I should have just got rid of it and that Jiju you killed would be alive, and all Charlotte Villiers's soldiers, and that other Tejendra on Earth 1, and the crew of that hovercraft on the ice world, and 'Appening Ed, and that other Everett, he'd just be another me, going to school and seeing friends and trying to get girls and playing football, and Annie and you would have a ship and lives back there on Earth 3, and okay, Charlotte Villiers would have my dad, but he'd be on Earth 3, and they'd treat him well, and maybe when she had the Infundibulum from him she'd let him come back."

"You think that?" Sen said. Her eyes were very blue and clear and burning with passion. "You really think that? Coves like Charlotte Villiers, they nanti let anyone go, ever. I seen the likes of her around Hackney Great Port. You done right, Everett. You the hero."

"I'm the hero. Okay. So, if I'm the hero, how come we're sitting in a wrecked airship surrounded by a trillion smart lizards who I've just given the ability to go anywhere in the multiverse? Is that what heroes do? If I'm the hero, how come everything around me goes to shit? How come everyone gets hurt? How come everyone dies?"

"Everett." Sen stood up. She had a look of determination on her face. "Come and sleep with me."

"What?"

Sen nimbly swung herself up into her hammock.

"Doss up here beside me. There's loads of room. Remember back on Earth 1, when I had the nightmare?"

"About being trapped in the Tower of Souls?"

"An' you came and I asked if you'd sleep with me down on the deck for company and all?"

"I did."

"Well, I think you needs that now but you're an omi so you won't ask, so I'm asking you. Come and doss with me, Everett Singh."

The hammock rocked and the hooks creaked as Everett slid in beside Sen. She was as small and wiry as a street dog, but she wrapped arms and legs around him, and her small body was warm, and Everett felt the deep shuddering breaths in his chest turning into little sobs— nothing big, nothing embarrassing, nothing he would be ashamed of. A bit of omi crying. Because she was so warm and close, and *there*.

Sen stroked his head.

"'S all right, Everett Singh."

The ship moved again around him. Through the porthole came the lightning flicker of the electric arc between the wall of the shaft and Palatakahapa. And Everett Singh shook in Sen's skinny arms and knew that however far he might be flung across the trillion trillion planes of the Panoply, he would never be alone.

Her hair was so mad and soft, and it smelled of Sen.

"Sen."

"What, Everett Singh?"

"There's a kind of . . . Like . . . well, way you smell."

"Are you saying I's a minger?"

"No, no. It's just—I really like it."

"That's good, Everett Singh."

Everett snuggled up close and tight against Sen.

"Sen."

"What now, Everett Singh?"

"That rugby shirt?"

"What about it?"

"Could you take it off?"

Sen gave a gasp.

"Get you! Cheeky omi. No, Everett Singh. You're a BB. My new BB."

"Is that like a boyfriend?"

"No! You omis! You never let it lie. BB—Bona Bitch. Best friend. The boys back in Hackney, well, they're never around long enough. And they're so full of themselves. All zhooshed up. Looking at themselves in the mirror more'n you."

"Best friend."

"Best friend I sleep with."

"Do you do that much?"

"Sometimes. Me and Jiri . . ."

"Who's Jiri?"

"Get you, Everett Singh, do I hear jealous? Another BB. A polone, Everett Singh. And stop you thinking that. I know what omis are like."

"You invited me in, Sen."

"I know. Everett Singh, the rugby shirt."

"Yes."

"When I says 'no,' I don't mean 'yes cos it's you' and I don't mean, 'not right now, maybe a day or two,' I mean *no*."

32

First came the light. A ray of pure white stabbed upwards through a crack at the center of the Sun Control Chamber. It struck the top of the dome and broke into a hundred beams. The central ray widened; the crack expanded into an iris. The holographic model of the Diskworld system split into six sections and slid away from the expanding hole. Sen giggled as an apparently solid section of World-wheel passed through her.

"Airship-shape and Hackney-fashion," Captain Anastasia ordered. Everett sucked in his stomach and pushed back his shoulders the way he had been taught in drama class, when he had been forced to do those embarrassing warm-up exercises. He'd never have imagined they would come in handy in an audience with the Empress of the Sun.

The light brightened to painful intensity. Squinting through the glare, Everett could see a brilliant object rising out of the hole: the Sunburst Throne. A model of her people's power. It was very, very cool.

The Empress of the Sun rose into the center of the Sun Chamber. Light beamed from the thousand spines of the throne. Just as Everett could bear no more light, the glare dropped to tolerable levels. The floor closed. The Throne extended a ramp. The Empress descended to floor level. The Jiju folded their hands in reverence. The room rang with a chorus of swooping whistles. Crest colors ran gold to blue, forward and back again.

Everett felt Sen slip her hand into his. Her fingers were small and warm and strong. Everett had woken early—in the half-light of the great shaft through the world, natural body clocks went haywire—

to slip out of Sen's hammock and creep back to his own latty. No one had seen him, but he felt guilty. He was still trying to work that one out: Sen had invited him to be with her, but Everett felt like he was the one who had taken advantage. Bona Bitch you doss with. He wanted to be more than that.

The Empress of the Sun raised a jewelled claw and a screen on a tall stand slid up out of the floor. The Jiju had modeled their Infundibulum exactly on Everett's iPad.

"They might have, like, at least filed the serial numbers off," Mchynlyth muttered.

The Empress of the Sun touched the screen. Light shone up into her face. Her eye membranes flickered. She sang a brief phrase in Jiju.

"I think that means, how do I get this to work?" Sen whispered.

Kax hurried to her mother. Long fingers moved over the screen.

"Oh God," Everett whispered. Sen squeezed his hand.

The Empress of the Sun looked at Everett. He saw in her eyes power and darkness and hate ten million years deep. She was terrifying.

"The Empress of the Sun thanks you," she said. "You have done a great service to the Sunlord Nation. A million years from now my people will be singing poems that praise the name of Everett Singh."

She still sounded like his mother. The Empress of the Sun returned to her floating throne.

"What do you want it for?" Everett asked.

Hisses of intaken breath all around the chamber. No one talked back to the Empress of the Sun.

The Empress whipped back to Everett. Her nostrils flared. She stared him down. But Everett was not afraid now.

"The safety and security of my people. What other desire does a monarch have?"

"Can we go home now? You've got the Infundibulum, you can send us home."

"You are guests. You were free to leave at any time."

The Empress of the Sun took her place on her throne. The light brightened until the crew were forced to shade their eyes. When Everett could see again, the throne was gone, the floor intact. The fake Infundibulum stood on its pedestal.

"Well, I think the show's over," Captain Anastasia said. "Let's get *Everness* airworthy and jump the hell off this world. No disrespect, Princess."

"You talked back to my mother!" Kax hissed to Everett as Captain Anastasia led her crew from the control chamber. "My mother!"

"I wouldn't have done it if she hadn't sounded like my mother," Everett muttered.

"You should hear what I say to my mother," Sen whispered.

"Your mother heard that!" Captain Anastasia thundered.

"Bona togs." Sen threw clothing at Everett. Jacket, ship shorts, boots. "Go and put some clobber on!" She had changed into her favorite slashed T-shirt, grey leggings, and pixie boots, topped off with her Airish-style cavalry jacket.

"What for? What's going on?" Everett said with two armfuls of gear.

"We's going home, ain't we?"

"We're what?"

"That's correct." Captain Anastasia stuck her head out of her latty. "Earth 3. As soon as Mchynlyth's charged the batteries up enough for you to jump us out of here."

"You can't go there!" Everett said. "I mean, what about my dad? What about Charlotte Villiers and the whole Plenitude after us? That's insane."

Captain Anastasia stepped out of the latty into the corridor. She straightened the waistband of her riding breeches, wiggled a foot deeper into a boot.

"I'll overlook your last comment as a spontaneous outburst of teenage angst," Captain Anastasia said with a sub-zero stare. "I must repair my ship."

"The Jiju have like sixty-five million years of tech. They can repair anything."

"They may well have, but they don't have airships and they especially don't have *Everness*. I'm taking her home to people who can make her well again."

"But . . ."

"No *buts* Mr. Singh. I'm taking her home, proper home: back to Bristol. I'll lay her low and get the Portishead Massive in to zhoosh her up bona and Bristol-fashion. Now that we've got rid of that bijou tracking device, we can out dance Charlotte Villiers and her groundpounders. Dress up warm and get to your station, Mr. Singh; we jump at our earliest convenience."

And with that Captain Anastasia skipped down the rattling, dented companionway to the bridge with the lightness and excitement of a teenager going to a party.

Dozens—hundreds, thousands—of objections rattled through Everett's head as he pulled on his leggings and ship shorts. Any Heisenberg jump left a trail in the quantum reality of the multiverse: Charlotte Villiers would know at once that *Everness* had returned to Earth 3. Captain Anastasia had briefed him on the raid on *Everness*. Charlotte Villiers could send a snatch squad from Plenitude to Diskworld—a few hundred kilometers of English West Country wouldn't faze her. And repairing the damage the crash and the Genequeen shipnapping had done didn't look like the sort of thing you could pay for with a charity car wash or a garage sale or even a quick crowdfund.

Everett's jaw and fists tightened at the thought of Charlotte Villiers—so brave, beating up a nearly fourteen-year-old kid; so noble, leaving her crew to be cut to pieces by the Genequeens. Captain Anastasia would never have abandoned her crew. He had seen the captain in kneepads with a brush, scrubbing away, scrubbing away, trying to get the blood out of every corner and crevice of her ship. And Sen—Everett was glad he had not seen her broken and bloody: the Jiju had put her back together again, sent their nanomachines into her lungs and through her veins, into every cell in her body, but what had those healing machines left behind? The changes, the differences, her ability to make the Genequeen staff obey her will—were they forever? Yes, he wanted more than anything to be off this artificial world, away from its terrible, brutal wars and rivalries, its history soaked in blood for sixty million years. Earth 3 was home to him now; but he couldn't feel the joy of finally going home.

The Jiju had the Infundibulum.

Everett was tightening the straps on his boots when a sudden commotion made him look up.

Mchynlyth's voice. Angry: he seemed to wake up angry. And another: a woman's voice. Angry: more than angry. His mother's voice. *Impossible.* Kax.

Everett rattled down the stairs to the cargo hold. Sen was a footfall behind him. She carried the Genequeen staff like a spear. Mchynlyth had a restraining hand on Kax's chest. Kax's halo was angry, splintering into sharp red blades then reforming again.

"Everett Singh!" Kax called. "Get this man out of my face. Get all your people! Now! My mother. The Empress of the Sun. I know what she's going to do with the Infundibulum!"

"For fifty million years we have battled each other. War after war; civilizations rising, fighting, collapsing. No side has ever been able to gain the ultimate victory."

The crew formed a circle around Kax. Mchynlyth squatted; Captain Anastasia stood, arms folded; Sharkey behind her, looked on with suspicion. Everett perched on the bottom step of the main companionway, knees pulled up to his chest; Sen sat on a section of engine casing. The Jiju staff lay across her lap. Kax stood in the center of the circle. She looked long at each human in turn.

"Until now. My mother has a plan that will bring about the final victory of the Sunlords. We win. Everyone, everything else loses."

"The Infundibulum," Captain Anastasia said.

"Yes."

"How?" Everett asked.

"We are the Sunlords. We make the sun dance to our command. We give the sun and we can take it away. And we can give too much sun."

"What do you mean?" Sharkey asked.

"A solar flare," Everett said. "Like the jets you use to move the sun up and down—you could send them in a different direction. Like outward. Across Diskworld—sorry, the Worldwheel."

"We can do much more than that. We can make the sun nova," Kax said.

"What's that?" Sen asked.

"It's like a star exploding," Everett said. "They flare off their outer layers. It's usually neutron stars . . ."

Sen cut him off with a small cry of horror. "But that would . . ."

"Incinerate every living thing on the Worldwheel. Yes," Kax said. "Trillions of deaths. It would be a sterile, uninhabitable waste for tens of thousands of days."

Everett did the maths in his head. "That's hundreds of years."

"But you'd die with them . . ." Sen said.

"But you wouldn't be here," Everett said. "You'd be somewhere else. That was the bit that was missing from the Empress's plan: you'd nowhere to go, no place to hide."

"Yes," Kax said. "And now the Empress, my mother, has what she needs to gain the final victory."

"The Plenitude," Everett said. "You'd go there. You'd invade, take over, wait it out for a few centuries or whatever, then jump back when the sun had died down and the whole Worldwheel would be yours."

"That is the plan."

"But in like, a few centuries, we could learn enough to fight back against you. Maybe even beat you," Everett said. "You couldn't risk that."

"No," Kax said simply and the meaning was clear to all. The Sunlords would exterminate every human from the Ten Worlds. And Everett had given them the weapon to do it.

No one spoke. There are no words when you have just heard the death sentence on humanity. Everett had given the Sunlords the axe to carry it out. It was too big, too hideous to believe. Kax, telling him the end of the world was here, in Everett's mother's voice. It couldn't be real. But Everett had never believed in belief. The universe didn't care what people believed.

Finally Captain Anastasia spoke. "Why are you telling us this? What do you think we can do?"

"You have the original Infundibulum," Kax said. "That's all I know."

"The sun gun," Mchynlyth said, uncurling from his crouch like a street cat. "I told ye, I told ye to use it on them Gene-genies! Punch a hole clean through that thing; open up a gate in that there Sun Chamber and let them see what a wee taste of real sun power's like. Burn the mother out of the sky!"

"We haven't got the power," Captain Anastasia said quickly. "And we're too close. We'd go up with it."

"Aye. And maybe that's the price," Mchynlyth said. "All of them, for the five of us."

But Kax was roused. Her crest rippled, changing from green to purple.

"Everett, what is this?"

Everett did not answer.

"Everett, sun gun?"

Kax stepped close to Everett. She cocked her head to one side.

"Everett, is this some kind of weapon?"

Everett felt sweat roll along the line of his collarbone, then down his ribs. He shot a glance at Captain Anastasia. She shook her head. Kax turned in a circle, facing each crew member in turn.

"Are you keeping something from me? Is this a threat to my mother and my sisters?" Kax's halo shimmered silvery black. The halobots flashed into hooked blades.

"No!" Sen yelled. She held the Genequeen battlestaff sideways, two handed, and thrust it forwards. The amber sphere sprouted spikes that flew from the head of the staff to hover in front of Kax.

Kax hissed, dangerous and totally alien.

"Sen," Captain Anastasia said. "Get rid of that thing."

"I didn't do it," Sen said. "It did it itself."

"Sen . . ."

"It does what I feel, not what I think!"

Everness jolted as if it had fallen into a hole in the air. Everyone went reeling across the cargo deck. Everett hit a container cleat hard. A huge thunderclap shook the ship. Blue lightning crackled along the struts and spars.

"Nobody touch anything!" Mchynlyth shouted. The electrical display vanished. Mchynlyth sprinted to his engineering cubby.

"We've lost the bottom half of my power connector!"

Sharkey was at a porthole, peering through cupped hands.

"We've lost more than that." His voice was steel grim. "The palace. It's gone."

33

Starlings swirled in an ever-shifting cloud over Green Park. Low winter sun glinted from the windows of the vehicles on Piccadilly. Charlotte Villiers lifted her short veil and enjoyed the blessing of the sun on her face. People stared at her old-fashioned costume. Take a good look, slovens. See what it is to dress with pride and discipline.

She turned to the peeling black door in the wall of dull red tile. She slipped off a glove and touched her hand to the door. Locks clicked. The door opened inward without a sound. Charlotte Villiers stepped through. The door closed and sealed behind her. It would open to only a dozen hands in all the Ten Worlds of the Plenitude.

A gust of musty, stale air threatened her hat. A train boomed far below, its noise amplified by the tunnels and shafts. Thousands of commuters rattled between Green Park and Hyde Park Corner every hour without realizing that they passed through an entire aban- doned station, walled up, shut away, forgotten. Down Street Station, closed 1932. Reopened eight decades later to house Earth 10's second Heisenberg Gate.

The elevator took forever to come. It was a cramped, rickety con- struction hoist—work was ongoing on old Down Street. The British government had set up base here, during the Second Global War of this world's twentieth century. Charlotte Villiers rode down the old elevator shaft. What was it these Earth 10ers had with tunnels and trains? But it was much more handy than that dank hole under the English Channel. And so convenient for Fortnum and Mason.

The elevator chimed. The safety barrier unlocked. The gate control was housed in a lower level of the lift shaft. Charlotte Vil- liers had requisitioned the Gate Command team that had overseen the disastrous mission to the Jiju Worldwheel. Keep one secret, keep a thousand secrets. The Jump Controller—Angharad Price: Charlotte Villiers made sure to remember her name—wore a sky-blue Earth 3 Gate Command uniform and forage cap. Her hair was tied back, her face and nails immaculate. Charlotte Villiers thought the look very smart and professional.

"We're just about to send Ebben Heer Daude back to Earth 7," Angharad Price said. "Will you be joining him?"

"No, I want to go back to my own London for a while," Charlotte Villiers said. "This one dispirits me. It's so scruffy and mean spirited."

"I'll set up the coordinates," Gate Controller Price said.

"You have been invaluable to me, my Heers," Charlotte Villiers said. The twin agents gave a bow. "Enjoy your time together."

"We have missed each other," began Ebben Heer. "Terribly, terribly," Heer Daude said. Charlotte Villiers had brought Heer Daude from Earth 4 as quickly as she could, but their voices, their hands, their faces, were drawn and thin and pale. Too much time apart. Worlds apart. *Can the loneliness kill you?* Charlotte Villiers thought, and for the first time wondered, w*hat happens if one of you dies before the other?*

The control room filled with light. The Heisenberg Gate occupied the entire width of an old access tunnel that led from the lift shaft to the former platforms.

"You are clear to jump, Ebben Heer Daude," Gate Controller Price said. The light faded. The Heisenberg Gate opened onto a jump room in the Praesidium Headquarters. The twins walked towards the gate— every footstep lighter, firmer, more eager. The gate opened, the gate closed.

"Locking on to Earth 3 now," Angharad Price said. The light from the screens made her face severe and otherworldly. *You are otherworldly*, Charlotte Villiers thought. *Literally. Have you see anything of this Earth beyond the black door in the red wall? The irony is, it's a faster commute home for you than any of those poor fools on the Piccadilly line. Faster, but not shorter.*

Again the old ghost station shook to the pressure wave of a passing train.

"In three, two, one . . ." Angharad Price pushed forward the lever. The Heisenberg Gate lit up.

And flickered.

And went out.

And lit again.

And flickered. Dancing light cast insane shadows across the control room.

"What's wrong?" Charlotte Villiers asked. Fear chilled her. She had never seen a gate do this before.

Angharad Price's eyes darted from screen to screen. She punched glowing buttons.

"Something is interfering with the quantum resonance field," she said. "This isn't possible. It's massive."

The Heisenberg Gate went dark. Screens blinked crazy with information.

"I'm picking up a massive quantum displacement," Angharad Price said. "Something's coming in. It's off the scale." She looked at Charlotte Villiers. Her eyes were wide. "It's right on top of us!"

Tens of meters of London lay between Charlotte Villiers and Piccadilly, but she looked up, as if she could see through them to whatever was unfolding over London.

"This isn't possible," Angharad Price said again. "Multiple Heisenberg events. Ten. Fifty . . ." Screen after screen flashed red warnings. "Thousands. *Thousands*. It's not just here. It's every single world in the Plenitude. Twenty thousand . . . One million . . . Ms. Villiers, two and a half *billion* jump gates just opened."

34

"There're *other* aliens?"

Everett M and Ryun sat on the park bench. Clissold Park was a good place to talk: open, public, easy to see friends who might ask, *what you talkin' about*? Serious-faced girls with scraped-back hair jogged along the gravel paths. Middle-aged men in beanie hats flung tennis balls from ball throwers for their dogs to catch. Single fathers wheeled baby buggies; kids swerved and dodged on BMX bikes.

"They're super-evolved dinosaurs from a plane where they didn't get wiped out by an asteroid," Everett M said.

Ryun pulled the collar of his Puffa jacket up around his face. It was a cold day but bright, and Stoke Newington was making the most of the sunlight in Clissold Park. The taxi had left the boys outside Bourne Green School, but they had kept walking. Mrs. Abrahams's office was on the street side of the campus. Everett M had used the tiniest flicker of enhanced Thryn sight to check if she had seen them walking past. She had. Everett M did not doubt that punishment would come. He could hunt down and exterminate nests of Nahn nano-vermin, but he was helpless in the face of Saturday detention.

"My life used to be simple," Ryun said. "Before, when you were, you know, him. The other one. Do you think we got all the Nahn?"

"I thought I had last time," Everett M said, stretching his legs out before him and sinking his chin to his chest.

Ryun sat up. His eyes were wide. He pulled a face.

"I don't feel good. I'm going to hurl."

He leaped up and went into the rhododendron clump behind the bench. Everett M tried not to listen to the retching. Ryun returned, wiping his mouth with a tissue.

"Oh, geez, that was like . . . green. I think that sushi was off."

"I don't think it was the sushi that was off," Everett M said. "I think it was the people. I used to love sushi."

"She didn't actually threaten anyone. She didn't actually say, like, your mum or dad, they're *dead*."

"She doesn't need to. All she needs is for us to know she's absolutely, completely serious. If she says a thing, nothing will stop her from doing it. She wants us to know there's nothing we can do."

Ryun's face twitched.

"It works."

"She did it to me, Ry. She smashed me to bits and sent those bits to the Moon and put them back together the way she wanted, and when it suited her she told me exactly what she had done."

Ryun huddled deeper in his quilted coat.

"We're in shit," he said quietly.

"Neck deep," Everett M said. "Do you know why I hate her most? Because she's laughing at us, because she knows we can't touch her. We do anything, and our families get hurt. All these things I can do, but in the end there's nothing I can do. People get hurt because of me."

"There is something you can do," Ryun said. "The real—the other—Everett's mum and his sister. They need someone to look after them. Me, I walked into this because I'm too nosey, but they don't know anything. They're like, *innocent*."

Everett M pulled out his phone and got up from the bench.

"Where you going?" Ryun asked. Everett M was walking away, faster with every step.

"There's someone else I need to look after," Everett M called back.

35

Her saw her in the Mermaid Café with her friends, legs curled up on the old cracked-leather sofa, with her Vietnamese coffee on the table, frowning at something one of her girlfriends had said. Although she was wearing a campy animal hat, she made it look good. Impossibly cute, but hot at the same time. Why did she have to look so cute?

And I'm going to walk in and nothing will ever be the same, Everett M thought. Her friends made it more difficult but at the same time better. He would have witnesses.

Aidan the dreadlocked barista nodded as Everett M entered. The bell on the door tinged. Everett M didn't sit down.

"You're standing," Noomi said when the girl chat finished. "Oh. Ev. No. School clothes. Points off."

He was shaking. He couldn't speak. His heart felt as if it were made of C46 and would explode at the slightest tap. Nothing had ever been this hard or this scary. Nanotech zombie Victorian skeletons were easy.

"Noomi, can I talk to you?"

She slapped the cushion beside her.

"Not . . . here."

Her eyes went very wide. She was fantastic and gorgeous and innocent. He was all the evil in all the universes. Everett gestured for her to come outside. They stood in the glass porch. That was good. Her GFs would see everything.

"You're weird even for you, Ev."

"Noomi, I don't want to go out with you anymore."

"What? Everett? Are you on medication?"

No, this was wrong: he shouldn't let her answer. If she answered, if she argued, he would weaken. Be quick and cruel and a total enemy. Kill the relationship now; kill it dead.

"No, I'm not. Do I have to be? You just have to decide everything. Like I can't do anything for myself. Like I have to be on medication. Like I walk in, and when you finally decide to talk to me, it's *Oh Everett, bad clothes, now be a good boy and sit beside me and talk to me?*

"Can I point out that you wanted to talk to me?"

"No, you can't," Everett said. "For once, you say nothing. That's the problem with you. You're always saying something, you've always got some opinion, and it's like so important that everyone knows it. Like no one else's opinion matters but yours always does. And can I point out: points? No points? I don't need you scoring me."

"Everett . . ."

"Shut up!" Everett M shouted. Noomi flinched. Inside the café, Aidan glanced up. Everett knew all the GFs had heard. "It's always about you you you, and do you know? I didn't see this for so long, but even that website, that was all about you. Who said you could take pictures of me? Who said you could talk about me? Like you just wanted me like a . . . like a doll you could dress up or something. Drag around and show off, like a bangle."

Everett M's brain burned; his heart beat strong and hard. This wasn't hard at all. This was so easy.

"Everett, what is this?"

"And another thing: you're fake. Everything about you is fake. Noomi: what kind of name is that? Ooky-cookie girly name. Your real name's Naomi. Naomi Wong. Fake name, fake clothes, fake fake attitude. Nothing about you is real." He spat the words out. There were more behind them: a torrent of words and abuse and spite. Noomi's friends were all staring.

"Everett. This is vile."

"You know? I don't care. It's you's vile, with all your games and tricks and things I'm supposed to know, and you get upset if I get them wrong but you'll never ever tell me how to get them right. You're bad through, bad and fake and sick."

Her hands covered her mouth. Her eyes were wide in horror.

"And because you always always *always* have to have the last word, I'm going now," Everett M said. "I'm gone. Shut up. Go away. Nothing you can say."

And he turned and he walked.

"Everett!" Noomi screamed after him. He kept walking. "Everett!"

Safe. She would never come near him again. And so she would be safe from him, safe from Charlotte Villiers, safe from the Order that could reach across worlds to hurt and harm and kill. He had done right but he was dying inside; a blackness devouring him like the Nahn, eating him from the inside out. He had not done right. He had done the worst thing he had ever done. Bringing the Nahn back from Earth 1; he had no choice. He would have died. And he had made that wrong right. He had tracked down and exterminated the Nahn infestation. But this had gone too far. He had said too much. The vile things had spewed out of him. And what was more unforgivable was that they were true. She was all of those things he had accused her of. She was kooky and self-centered and astonishingly selfish and really into how things looked, and she loved to play games with people, and that pissed him off, and at the same time they were the things he really liked about her. They annoyed him, but he adored them. The things that made him smile when he thought about them. The things that turned his heart over. The things he wanted more than anything else. He almost stopped to turn back, but he knew he shouldn't. He had made sure that she would never forgive him. He had made himself a monster. But she would be safe. Charlotte Villiers would never come near her.

Everett M walked on, his eyes like black holes, his heart filled with thunder. *That's another one I owe you, Charlotte Villiers.* That was one name for the darkness. He had another: anger. The darkness filled up his sight. He couldn't see . . .

The darkness was *real*.

Everyone on Green Lanes had stopped in their tracks. Every car, every truck, every bike and bus was stationary. It was afternoon but dark as midnight. Everett M looked up.

36

Silence is not an absence, a state of no sound. Silence is solid. Silence is real. Silence can be heard. Charlotte Villiers heard it the moment the elevator motor switched off and she opened the cage. London, totally silent. It was the most terrifying thing she had ever heard.

The locks opened to her touch. Charlotte Villiers stepped out into the silence. Piccadilly was at a standstill. Not a bus, not a van, not a taxi or car moved. Not a motorbike or bike courier or cyclist. Not an office worker or a shopper or a Chinese tourist or a traffic warden. Every human on Piccadilly, on foot or in car or bus, was looking up.

Silence and darkness.

The object hovered three thousand feet over London. It blocked out the sun. Its shadow was dark as night. Camera flashes flickered in the crowd. A thousand hands held up a thousand phones and iPads, taking photographs, shooting video.

An underground train rumbled far below. On any other day, it would not have been heard. It broke the silence. In an instant, London found its voice again. Phones ringing, people making calls: *hello hello?* It's *massive*; car radios blaring, horns blaring, people blaring; people talking, people shouting, people all asking the same question. *What is it?*

"It's a Jiju city ship!" Charlotte Villiers called from the side of the footpath to anyone who would listen. "It's not just London, they're everywhere!" The people standing by their cars gaped. The radio reports were confirming what the mad shouting woman was saying. "It is the end of your world! The Jiju are here."

37

The view from the bridge destroyed any doubt or hope. Where Palatakahapa, the palace of the Empress of the Sun had floated, glittering with ten thousand windows, was now void. Nothing. Dead air. Everett could see across twenty kilometers to the pinprick lights at the far side of the shaft through the world. The slender bridges were snapped and dangling like cut threads. The four streamers of lightning below arced without interruption across the great pit.

"Where did it go?" Sen asked.

Kax stood at the great window, hands against the cracked glass.

"Where do you think?" she said in a voice like winter. Everett shivered. He hated Kax using his mum's voice. The tone of voice she had used was exactly the same one his mum had used to tell Everett that his dad was gone, that he wouldn't be back, that they were splitting up. The End of Everything voice. "My mother has initiated the Final Victory. It's not just Palatakahapa. It's every single Sunlord city. The invasion has begun. And she has left me . . ."

The realization hit Everett like a body blow.

"The sun!"

"Yes," Kax said. She turned from the great window. "The order to fire the nova sequence would have gone out at the same time that the cities jumped off the Worldwheel."

"Mr. Singh, get us out of here!" Captain Anastasia snapped. "Now!"

"He cannae," Mchynlyth said in a quiet voice of bone-deep shock. "He disnae have the power."

Everett tapped up the Infundibulum. The JUMP button was greyed out.

"Heisenberg jump is not available," he said.

"Mr. Singh, we need answers," Captain Anastasia said. Her voice was supernaturally calm.

"It takes eight minutes twenty-six seconds for the nova message to get from here to the sun," Everett said. "It's a speed-of-light thing. And it'll also take eight minutes twenty-six seconds for the blast to reach us."

"About two minutes since Palatakahapa disappeared," Captain Anastasia said. "Fourteen minutes before the sun blows up. That's enough. Mr. Mchynlyth, have we power for the impellers?"

"Fart in a hurricane territory," Mchynlyth said.

"A fart in a hurricane will suffice. Sen, fire up the impellers. Gentlemen, to engineering. Kax, I need every hand. If you please, ma'am. Break out the lightning array. I'm taking her down." Captain Anastasia pointed at the blue electric arc. "Into *that*."

"You can't!" Sen cried.

"Take her in, Miss Sixsmyth," Captain Anastasia said in her sternest tone of command. "Gentlemen, reptiles, you're still here."

"The lightning array," Everett said, chasing Mchynlyth up steps, walkways, ladders, up between the gas cells into the heights of the airship. "Isn't that where you fly into a thunderstorm to recharge the batteries?"

"It is," Mchynlyth said. They were on a crawl way pressed up tight against the top of the ship, so low even Everett had to crouch.

"Like, the thing where if it goes wrong, it can burn up your airship?" Mchynlyth's face was purest disbelief.

"Laddie, the sun—the *sun*—is about to explode and blow our dishes to the Dear. A wee sense of proportion here." And he was gone, scuttling like a crab down the cramped passage. Everett's thighs complained with cramp as he scurried after the chief engineer. Mchynlyth stopped under two large brass wheels set into the ceiling.

"Haul for all your might, lad!" Mchynlyth grabbed a wheel. Biceps, neck sinews, collar bones bulged as he wrenched the wheel round.

Everett's watch beeped.

"Six minutes to Sunburst." He had thought of the name on the race up the stairs from the bridge to the top of the ship. The end of the world and he still couldn't resist making up a name for it.

Mchynlyth banged his fist against the skin.

"You know? I really, *really* do not need the final friggin' countdown."

"Sorry."

"Bugger sorry. *Heave.*"

Everett grabbed the wheel and threw his weight onto it. It wouldn't move. He took a deep breath and tried again. Every muscle screamed. It was agony: crouching cramped, arms up.

"Gaaahhhh!" Everett cried. With a squeal the wheel shifted.

"Turn! Turn!" Mchynlyth yelled.

Everett hauled on the brass wheel. His watch beeped again. Four minutes to Sunburst.

Mchynlyth held up a hand.

"We're moving," he said. "We're moving! Haul for Jesus and Krishna and the Dear!"

Sen felt it in her fingers, she felt it in her toes: the familiar vibration she had not known for so long now: the throb of the impellers. The constant welcome tremble that said you were on an airship, a living, breathing machine with a life and a great heart, like a lion. The vibration was weak, but the ship's heart was beating again. Sen lifted her hands from the engine-start levers. She felt as if she had worked magic: brought the ship back to life with a healing touch in the same way the Genequeens had healed her. But she could not put those hands on the steering yoke. The lighting arc below her blinded her, paralyzed her with fear.

"Take us down, Miss Sixsmyth," Captain Anastasia said. She stood by the great window, hands behind her back, feet apart, looking out: her customary stance of command. That stance said *I am master and commander of an airship again.* Sen reached for the yoke then recoiled. She saw the wreck of the *Fairchild,* as she had seen it so many times in so many falling, screaming nightmares. She saw her parents' ship spin end for end through the stupendous storm off the Azores, the lighting array unfurled like sails, one above, one below. She saw the lightning strike. She saw the killing arc. She saw the ship catch and burn.

She saw it happen again. She saw everything end in fire. She couldn't do that to the ship. But if she didn't . . .

"Miss Sixsmyth! We have twelve minutes before the nova hits us!"

Either way, it ended in fire. Sen whimpered. Everett had talked about choices between evils. All the evils in all the worlds were here, underneath her fingers. But the two crossing arcs of blazing blue light filled her eyes and her mind.

"Sen! Don't make me take the controls from you!"

She could not touch the steering yoke. The ship would scream at her betrayal if she touched it.

"Sen! Listen to me! *The Fairchild.* I was the pilot. Never forget that. I was the pilot. I took her into the storm. And I made a mistake. Sen, I flew that ship to its death. It was too much for me. And I can't do this. You can do it. Only you can do it. You're a better pilot than I ever was. Only you can save *Everness!*"

"No!" Sen shouted as she seized the control yoke. Slowly; very slowly, so slowly it hardly seemed like movement at all, *Everness* crept forward on the last whispers of energy in her batteries.

He was failing. He was in pain. It hurt too much. Every muscle was on fire, dipped in liquid lightning. Pull. Pull. Pull. Did this wheel never come to an end?

"Come on Mr. Singh!" Mchynlyth yelled.

With the last of his strength Everett hauled the brass wheel round. There was a moment of resistance when he felt his muscles might fail, then the wheel clicked into place. Mchynlyth locked his wheel.

"She's up. Now, let's scarper. You don't want to be up here when we hit the lightning."

"Have you ever done this before?" Everett asked.

"No. But I have a very strong imagination. It's a Mchynlyth family trait. Anytime you like, Mr. Singh. Nae rush."

Everett covered the last meters of crawl way on hands and knees, body contorted with pain. He hauled himself upright. The stairs went down and down forever between the ballooning gas cells.

"Oh God."

"Ach, come on, you're young, you're fit," Mchynlyth said. He pushed past Everett and took the steps at a canter. Everett's watch pinged. Another two minutes closer to Sunburst.

"Power at fifteen percent, Ma."

"Hold us steady."

Sen held *Everness* straight and true for the place where the two arcs crossed. The great window was a wall of searing electricity. Captain Anastasia stood silhouetted against crazy lightning, black against blue.

Everness shook. Sen trimmed the attitude controls. Her air mojo was back, the inborn Airish gift for feeling the winds, thinking in three dimensions, reading the atmosphere. She reached inside her jacket and felt out the contours of the Everness tarot. She slipped out the top card and peeked at it.

Empress of the Sun.

Sen flicked the card across the bridge. Another draw: a solitary tree within a circular wall at the top of a hill. *Lone Tree Hill.* Does the wall keep the tree safe from the world or the world safe from the tree? People, events, circumstances can flip in an instant and still be the same.

Was the tarot speaking to her again or were the visions and skills the Jiju had put in her head muddying her ability to read the deck? Or was the Everness tarot saying that sometimes all an oracle will tell you is the absolutely obvious. Save the ship, Sen Sixsmyth.

"Lightning array is operational." Mchynlyth's voice, suddenly at her side.

Everett slipped behind his station next to Sen. He nodded, gave her the briefest, sweetest, most pain-filled smile. Then he turned all his attention to his comptators.

"'The Lord thy God in the midst of thee is mighty; he will save.'" So Sharkey was here, too.

Everness shook again, more powerfully. Electricity sparked from every exposed metal surface. In the corner of her eye Sen glimpsed Kax. The Jiju princess's halo was pulled in tight to her head. It shone almost as blue and bright as the lightning.

"Take us into the heart of the storm," Captain Anastasia ordered.

"Aye, ma'am." She pushed the steering yoke forward. Creaking, groaning, whining, shuddering from mismatched impellers, *Everness* answered the helm. The great window was a wall of lightning. Sen could feel every heartbeat; every muscle in her body ordered her to twist the steering yoke, take the ship up and away. She held true. She held firm. She held her course.

Everness jolted. Sen gave a small, animal cry but kept her grip on the yoke. The ship was shaking now, like a dying, thrashing thing. They were in the heart of the plasma stream.

"Charge her up, Mr. Mchynlyth," Captain Anastasia ordered. Mchynlyth threw a brass lever and the bridge came alive with lightning. Sparks cracked from every bolt and rivet. St. Elmo's Fire danced along every trim and fitting. The bridge was filled with a cacophony of cracklings and fizzings and hissings.

"'And the temple of God was opened in heaven, and there were lightnings, and voices, and thunderings,'" Sharkey said.

"Try not to touch anything," Captain Anastasia shouted.

"Aye right," Mchynlyth muttered.

"Captain." Everett's voice was small and quiet and almost lost in the blazing thunder inside the bridge, but his tone turned every head to him. "The sun just exploded."

"How long have we got?" Captain Anastasia said.

"Eight minutes twenty-six seconds," Everett said.

"What's the state of our batteries?" Captain Anastasia asked.

"Twenty percent," Mchynlyth said.

"Sen, hold position."

Everness lurched and dropped. Sen yelped as her feet left the ground. The ship yawed. She fought to regain her grip on the steering yoke.

Sharkey was scanning those monitors that still worked.

"We're arcing from the lightning array to the hull. Burn through in section upper 6."

"Hold her steady, Sen."

"Thirty-three percent," Mchynlyth said.

"Mr. Singh, make whatever preparations you need. I want Heisenberg jump the instant we have the power."

"Aye, ma'am. Sunburst plus two minutes."

Captain Anastasia bit back an oath.

Lightning danced around Everett, floor to ceiling, as he powered up his equipment, computer by computer. The Panopticon. The Infundibulum. The jumpgun. Slow and steady. One careless move in this electrically charged environment could cause an arc. An electric arc could burn out the processors in his computers. Dead computers was dead Everett, dead everyone. Slow and steady and try not to think of the wall of light and heat racing at the speed of light across the innermost edges of Diskworld. Everett could imagine that all too well. He had touched the very stuff of the sun, turned it to a weapon in his hand, and its power awed him. He had loosed the tiniest piece of it on Imperial University in Earth 1. This was the entire sun blasting off its outer layers. The light and heat would be enough to kill—there would be no warning, not even a flash of light racing across the world. The wall of sun stuff would blast everything to free-floating atoms. Trees, living creatures, seas rivers lakes, cities, the rocks themselves. Could even the fantastically strong substance of the Diskworld resist the energies of Sunburst? The Sunlords believed so: after the lava cooled and the water vapor rained out, they would return and reseed and restock their world.

Everything dying, everything twisting and burning in the killing light.

"Sunburst plus four," Everett said. The Panopticon was live. Everett blinked as the screen filled with Heisenberg jump points. Thousands of them. Millions of them. More than the stars in the sky. On every one of the Known Worlds of the Plenitude. An invasion. His world; his home: he had to know. Everett tapped up the parameters for Earth 10. They were all over it. Every single human city had a Sunlord city-ship hovering over it. And Palatakahapa, the center of it all, stood over London. His London.

The Infundibulum was active now. Everett looked from Infundibulum to Panopticon, Panopticon to Infundibulum.

"Sixty-two percent," Mchynlyth intoned.

"Burn throughs in lower and upper hull quadrants," Sharkey said.

"Hold her steady, Sen."

Everett glanced at Sen. Her face was tight, her muscles rigid as cables as she fought to hold the bucking, quaking airship in the plasma stream. Sweat ran into her eyes; she flicked it away.

"Ma'am, I have an idea!" Everett said.

"Make it a good one, Mr. Singh," Captain Anastasia replied.

And the Jump Controller went from grey to green. The controls were live. Everett swept code from the Panopticon into the controller. The JUMP button lit up.

"Heisenberg Jump in five . . ."

"Four minutes to spare, Everett," said Captain Anastasia. "You're losing your touch."

"Three . . ."

The wall of killing light racing towards him across the endless plains of the Worldwheel, flashing everything to vapor. Billions of deaths.

"Two . . . One . . ."

Everett hit the JUMP button. Light from beyond the universes flooded the bridge.

And *gone*.

38

N o *voom*.

Everness departed, *Everness* arrived.

Palatakahapa hung over London. Cold, clear January light showed it in all its might and monstrousness. Pinnacles and buttresses like a thousand mashed-up cathedrals; spines and spires like some creature from the bottom of the darkest sea; ribs and spars and vents like the oily body of some obscenely elegant movie alien. An iron crown ten miles across: from Acton to Canary Wharf, from Hampstead to Streatham, London could be in no doubt who its new overlords were. Three million people cowered in its shadow.

"Coms are crazy," Sharkey said. "Two hundred channels of screaming."

"Belay coms, Mr. Sharkey," Captain Anastasia ordered.

The entire crew was on the bridge as fighter aircraft flashed over the airship, close enough to set *Everness* trembling with their jet exhaust.

"Are those *air-o-plans*?" Sen said.

"Mr. Singh, where have you brought us?" Captain Anastasia said.

"My world," Everett said. "My home. I've got a plan—but it only works if I can get to Palatakahapa. And that's here. Over my London."

They were all drawn from their posts to the great window. The sight was awesome. *That's a word we use too much*, Everett thought. A new phone or a movie trailer or hi-tops and we say *awesome*. That's just *stuff*. The flying palace of parallel-universe smart-o-saurs hovering over London. Now that's awesome. *I look, and I feel awe.*

Everett had jumped *Everness* in over White Hart Lane football stadium. He had done the math quickly but carefully: far enough away from Palatakahapa to avoid the danger of jumping one material object inside another; close enough to be able to see pieces of snapped bridge and sheared architecture that continued to crumble and fall to the streets of Stoke Newington three thousand feet below. *Everness* hung half a kilometer from the northeast sector of the Palace. It dominated the great window. Abney Park, Stoke Newington, Clissold Park, the Emirates Stadium, Bourne Green School, all lay under the shadow of the Empress of the Sun.

"My mum is down there," Everett whispered. "My sister, my Bebe, and my cousins. All my friends . . ."

"My mum is in there," Kax said. She blinked at Everett. Her halo was obsidian dark. "I felt them all, Everett. I heard them, in here." She touched the corner of her jaw where the Jiju small ears sat. "Everything that walked or swam or flew or burrowed. One short cry, and gone. Turned to ash, the ash turned to dust, the dust to atoms. Every story and song and building and poem and game and toy and painting, every piece of knowledge and wisdom: gone in the blink of an eye membrane. Sixty-five million years of Jiju civilization. We are the last of the Jiju!"

As Kax spoke the skin of her face darkened into a deep indigo stripe that ran from the edge of her crest to her chin and around each eye.

"Kax, your face . . ." Everett said.

"It's what you call *crying*."

Captain Anastasia beckoned Everett away from the great window, summoned her crew with the crook of a finger.

"Everett," she whispered. "What is your plan?"

"Do you remember the battle of Abney Park?" Everett said. "Do you remember how we got away from it, Sen?"

"You called up a gate on your telephone-comptator thing.

You dialed it up behind a tombstone and we jumped through," Sen said.

Everett held up his iPhone.

"The Jiju copied the Infundibulum. Exactly. In every detail. Which means . . ."

"You can control their Infundibulum," Mchynlyth said. "But there's a muckle of them Jiju city-ships out there. And that's just your world here, laddie. Buggerello for our world."

"They're all routed through the one command point," Everett said. "That's how they all jumped at the same time. Because they got the command from the Empress."

"You'd just need to send the command to the one . . ." Sharkey said.

"And they'd all go," Everett said. He waggled his phone. "And I have a signal!"

"Go where?" Captain Anastasia said. Her voice was flat and hard. "Where would you send them?"

Everett swallowed.

"Back," he said.

Everett saw Kax's face change color and her crest lift the split second before the halo fired an arrow at him. A flash, a loud clang, and the arrow was embedded in the ceiling. Sen clenched her fist. A boomerang flew back to her hand. A wave of the hand and the boomerang came apart into its component bots and fused with the buzzing swarm of bots at the head of her Genequeen battlestaff. She rounded on Kax.

"You will not send my people to the fire," Kax said. "My mother, my sisters. You will not send them back to the fire."

"You don't touch Everett!" Sen shouted. Kax hissed and dropped into combat crouch. Sen grabbed the battlestaff double handed and lifted it above her head. "I can work your toy. Good as you. And there's only one princess on this ship, and guess what? Ain't you."

"I will cut you and gut you from top to bottom, ape," Kax shrieked.

"Mr. Sharkey, restore order!" Captain Anastasia shouted.

The shotgun blast was deafening in the confined space of the bridge. Woodchips and shotgun pellets snowed down on Everett. The air reeked of spent cartridge. He had fired one gun into the ceiling. The other he trained on Kax.

"There will be no cutting no gutting and absolutely no princesses on my ship," Captain Anastasia thundered. "There has been enough violence. Enough killing. Enough blood. I am sick of it. Mr. Singh: I will not be party to genocide. You would send billions back into the exploding sun. You would exterminate the entire Jiju race— all except one. She's there, in front of you. The last Jiju. Everett, you would be no different from the Empress of the Sun. No different at all. There has to be some solution that doesn't kill billions. Come on, Everett. Think fast. Think better."

Sen held the battlestaff level. Kax's halo rippled. Sharkey's gun was steady and sure.

Think, Everett. Think.

Everett stared at the weapons he held. The Panopticon. The Infundibulum. His phone. The jumpgun.

Not a thing in his head. Just staring, not seeing.

Ten worlds. Billions of lives. Human and Jiju.

No one moved. Time chilled and froze over.

Think, Everett. Think!

And then he saw it. It was right in front of him. It always had been.

"I can do it," he said. "It still just takes one phone call."

"My people," Kax said.

"I won't send them back. I promise you."

"What will you do?"

"I'll send them everywhere. The jumpgun. That was the clue. It sends objects to random parallel universes. I can do that. I can send a command through for the Empress's Infundibulum to send every single one of the Jiju city-ships into a random parallel universe."

"Do it, Mr. Singh," Captain Anastasia said.

Kax growled deep in her throat.

"You move, you so much as twitch, and my wrath shall wax hot against thee," Sharkey said.

"They'll live," Everett said.

"Can you promise that?" Kax asked.

"No one can promise that," Captain Anastasia said.

"I dinnae ken if this is important," Mchynlyth said, "but the lights are going out."

"What?" Everett raced to the great window. The shadow of the Sunlord Mothership was so deep and profound that London's street-lights had switched themselves on. Now, before Everett's eyes, the city was blacking out, street by street, district by district. Islington to Canonbury, all along the Balls Pond Road. Shacklewell to Albion Road. Stoke Newington to High Street.

"My mother is drawing on your power grid to keep Palatakahapa aloft," Kax said.

"No!" Everett shouted. "No no no no!"

The iPhone in his hand flashed signal bars. They dwindled to one bar then went out.

"No!" Everett stared at the dead phone.

"Your tone concerns me, Mr. Singh," Captain Anastasia said.

"I've lost signal. I can't do it remotely! I'll have to open up a jump point right into the Sun Chamber."

"And go in there," Captain Anastasia said.

"Yes. But I have to be the one who does it."

"I will be with you," Captain Anastasia declared.

"'I am with you always, even unto the end of the world,'" Sharkey said.

"I'm with ye," Mchynlyth said.

"I'm not being left out of this," Sen said. "We's *crew*."

39

"I need your velo."

The unshaven young man in the yellow motorbike helmet stared at Charlotte Villiers as if she had beamed down from the Jiju city-ship.

"Your bike, whatever you call it. I need it."

It was a small, light, motorized bicycle with a boxy cargo area behind the seat. Domino's Pizza. Some kind of fast-food delivery service. The initial shock of the Jiju city-ship's appearance had passed. Piccadilly was coming to life again as a hundred drivers and a thousand pedestrians each decided that they needed to get away, get home, get to family and loved ones. Get out of London. Engines revved, cars moved and shunted, horns blared. The street was locking up into a massive, panicked traffic jam. There would be violence soon. Charlotte Villiers could not be trapped here. Everett Singh could have already arrived over Stoke Newington. This time she would not need soldiers or force of arms. She would not need Everett's treacherous alter or threats against his family. She would not even need to take it from him. When she told him what she could do with it, things he had not even dreamed—how she could destroy the Jiju—he would give it to her. But she needed to get there. She needed to get out of grid-locked Piccadilly. Then she saw, five cars down, the startled pizza-delivery guy with his moped.

"Give me the velo!"

"It's not mine. The pizza company will fire me," the pizza man said. He had a strong Russian accent. He grabbed the handlebars firmly.

"You stupid, stupid man. The fate of universes hangs in the

balance." Charlotte Villiers took the gun from her bag. "I need your velo."

He stepped back, hands up.

The velo was quick, agile, and stupidly good fun to ride. Charlotte Villiers hitched up her skirt a few centimeters to free her legs, twisted the throttle, and skidded off along the footpath. The horn was a petulant buzz: it was the sight of the moped charging towards them that made the pedestrians scatter. She clapped her hat to her head, pulled down the net veil. Along the pavements, weaving through the traffic-jammed intersections, driving at full speed, horn blaring, the little klaxon blaring at the stupid sheep people milling around lost, confused, not knowing what to do. Past the statue of Eros in Piccadilly Circus beneath the shining neon signs. Up Shaftesbury Avenue, dodging under the awnings of Theatreland—all the shows still advertized their wares in neon and glitter. Above her the underside of the Jiju city-ship crawled with blue electric fire. Charlotte Villiers drove on, north by east, Oxford Street to Theobalds Road, Finsbury to Shoreditch, ever closer to Stoke Newington, followed every meter of the way by a strong smell of pepperoni and double-cheese pizza from the delivery box.

40

The pinpoint of blinding light opened into a disk that opened into a gate. The crew charged out into the Sun Chamber. The Heisenberg Gate closed behind them. Sharkey swept the room with his shotguns. Captain Anastasia dropped into savate stance. Sen menaced with the battlestaff.

"Feeling a wee bit exposed here," Mchynlyth said. "An old Punjabi-Scots fruit wi' anger-management issues; it's no exactly a superpower, is it?"

Sharkey threw him a shotgun.

"The end with the two holes points away from you," he said.

"Where is it?" Everett stood in the center of the chamber. "The Infundibulum, where is it?"

The chamber was empty. The control desks, the Jiju who had operated them, the model of Diskworld's sun, and the Sunlord mechanisms that had finally destroyed it: all gone. The thin stand that had supported the Sunlord Infundibulum, the tablet computer itself: gone.

There was nowhere it could be, but everyone looked, everyone searched, everyone scanned the room.

"Maybe, like, if the Empress of the Sun came out of the floor, maybe it went back in the floor," Sun suggested.

"Sen, you've got a . . . *connection* with the Jiju," Captain Anastasia said, as if the words tasted like dog shit in her mouth. "Can you work something?"

Sen pressed her hand to the floor.

"I can feel something," she said. "It don't like me. I's the enemy. The Genequeens." Sen stood up quickly, eyes wide. "They're all dead! Oh the Dear, all of them."

"Sen, here." Captain Anastasia held out a hand. Sen took it. The moment of contact was love, reassurance, hope. "It's okay, it's okay."

"Maybe Kax?" Sharkey said. "She's royal blood and all that."

"Aye, like you'd trust yon lizard," Mchynlyth said. "She'd never have arranged all this just to lure us in here and spring some sort of trap, would she?"

"Kax stays on the bridge," Captain Anastasia said. "Everett . . ."

"Simple," Everett said. While Sen had been searching, he had been looking at his phone. The mobile network might be down, but there were other ways that phones and tablet computers could communicate. It all depended on how slavishly the Sunlords had copied Dr. Quantum. A few taps. He almost yelled with delight when the DEVICE AVAILABLE icon lit up. Everyone else held their weapons. Everett held up his. "Bluetooth! Oh yeah! Brilliant or what?"

"Blue what?" Mchynlyth said.

"It's a phone thing," Everett said.

"This is a strange and perverse plane," Mchynlyth said. Sharkey held up a hand.

"By the pricking of my thumbs something Jiju this way comes," he said, aiming his shotgun single handed at the door to the Sun Chamber.

"Everett, how much time do you need?" Captain Anastasia asked.

"I need to get into the Infundibulum and then write some code," Everett said.

"Time!" Captain Anastasia shouted.

"Five, six minutes?"

The adults looked at each other. Captain Anastasia shook her head.

"Sharkey, Mchynlyth . . ."

"Aye, ma'am," each of the men said.

"Sen, keep him safe."

"Ma?"

"Keep him safe. Everyone is expendable here except Everett."

Now Everett could hear the drumbeat of running claws, a swelling choir of bird voices. He would never hear the dawn chorus of songbirds the same way ever again.

White light flooded the Sun Chamber: a blazing atom exploding to a circle of white light. Kax dropped out of the Heisenberg Gate into a crouch on the floor. Her halo spun like a buzzsaw.

"What?" Everett said. "How?"

Kax tapped his iPhone with a fighting claw, then her head.

"Clever, but not so clever, Everett Singh. Earth 10 stuff is easy. Captain! My sisters will cut you to pieces. Leave them to me. We are eggs, we are blood, we are princesses. Save yourselves."

"But your people . . ." Everett said.

"You waste thought, Everett Singh!" Kax hissed. "We are bad, we have done the greatest wrong any creature ever did, but we do not deserve to die. The Sunlords need to find a better way. Maybe apart, we can find it." Then she bowed in the human way to Everett, touched her crest in the Jiju way, and charged down the corridor.

"Kax!" Everett yelled. "Kax!"

"Code!" Captain Anastasia commanded. Everett's fingers flew over the key display. He hissed and swore at every missed key. Stupid, stupid fiddly smartphone keypads. For thick people who pointed at things. The jump codes were easy. A simple arithmetical function could generate the coordinates for each of the city-ships in a fraction of a second. Like all the sticky situations Everett had ever seen in movies, getting out was the tricky bit. Done. But there was one last piece he had to write himself. He had to close and bolt the stable door. He had to make sure that the Sunlords stayed in their billion different exiles.

"Everett," Captain Anastasia said.

"Just one last piece of code." No time to test it, of course. He had one shot: one shot made up of three parts, and each of those parts had to work right the *first* time.

Then he heard something. Not a noise. Something in his head like a noise, but more like an absence of noise. He could not say what it was, but the un-noise was louder than any of the noises and voices in the Sun Chamber.

Everett snapped his head up from his iPhone to the corridor.

"Kax."

He knew. He didn't know how he knew, but he knew. Something was gone out of him. Something forged in a forest clearing in the shadow of thousand-foot trees: all ashes now, and the terrifying, magnificent creatures that lived among them. Dust. Gone. Something that touched mind to mind, Jiju to Human. Gone.

"Kax!"

"Everett," Captain Anastasia said gently.

"Sorry. Yes. No. The return gate should be here about . . ." Once again, blinding light as a disk of light opened into a Heisenberg Gate leading to the welcome bridge of *Everness*. "Go go go, I have to send the code. There's a five-second delay. And I put in a command that will erase the Infundibulum files on every Jiju computer. Just to make sure they can't come back. Or when they do, we're ready for them. Go!"

Sen was last through the gate. Her on the bridge; Everett in the Sun Chamber. Rattling claws, close now: the birdsong had become a war shriek. He hit the SEND button as Jiju warriors burst into the Sun Chamber. Their halos were rings of fierce blades. Everett saw a whirlwind of swords fly at him. Sen lifted the Genequeen battlestaff then threw it at the Sunlords and with her two free hands grabbed Everett by the waistband of his ship shorts and hauled him back onto *Everness*. Everett hit the deck hard.

The Heisenberg Gate closed.

"Three," Everett counted, struggling to his feet. "Two . . . One . . ."

41

A thousand people stood motionless on Green Lanes. School kids, grandparents with baby buggies, young women with plastic shopping bags, Hackney Council workers in yellow hi-viz, street runners and old ladies. Cars stopped, trucks and buses came to a standstill. Cyclists paused to stare. From down the road came the bang and crunch of one car shunting into another. Drivers and passengers got out. People came out of shops and cafés, businesses and offices. Everett could see workers at upper windows all along the street, all staring upwards.

Everett M stared at the thing in the sky. Black stalactites, upside down towers, buttresses, and inverted domes; millions of glowing windows. It was a thousand Gothic cathedrals, ten thousand Disneyland castles turned upside down and mashed together. In an instant the world of every one of those thousand people on Green Lanes, those millions of people all across London, was turned upside down. Whatever they were thinking, whatever they were feeling—their problems, their joys, their heartaches, their heartbreaks, and the hearts they had broken—were all swept away. There was a thing in the sky, so big it hid the sun. Whatever they were thinking and feeling didn't matter anymore. He clenched his fists, willed energy into the Thryn weapon systems. The power excited him as it always did. Everett M's hands flew open. The power ebbed away. The thing hanging over London blacked out the entire sky. It was miles across. He realized that his finger lasers, EM pulsers, speed, strength, and enhanced senses would make him no more effective against the invader in the sky than anyone else on Green Lanes. There was nothing he could do. But he had to do something. He was supposed to be a hero.

"Screw you, Charlotte Villiers," Everett M said.

Whatever he did, it would not be what she wanted.

Everett's phone played Swedish House Mafia: Ryun's ringtone.

"It's the Jiju, isn't it?" Ryun said.

"It's the Jiju."

"The size of that thing . . ."

"Ryun, I need to call my mum. I don't know how long the network will stay up."

"Sure, sure."

"Ry, get everyone you can and get them out of London."

"My dad's at work . . ."

"Do what you can. Ry. Have to call Mum. I'll be in touch."

Everett M thumbed Laura's number.

"Everett, where are you? Are you all right? Come home right away."

"Mum, is Vicky—Victory-Rose at Bebe's?"

"No, she's with me love. Everett, get home."

"I'm coming. Mum, we should get out of London. Go down to Aunt Stacey's." On Earth 4, Laura's sister lived in Basingstoke, a place Everett M had always found so boring that it reversed into being weirdly interesting. Right now it was the safest place he could think of. Aliens never invaded Basingstoke. But first they had to get out of London. And that could be the big problem.

An argument had broken out where the cars had crashed. The window of a charity shop suddenly shattered and collapsed into sugar glass. The noise aroused the crowd. Car horns blared, drivers tried to maneuver their trapped vehicles free. A cyclist clipped the wing mirror of a car as he tried to weave a careful route through the clogged traffic. Another argument broke out. An old lady gave a cry, a woman shouted about her baby, mind her baby! Panicked voices were raised. The panic spread from person to person, and suddenly the thousand people on Green Lanes gelled into one thing: a crowd. They wanted out, they wanted away, they wanted home. The mob milled then surged. Another shop window went in. Through the heads Everett M glimpsed Noomi's face, scared, trapped in the porch of the Mermaid Café by the press of people.

"Mum, I'll be there in a minute. There's something I need to do first."

"Everett . . ."

"I'll look after you. Really."

Everett M closed his eyes, thought power into his enhancements and in single bound jumped onto the top of nearest car.

"Hey!" The driver of the Peugeot yelled as Everett M leaped lightly from car roof to car roof.

"What the . . ."

"What's he doing, what's he doing?"

"You can't do that . . ."

But most people were yelling at each other, pushing and shoving and stretching arms between jammed bodies, reaching for . . . reaching for what? Everett couldn't see anything they could seize hold of, grip as a strong anchor. A distraught woman with a double buggy was marooned in a shop doorway, weeping openly, terrified. Green Lanes were littered with shattered glass from shop fronts and car windows.

Why are they doing this? Everett M thought. There's an alien city-ship in the sky and they're smashing everything up. He raced from car to car, fast and light and strong with his Thryn enhancements. The Jiju are up there in whatever that thing is, and we turn on each other. Everyone for her or himself.

"The kid . . ."

"Stop the kid . . ."

"He can't . . ."

Everett dropped off the roof of a Mini in front of the Mermaid Café, pushing people out of the way. A shaven-headed man in a zip-up jacket over a hoodie rounded on him, shoved him hard. Everett stood firm as a mountain. The man boggled, tried to push Everett M over. Everett M planted a single hand on his chest and held him off.

"No," Everett M said. He fed power to his enhancements and pushed the crowd apart as if they were water.

"Noomi!"

She looked up at the sound of her name. Everett M arrived in the café doorway.

"Are you all right?"

"They all left me," she said. Her eyes were wide with shock. "My GFs. They just . . . left me. They just left me."

"I'll get you home," Everett M said. "I promise. Noomi . . . all those things I said. I had to say them. But they're not true. I only said them to make you safe."

"Everett, this is not a good time."

The crowd was jammed solid now and descending into panic. Panicked mobs were terrifying things. People could get hurt. People could get killed. The screaming of an old lady, the scared mother with her twins; how Everett M wished he could help them. But he couldn't save everyone. That was the other side of power: guilt. The ones you can't do anything to help.

"Noomi, put your arms around my neck."

She did it without question. Everett M scooped her up in his arms and with a flicker of Thryn technology jumped back up onto the roof of the abandoned car.

Noomi's eyes were wide with amazement.

"Everett . . . you can't do that. People can't do that."

"Hold tight."

With Noomi in his arms, Everett M ran from roof to roof, between the surging, scared people, down Green Lanes. The big junction at Newington Green was a mass of clogged traffic and panicked people, surging, pressing, trying to find a way out. As Everett made a jump to the top of a bus the street lights went out. The screaming started.

"Whoa," Everett M said, and "hold on," as he blinked up his Thryn night vision. He fed power into his leg augments to make a leap from the bus to a white van to the top of a truck. He ran along the sagging soft top of the truck, dropped down onto the cab, then to the street.

"Albion Road," he said.

"Okay, you can put me down now, Everett."

Albion Road flickered with the beams of dozens of cell-phone flashlights. Everett M's phone played "Miami 2 Ibiza."

"I'm on the M25. There's another one of them up over Hemel Hempstead. The lights are all out. I've got the night-vision gogg—"

The phone went dead. In Everett M's Thryn vision, Noomi's eyes and teeth glowed. Albion Road was full of infrared ghosts.

"I can see your mum and dad. I can take you to them."

"Everett." Noomi punched him lightly on the chest, a kitty-paw punch. "Thank you for rescuing me. But I don't want to be the girl who needs to be rescued. So: yay! Points. But also, no points."

"Oh." And right there—in the dark, in the madness, in the roar of scared, confused people down on Newington, with a Jiju city-ship hanging overhead and who knew how many others all over the country, all over Europe, all over the world—Noomi's words seemed the worst thing.

"Deal, Ev. You rescue me; at some point, maybe not this week, maybe not this year, maybe not running about and jumping and all that, I will rescue you." She held out a hand. Her face was very serious.

"Deal."

"One thing: who are you?"

Everett M swallowed. This was the hard thing.

"Minimum standards: truth, honesty, caring?"

"Minimum standards."

"Remember that first homework date, when I said I was an alien cyborg double agent from a parallel universe?"

"And you'd replaced the real Everett Singh. Ev . . . No."

"Yes. That's why . . ."

She touched a finger to his lips, finding them effortlessly in the dark.

"I don't want to believe this but I think I kind of have to."

"Don't let anyone know. It's not safe."

Noomi tapped her finger against his lips.

"Ssh."

"Noomi, those things I said, I'm sorry . . ."

"I felt the worst ever, Everett."

"I said terrible things to hurt and push you away . . ."

"Yes, you did. You're not completely forgiven. Maybe about seventy percent. But this isn't the time, Everett."

"I got secrets that hurt people. People who get close get hurt."

"Ssh. I knew there was something. Parallel universe. Wow. That's weird, but no weirder than what's going on right now. I like this Everett better. I have to go now." Noomi lifted her finger from Everett M's lips. He tasted salt and cherry. The world was ending; this time tomorrow London could be ashes, they could all be dead, but in five words Noomi had filled up Everett M's universe with heart and hope. *I like this Everett better*.

"Mum!" Noomi shouted. "Dad!"

Glowing figures turned down Albion Road. Cell-phone lights danced towards Noomi.

"What about you, Everett?" Noomi said.

Truth crashed in around Everett M. His mum, Victory-Rose. They didn't know where he was, if he was safe, if he was coming back. *Get out of London*, that was the last thing he had said to his mum. But the phones were down, and now he could hear sirens in the distance and the roar of aircraft, and the Jiju ship was crackling with blue lighting. He had to get home.

"My mum," Everett M said, and he started to run. No holding

back. He opened up his Thryn enhancements to the last click of the throttle. Already he could feel the cold tightening its grip around his heart and vital organs. He was burning his own body fat. Everett M pushed every piece of Thryn tech to its limit. He ran faster than any Olympic athlete, leaping cars, hurdling walls like a Parkour star, racing down back alleys, navigating by night sight.

"I'm coming!" Walford Road. Stoke Newington High Street. Across the Common: his old running ground, when he was hunting the Nahn. Roding Road. And there was light, sudden light, all around him that forced Everett M to a skidding halt. Blinding light. Painful light. Everett M blinked down his Thryn night vision. The Jiju ship was gone. He looked up into a clear, late-afternoon January sky.

There. A thought turned on Thryn magnification. An airship—a wreck of an airship—in the air to the northwest. He had told Ryun a lie about the magic airship he could call up when the world was in danger. No lie. There it was. Over White Hart Lane. A Spurs fan. It could only be one person. And Everett M was in no doubt that his alter had swept the Jiju from the sky.

We'll meet another time, Everett M thought. *I have more important things to do right now.* His mum—no, the other Everett's mum—Laura: whoever: her, was standing at the car, hands to her face, weeping in joy at the sight of her boy coming up Roding Road. *And whenever we do meet, alter-Everett, it won't be as enemies.*

"Mum," he said.

42

Charlotte Villiers blinked in the sudden clean, brilliant sunlight. Weak winter sun, but it felt pure and holy on her upturned face. A sky so clear she could see all the way to the edge of space. She had no doubt that the same instant the Jiju city-ship had vanished from over London, every other city-ship had disappeared from each one of the Ten Worlds. And she had no doubt who had done it.

The boy was good. Perhaps as good as her.

Charlotte Villiers had ridden the stolen pizza-delivery moped into the center of the little park. She whipped a small, exquisitely tooled Earth 3 monocular from her bag and scanned the sky. Her red lips formed a smile. It had taken her only a moment to find the airship floating over the soccer stadium. It was a wreck, a flying hulk, held aloft by gas and hope.

You'll need to get that repaired, Captain Sixsmyth, Charlotte Villiers thought. *And I'll be waiting for you.*

Sirens on Stoke Newington High Street. Blue lights: police, and dark green military vehicles. Helicopters rattled overhead. Charlotte Villiers could smell burning. People were coming out of their houses, off the stalled buses, into their gardens, onto their streets, drifting toward the common to look up at the sky. They held up their cameras and phones and tablet computers to take pictures of a deep, blue January afternoon.

Now everything is changed, Charlotte Villiers thought. Your politicians cannot lie and dissemble and obfuscate in the face of a billion home videos all across the world. The truth that you are one Earth in a Panoply of trillions of parallel Earths can no longer be hidden. The age of the Plenitude has dawned. And I can use the shock and

266

the awe the Jiju have left behind them. I can extend the influence of the Order and make this world my own. Not just this world, all the Known Worlds. These people have learnt that the multiverse is big, bigger than they can possibly imagine, and their own ten worlds are one tiny corner of a corner of it. For an instant, they saw reality. They saw the deep shadows out there. They're frightened now. Frightened people are easy to control. *You saved the Plenitude, Everett Singh, but you are its gravest threat. And so you have handed me the war. I will make sure that there is no home for you in the Ten Worlds. I can turn the Praesidium against you with the slightest application of my power. The Plenitude of Known Worlds will hunt you down all the days and all the nights without tiring, without sleeping, without pity, without mercy, worlds without end. I have won.*

In the center of Stone Newington Common, with the people from the streets moving in around her, Charlotte Villiers lowered her monocular and very slowly, very deliberately clapped her gloved hands together.

"Bravo!" she cried. "Bravo!"

The gathering crowd could not understand Charlotte Villiers's very private applause but they joined the gesture enthusiastically, clapping and cheering and whooping and waving at the clear sky.

A distant flash on the skyline. Charlotte Villiers raised the monocular again. The airship was gone. She must get back to Down Street. She had a meeting of the Order to chair, on another world.

43

Sen lurked in the latty doorway, teasing her hair into its maximum Afro magnificence with a long-pronged comb. She wore a crop top under her formal ship jacket and had pulled her gold shorts on over leggings, a look she had picked up from Everett's world. A gold shush-bag and mint-ice eye shadow and lipstick completed the look and said *come out with me, Everett Singh.*

"Oh wow," Everett said. She was an ice ghost, hot-cold.

Sen posed, stuck her butt out, shook her shoulders.

"I scrubs up bona with a bit of slap."

Everett did not want to say that he found Sen a little intimidating and a lot too grown up in party gear.

"Are you going somewhere?" he asked.

"Might be. Bristol's bona. Not as bona as Hackney, but that's coz I's not a Bristol girl, I's a Hackney polone."

In the empty skies over London, Earth 10, Captain Anastasia had given Everett an Earth 3 map reference. Even as the Royal Air Force Typhoon fighters had banked to make a run on this final, lingering alien invader in London airspace, Everett had made the calculations, fired up the jump controller, and with the last power in the batteries opened a Heisenberg Gate to bring *Everness* in at three thousand feet over Portishead.

"They're gone here, too," Sen had exclaimed, then added, "not that I's doubting . . ."

"They're gone everywhere," Everett said. It was true, every way that sentence could be true.

"Take her low, take her slow, take her home," Captain Anastasia said. Her voice was very, very tired, her skin grey with fatigue.

Sen gently moved the thrust levers. Groaning, protesting, loyal, *Everness* answered. Captain Anastasia guided her ship slowly up the Avon. The Clifton suspension bridge slipped under Everett's feet. He had been to parallel universes, he had been to the Worldwheel of the Jiju, mighty beyond the comprehension of a human mind, now a glowing disk of red-hot exotic matter, but he had never been farther west in England than Leigh Delamere services on the M4. Airships lined the river, moored four to a docking tree. The radio crackled: greetings, repartee from the other airship captains and Sion Hill control. The main channels were still full of bafflement and amazement and merriment at the Jiju invasion and its defeat— as sudden and total as it began. Where had they come from? What were they? Where had they gone? Would they come back again? The prime minister would make a statement at seven o'clock that night. On the secret, shushy Airish channels, rumor and specula-tion ran amok. And in the midst of it, Captain Anastasia Sixsmyth's return to the Floating Harbour was noted and celebrated and gos-siped widely, especially among those who might be able to repair a wrecked ship on the quiet for a price. Captains flashed their search-lights, sounded their foghorns like the cries of lonely deep-water creatures unknown to human science.

"You're going out in that?" Everett asked.

Sen rolled her eyes. "We's had this before. Yes, I's going out in this. No, you's not my mother."

"Where is your mother?"

"Visiting her mother."

"Sharkey and Mchynlyth?"

"Mchynlyth's talking engineering with the Portishead omis. Sharkey's like as not trolling for polone trade. Come with me, Everett Singh. I'll show you Bristol. We'll have fun! You deserve it. You saved the universe. The least I can do is buy you a buvare. You like buvare beer? Doesn't matter. You will. Zhoosh yourself up. Put on some of that clobber I'd bought you. I'll take you to Sewards. There's prize fighting. Bare knuckle. Bonaroo."

But Everett could not catch Sen's party mood.

"I'm sorry, Sen. You go. I can't get it out of my head."

Sen pulled down the seat in the back of the door and perched on it.

"Get what out of your head, Everett Singh?"

"Get *them* out of my head. All the Jiju. I would have sent them back, Sen. I would have sent them back to the fire. The captain stopped me. How could I have done that? What am I like?"

"You didn't."

"But I would have. Like a thought. And she was right: that would have made me no different from the Empress of the Sun."

"The Empress is the bad one. She's the villain. She killed all those people. I know, Everett. I felt it. It's fading now, but it's still in there. I'm bijou scared it always will be."

"You say that; she's the villain. I know that. But am I the hero?"

"We're here. We're alive. The ship is here. You have the Infundibulum. The Jiju are gone. I don't know where, I don't care where. They's gone. You beat them, Everett. You are the hero."

"I saw things in me I don't like, Sen. I did things . . . It's like—in school, I used to see guys having fights. I was thinking about when Kax killed her rival. They had fights, and they were your mates, but I never saw them the same afterwards."

"I like fights," Sen said, then saw Everett's doubt and vulnerability. "Sorry."

"It was like I'd never known them at all. Sen, I think I'm one of them now. I'm a fighter, and nothing can be the same and I don't know who I am."

"Everett, you're always Everett. I'd know."

"It's like, that other me—my alter. I never could understand where that anger and fight came from. I can understand that now. I've done that."

"I might give you a hug, Everett Singh, but you have to promise not to mess up my riah."

Everett held a hand up as Sen stood and opened her arms to him.

"Wow," she said and recoiled.

"I'm not worth it, Sen. I don't deserve it."

"Doesn't matter."

"It does matter. It matters to me. And Sen, you remember, when I asked you if you'd take your rugby shirt off? I shouldn't have done that. It wasn't right. It wasn't good."

"I's not good?" Sen said, pretending to be outraged.

"No, that's not what I mean. In my world, girls your age, guys my age . . . we shouldn't."

"Everett Singh, remember, it was me said no, but you did no. No should or shouldn't about it. Do or don't do. No word for *should* in palari, Everett Singh."

"I'm not the good guy."

"No one is. We're good and bad, young and old, heroes and villains. That's the way of the Dear."

"Not where I come from."

"Not in most places here either, but where I comes from, we're all those things. Black and white. Come on."

Everett shook his head.

"I got stuff to think about."

"All-alonio on a big, cold airship? No. That's not right. You come out with me, Everett Singh. Even if we just do this little thing I need to do."

"Little thing?"

With a sleight of her hand Sen conjured an Everness tarot card. She flipped it face up. *The Sun Empress.* Empress of the Sun. The cheerful plump woman on the throne with two wands.

"I's retiring this card. I want her out of my deck. All the stuff the Genequeens put in my head, I put them into this card."

Everett could not begin to imagine how that could work in any real, physical way, but it was vital to Sen. It was how she saw the world, with added colors and shades.

"When she's gone, the cards will speak again. True. I's going to drop her in the Floating Harbour. You coming, Everett Singh?"

Everett shook his head.

"Well, I can send her to the water meself. I just thought . . . Nah . . . Everett, hug. I's not leaving this latty until you get one."

Everett stood up. He ached, inside and out. He let Sen wrap her arms around him. She was small and skin and bone and wire like an airship but she was warm and sweet and fierce and most of all there. He slipped his arms around her. She held him long and tight and close and without saying a word. He knew she would stay there as long as he needed. He breathed in her sweet, musky Sen scent. Everett tried to imagine the city-ships of the Sunlords, scattered across a billion random parallel universes. There might be people in those parallel universes. He had just sent them an alien invasion. There was no right solution. Only a choice between evils. He had chosen for his own people at the price of strangers in unknown universes. He did what he had to do. The Empress of the Sun had been the villain, the Big Evil. Everything he had done, he had done because of her.

You didn't exterminate your civilization, Everett Singh. You didn't commit the genocide—ecocide, panicide. You didn't invade the Ten Worlds with a billion city-ships.

Kax . . .

He buried his face in Sen's hair.

"Hey! Don't muss the riah," Sen murmured.

"Yes," Everett said.

"What?"

"Go out. Yes, I will, yes."

"Yes!" Sen slipped from his embrace and skipped into the corridor. "It'll be fun, Everett; the bars and the music clubs, and the prize fighting . . ."

"Maybe not the prize fighting . . ."

"What's wrong with prize fighting? Big men hitting each other. Bona. You'll love it. Now, stand back." Sen pushed Everett aside and went to the cubby where he kept his clothes. She rooted through ship shorts and shirts, socks and leggings and T-shirts. "I'm gonna dress you up proper *so*."

"Sen."

The tone in his voice made her look up, startled.

"What?"

"Nothing. Just. This." Very quickly, very lightly, soft as morning mist, he kissed Sen on her green-ice lips. Her eyes widened then she shook her head and laughed.

"Nah, Everett Singh. Zhoosh up. Let's go: Bristol-fashion."

44

Paul McCabe was the last to leave. Long after the rest of the committee had departed, he lingered in Charlotte Villiers's apartment, commenting on her view of the Thames, the lights of the airships moving slowly over London, the quality of her porcelain.

"Ming?"

"Qing. Kangxi." He knew nothing about Middle Kingdom china.

Even after Charlotte Villiers had thanked him for his contribution to the meeting, making it clear that business was finished and he was intruding on her own time, Paul McCabe found a sudden interest in the etchings in her lobby.

"They're from Earth 5," Charlotte Villiers said. She immediately regretted the comment as Paul McCabe began to intently study the street scenes of an alien London.

"I do like the way the artist has caricatured the people into different types," he said.

"It has nothing to do with caricature," Charlotte Villiers said brusquely. "Earth 5 has five different species of humanity." If she said any more he would be there all night. Such an intensely dull man. Friends—if he had any—must dread him coming to parties. First to arrive, last to leave. "Now, I have private business . . ."

Lewis brought coat, scarf, and gloves, called a cab to take Paul McCabe to the Tyrone Tower, held the door to make sure he left, and saw him to the elevator.

"Lewis, you are a treasure."

"Thank you, ma'am."

"I won't be needing you again tonight."

Charlotte Villiers resisted the urge to wipe Paul McCabe's greasy fingerprints off her porcelain.

She heard Lewis close the front door and waited for the clunk and whir of the elevator. The meeting of the Order had surpassed her expectations. There was nothing like an alien invasion to concentrate minds. Earth 3 had quickly returned to normality. The papers and television were already calling it the Thirty-Minute Invasion. Cities in the sky: had they been real or some mass quantum hallucination? Had worlds merely overlapped for a few minutes of uncertainty? Could anyone really be sure what had happened in that insane half hour? Whatever had happened, it was over now. The electricity was back on, the sky was empty, and there were January bills to pay and work to be done and the weather was still terrible. From the window of her penthouse apartment, Charlotte Villiers looked down on the traffic of night-time London; the shuttling trains, the people on the streets and in the brightly lit restaurants and theatres and cinemas, the pilot lights of the boats on the Thames, the ever-shifting patterns of the airship lights high above the floodlit angels and gods of London's towers. Nothing was different but everything was changed. The worlds would never be the same. Earth 4 had fought the Jiju. The Thryn Sentiency had opened jump doors into the city-ships. A million Madam Moons had battled Sunlord warriors. Charlotte Villiers could not begin to imagine the carnage. Earth 3's radio and television were filled with speculation on why the Jiju city-ships had disappeared. Charlotte Villiers knew, and now so did the Order. Soon, the Praesidium would know, too.

The clock on the sideboard chimed eleven.

It was almost time.

Charlotte Villiers's apartment was twelve spacious rooms in a residential block on the Southwark Shore. Double doors, tall windows, high ceilings, filled with light and air. One room, next to the second guest bedroom, was kept shuttered and sealed. No one but Charlotte Villiers was permitted to enter it. Not the cleaner, not even Lewis. Charlotte Villiers took a key from her bag and opened the door. The room was not large, little more than a box room. Most of its space was filled with a metal ring. Three mahogany steps led up to the ring. Before it stood a console, beautifully made from the same dark mahogany. It was inlaid with a brass panel and an ivory keypad. Charlotte Villiers took out a handkerchief and wiped dust from the controls. Her gloved fingers pressed out a sequence of keystrokes. And the metal ring filled with blinding light. Charlotte Villiers slipped on a pair of dark glasses. More keys. The light cleared to open a window onto an elegant drawing room, heavily furnished and draped, lamp lit and warm.

Charlotte Villiers walked up the steps into the living room. The Heisenberg Gate closed behind her.

She stepped down from the gate and looked around her. The warmth of a coal fire. Light glinting from cut glass decanters. Ancestors glowering in smoke-darkened portraits. Tree branches thrashing in winter wind beyond stained-glass windows. Perfumes of bees' wax, old wood, wood smoke, and books.

A butler in striped trousers and a frock coat peered into the living room, saw Charlotte Villiers, and entered formally.

"I thought I saw the light. Welcome home, Madam Villiers. It's been too long."

"Thank you, Baines. It certainly has been too long."

"I trust your business was successful?"

"If you count fighting off an invasion of the Ten Worlds by intelligent dinosaurs a success, then yes."

"Sounds frightful, madam. Thank the Dear nothing like that ever troubles us here. Ours is a quiet plane."

"Long may it continue, Baines."

The grandfather clock struck the quarter bell. Charlotte Villiers slipped her dark glasses into her purse.

"Have to hurry, Baines."

"I'll have tea ready for your return."

"Whatever would I do without you, Baines? I do have the most marvelous hot chocolate recipe. I must give it to you."

Eight minutes. Charlotte Villiers opened the door to the servants' stairs and went down the spiral to the old kitchens. Plenitude business had kept her away from the last two Manifestations and she hardly thought of the house in Cambridge as home anymore. Home was her Southwark apartment, warm and comfortably furnished to her taste. Home was London. Home was Earth 3. This plane, this world on which she was born and from which she had ventured, taking her father's theorems and making them real, she now thought of as Earth 3a.

The laboratory occupied the old kitchen, butler's pantry, and wine cellars. Lights flickered: the Manifestation was building, drawing power into the rift between universes. Charlotte Villiers knew that her neighbors in this leafy, academic suburb had complained repeatedly about the intermittent electrical supply and why it always failed at twenty-three minutes past eleven at night, every six weeks two days.

Baines kept the equipment scrupulously clean but never touched the big, velvet draped object in the center of the floor. Charlotte Villiers whipped off the covering cloth. The portal was an empty frame, two uprights, two cross pieces, tangled with cables and power conduits. A doorway to nowhere. A doorway to everywhere. Comptator screens blinked behind magnifier lenses and went dark. Around the house light bulbs would be dimming in the chandeliers. Old dusty candles, dripping and black wicked, stood in heavy brass holders on the desk. Charlotte Villiers lit them one by one. She could feel the gathering energies in the air. Dust rose into the air. She could feel the hairs on the back of her neck stir.

"Make it work," had been her father's last words to her, dying in the gloomy four-poster bed upstairs. "All I've done is glimpsed. Shadows of shadows. Glimpses! You must go. Go and see."

I've done more than that, Daddy, Charlotte Villiers thought. *I've seen, and I've gone. I've seen wonders. I've seen terrors. I've seen worlds beyond imagining and power beyond believing. I've seen all power. Ultimate power. I've seen the power hidden inside those equations that allowed you to open up your magic lantern and show me those faint, haunted images of life on another Earth, I've seen the Pleroma.*

One minute.

Candles were the only light now. Their flames bent towards the gateway, which shone a ghostly blue.

"Oh, my love," Charlotte Villiers whispered. "I've been away so long. Forgive me."

The clocks all stood at twenty-three minute past eleven.

Charlotte Villiers put on her dark glasses.

And the gateway blazed with boiling blue light.

Charlotte Villiers came closer to the gate until her face was centimeters from the plane of warped blue. Blue lit her face. The blue lightning of the place between the planes crackled in the lenses of her glasses. A wind from beyond the universe streamed her hair back from her face.

The Rift. A hole torn between worlds, between all worlds. A wound in reality where all the planes touched and bled into each other. And down there, *in* there, at the heart of the Rift, the Pleroma, the heart from which all reality flowed. And in there, in the heart of the heart of everything, Langdon Hayne.

Charlotte Villiers remembered the night they had opened the gate. Her father's lifelong work, left incomplete by the cancer that had eaten his bones and dreams, made real. Years of study, research, dedication, work work work; she the finest mathematician her college had produced in a century, he the engineer who could turn those theories into metal and electricity and fundamental physical forces. One flick of the switch would open the gateway to that other Earth her father had shown her on his Quantic Lantern, a world so very like this one that it took long and careful study of the recorded images to see that they were different worlds. One flick of the switch and that world was a single step away through the Villiers Gate.

She remembered the excitement, the trembling rush as they looked at the switch and asked each other: *Shall we, shall we?* And then decided to do it together, two hands on the lever. But they could not go through the gate together. Someone had to operate the controls.

You go, she had said.

No, you go, he'd insisted, *it's your idea*.

They had tossed a coin. Leave it to indeterminacy. He had stepped into the rippling light.

The clocks had all stood at twenty-three minutes past eleven.

"Langdon?"

And he was there, a face buried in the folds of endless blue, like a man coming up from deep water or a child wrapped in warm blankets on a cold night. Colder than any night, out there, trapped between worlds. So close she could touch him; faces millimeters apart. But she never could touch him. To cross the threshold would be to fall under the pull of the Rift, to be scattered among the Panoply of worlds, without even the tiny comfort of this one moment, every few weeks, at the precise time Langdon Hayne had stepped into the open gate. And Langdon Hayne had fused with the Pleroma, the quantum reality that was the fundamental structure of the multiverse. Nowhere and everywhere.

Her fingers hovered over his face.

"My love," she said. He smiled. He could not have heard her, but he could read her lips, her eyes. His lips formed words, *I love you too*. And them the blue light folded over him and pulled him away. He was gone, whirled off to another random universe, a ghost gibbering in the walls of the world.

"I will bring you back, my love," Charlotte Villiers said. She knew her mistake now, and she knew how to make it right. Her father's calculations had been out by whole orders of magnitude. The worlds were brought into contact not by force ripping apart the fabric of reality, but by the subtle matching of energies, like musical instruments coming into tune with each other. The first gate had punched a hole clear into the Pleroma itself. But the Pleroma, the very stuff of reality, could be manipulated. Everything was mathematics ultimately. The Infundibulum was a tool for tuning the multiverse itself. Everett Singh and his father had not realized the implications of their machine: jumping from any point in any universe to any other was only possible because the Infundibulum could access the Pleroma. A tool that could chisel Langdon Hayne free from the Pleroma was a tool for the control of reality itself.

The candles gusted and blew out in the wind from beyond as the gateway blinked out and closed. The lights flickered and came back on. The laboratory hummed to the sound of comptators rebooting.

The clocks read twenty-five minutes past eleven.

Charlotte Villiers drew the heavy velvet covering over the gateway.

Work first. The Plenitude had come close to disaster. In the disaster was her opportunity. The Order was unified and strong. There had never been a better time to make a bid for power. Ibrim Hoj Kerrim knew too much. She would neutralize him, in time. And Everett Singh was now a hunted enemy across all the Ten Worlds. There was much to do, opportunities to be taken quickly. She would return to Earth 3 this night. After Baines's tea. Next time, she would have him prepare the Blond Bear Café's hot chocolate recipe. The Earth 7 cuisine was quite exceptional.

"I will bring you back," Charlotte Villiers said to the rectangle of rich fabric. "I promise."

PALARI

Palari (polari, parlare) is a real secret language that has grown up in parallel with English. Its roots go back to seventeenth-century Thieves Cant in London—a secret thieves' language. It's passed through market traders and barrow-mongers, fairground showmen, the theatre, the Punch and Judy Show, and gay subculture. Palari ("the chat"—from the Italian *parlare*, "to talk") contains words from many sources and languages: Italian, French, *lingua franca* (an old common trading language spoken across the Mediterranean), Yiddish, Romani, and even some Gaelic. It's taken in words from Cockney rhyming slang—"plates" for *feet*, from "plates of meat" = "feet"; and London back-slang—"eek" is short for "ecaf," which is "face" backward. Many words from palari/polari have entered London English. In Earth 3, palari is the private language of the Airish. In our world, polari still survives as a secret gay language.

GLOSSARY OF PALARI:

alamo: hot for someone
amriya: a personal vow, promise, or restriction that cannot be broken (from Romani)
aunt-nell: listen, hear
aunt nells: ears
barney: a fight
bijou: small/little (means "jewel" in French)
blag: pick up/beg as a favor/get without paying
bona: good
bonaroo: wonderful, excellent

buvare: drink (from old-fashioned Italian *bevere* or Lingua Franca *bevire*)

Buggerello: expression of distaste or impatience, entirely of Mchyn-
    lyth's devising.

cackle: talk/gossip/speak

charper: to search (from Italian *chiappar*to catch)

charver: to have sex

chavvy: child

clobber: clothes

cod: naff, vile

cove: friend/person/character

dally/dolly: sweet, kind

dish: bum, arse

divano: an Airish ship's council.

dona: woman (from Italian *donna* or Lingua Franca *dona*), a term of respect

dorcas: term of endearment, "one who cares"; the Dorcas Society was a
    ladies' church association of the nineteenth century, which made
    clothes for the poor

ecaf/eek: face (back-slang); *eek* is an abbreviation of *ecaf*

fantabulosa: fabulous/wonderful

fruit/fruity: Hackney Great Port term of mild abuse

gafferiya: Airish tradition of hospitality and shelter for travelers (from
    Thieves' Cant *gaff*)

ground-pounder: a non-Airish person

lally-tappers: feet

latty: room or cabin on an airship

lillies: police (Lilly Law)

manjarry: food (from Italian *mangiare* or Lingua Franca *mangiaria*)

meese: plain, ugly, despicable (from Yiddish *meeiskeit*: loathsome,
    despicable, abominable)

meshigener: nutty, crazy, mental (from Yiddish)

naff: awful, dull, tasteless

nante: not, no, none, never (Italian: *niente*)

ogle: look

omi: man/guy

Palari-pipe: telephone/in-ship communication system ("talk pipe")

polone: woman/girl

sabi: to know (from Lingua Franca *sabir*)/understand

scarper: to run off (from Italian *scappare*, to escape or run away)

sharpy: policeman (from "charpering omi")

shush: steal/stolen goods

shush-bag: holdall/backpack

slap: makeup

so: to be part of the in-crowd/Airish (e.g., "Is he so?")

tharbyloo: there below

troll: to walk about looking for business or some kind of opportunity

varda: to see/look at (from Italian dialect *vardare* = *guardare*—look at)

zhoosh: style, make a show of.

ABOUT THE AUTHOR

Ian McDonald is a science fiction writer living just outside Belfast in Northern Ireland. He's the author of over twenty novels and story collections—both adult and YA—and has also written for screen and stage. He's been nominated for every major science fiction award, and even won a few. *Empress of the Sun* is the third part of the Everness series.

SOMEWHERE IN THE PANOPLY OF ALL WORLDS ...

Light!

Light: all around him, enfolding him, shining through him so hard and so long he could feel it bleaching the organs inside his body. Embedded in light. Being *light*.

The primal light, the light that shines between universes. How long had he been here? Meaningless question. There was no time here. No space. He was everywhere, he was nowhere; he was everything, he was nothing.

And then the light splintered, like a window in a bomb blast, and darkness burst through. He fell into darkness. And the darkness was good. It was great and soft and endless.

This is what death is like, he thought.

"Is he alive?"

So, not dead then.

"Vital signs are all good, First Minister. Of course, there's no guarantee there's anything in there."

I can hear you! I'm trying to talk to you! I'm trying to speak. Listen to me, listen to me, can you hear me?

"How long was he in there?"

"Technically, in the Planck state neither time nor space exist. It's not really a meaningful question."

"For me, please, professor. I'm not a scientist."

"Nine days after solstice. We weren't even sure what it was. Certainly not a human. All we had was a weak resonance. We locked on to it and abstracted the pattern. It took us until now to entangle it with our universe."

"The pattern . . . And he comes from?"

"Another universe."

"Another universe. How can I tell you the chill those words strike into me? Wait. I saw his lips move."

"I can hear you."

"Nurse, bathe his eyes."

"Who are you?"

Soft sweet wetness dabbing at his eyes, wiping away crusted scales and scabs.

"I am First Minister Esva Dariensis of the United Isles. You are in a hospital."

He opened his eyes. Cried out. Light: true light, real light. He blinked the painful light away. A fluorescent tube on a ceiling, and faces looking down at him; a man in a high-collared suit, a well-dressed woman, a woman in a white cowl. Beyond the light: another light, a great window. He struggled up on his elbows, drawn by the light of the world outside the world. Towers, endless skyscrapers, pinnacles and glittering glass; the contrails of aircraft, ribbons of high cloud, arcs of light moving across the high blue sky.

"Where am I?"

"You're on Earth."

"Earth? Earth? Then what is *that*?"

He lifted an arm to point. Beyond the city skyline, beyond the aircraft and the clouds and even those higher, mysterious moving lights was another blue world hanging in the sky, so huge he could not blot it out with his open hand. A world of sea and green forests, brown deserts, white snow, coiling clouds.

"Easy, easy."

"You've had a shock."

"You're safe now."

"Easy, easy."

"Your name . . ."

"Can you remember your name?"

"My name," he said, still staring at the other world in the sky, "my name is Tejendra Singh."